STINGER

Ian,

ENJOY !

AN INTERNATIONAL THRILLER

GREGORY D. LEE

Black Rose Writing | Texas

First printing

The author grants the final approval for this literary material.

This is a work of fiction. Names, characters, businesses, places, events, and incidents are either the products of the author's imagination or used in a fictitious manner. Any resemblance to actual persons, living or dead, or actual events is purely coincidental.

ISBN: 978-1-68513-385-6
LIBRARY OF CONGRESS CONTROL NUMBER: 9781685133856
PUBLISHED BY BLACK ROSE WRITING
www.blackrosewriting.com

Printed in the United States of America
Suggested Retail Price (SRP) $22.95

Stinger is printed in Minion Pro

*As a planet-friendly publisher, Black Rose Writing does its best to eliminate unnecessary waste to reduce paper usage and energy costs, while never compromising the reading experience. As a result, the final word count vs. page count may not meet common expectations.

I dedicate my debut novel to my beautiful wife, Virginia,
who has put up with me for over fifty years.

PRAISE FOR *STINGER*

"Prepare to be swept up in a fast-paced thriller blends relentless action, shocking revelations, and moral dilemmas. *Stinger* is a riveting tour de force that will leave you questioning the sacrifices made in the name of justice."

–Cam Torrens, award-winning author of *Stable* and *False Summit*

"A superbly written work of thriller fiction! The author immediately draws the reader in and never let's go. *Stinger* is absolutely believable, a story about what might have been shortly before the death of Saddam Hussein. A breathless opening depicting a kidnapping, and the heroic efforts of American government agencies which orchestrated a daring undercover deal. A real whodunit! Gregory D. Lee's many years of experience in law enforcement is evident in this fantastically believable story which is highly entertaining and credible."

–Christopher Amato, author, *A Letter from Sicily,* and
Shadow Investigation

"*Stinger* by Gregory D. Lee is a pulse-pounding immersion into a world of spy craft, intrigue, and twisted conspiracies. The suspense built from start to finish as this reader struggled to winnow out the good guys from the bad guys, never sure which was which. As the tale progressed, I grudgingly began to root for the unlikely hero. No James Bond, he, but improbably clever, as he stumbles along from crisis to crisis in his quest to free his sister and mother from their terrorist (?) kidnappers. Much of the action takes place in the Middle East, and Lee's depiction of the region is spot-on. Take it from one who lived and worked there for 20 years. A stiff Stoli is recommended to take the edge off the suspense, but anyway you approach this adventure, you will not be disappointed. Fans of Le Carre and Fleming will feel right at home with this 5 star read!"

–Bill Schweitzer, Author of *Doves in a Tempest*

"Gregory D. Lee knows his stuff and has a story to tell! *Stinger* is relevant – and frightening – today. His varied background and real-world experience provide gritty detail that others can only imagine. He also delivers fascinating insights to how some government agencies really operate."

–**Philip H. Madell, Esq, President, National Counter-Intelligence Association former Special Agent, U.S. Army Counter-Intelligence**

"*Stinger* will leave you wanting more! Gregory D. Lee's new thriller masterfully combines the intrigue of espionage into a fast-paced page turner. The characters are complex and compelling, and the plot is full of twists and turns that leave you wondering what will happen next. His vast wealth of experience is apparent on every page of the book."

–**Gary Edgington, author of *Outside the Wire***

"Outstanding! *Stinger* is so well crafted and a very enjoyable read. Captivating from the first page, engaging and fast moving. It could not be put down."

–**Victor Guerrero, FBI Supervisory Special Agent (Ret.)**

"A walk-off grand slam home run! In his debut novel, Gregory D. Lee uses his 40+ years as a military and law enforcement professional to write a scintillating international thriller. Lee integrates espionage, police procedure, criminal investigation, terrorism, U.S. bureaucratic competitiveness, multiculturalism, and historical events into unexpected surprises—a real page-turner! The intrigue, deception, maneuvering, betrayal, disappointment, and exhaustion are palpable and rebarbative. Hoping for a sequel."

–**James Spurr, Special Agent (Ret.) U. S. Drug Enforcement Administration**

"*Stinger* is a nonstop thrill ride with twists and turns, engaging you until the final pages."

–**Dr. Gary Gerlacher, author of *Last Patient of the Night***

CHAPTER 1

Beirut, Lebanon
Monday, January 27, 2003

Amir Rahimi cursed when he glanced at his Rolex. Where the hell are they? He took one last drag from his cigarette and flicked it out the driver's window of the Land Rover, where it landed next to five others. He ran his long fingers through his trimmed graying hair and examined his nicotine-stained teeth in the rear-view mirror.

One of the Pakistani Khan brothers, Tariq, seated in the back seat of the car, complained. "How much longer do we have to wait for them?"

"Yes, how long?" his brother, Iqbal, said, squirming in the front passenger seat.

"Until I say it's time to go!" Rahimi snapped. He was determined to go through with his plan. He refused to accept any whining, especially from the likes of two former Pakistani-Taliban militia men whose military skills were the only reason they were worthy of his company.

"I don't want to hear another bloody word from either of you," Rahimi blurted.

• • •

Halfway into the third hour, a frail old lady and her thirty-year-old daughter emerged from a once charming high-rise apartment building that had never been fully renovated after the Lebanese civil war.

Rahimi's hunch the women would walking to the local open-air market this afternoon proved correct.

"Here they come," Rahimi said. "Get ready!" Tariq, who had a scruffy beard and mustache, grabbed onto the door handle. Iqbal, who only sported a bushy mustache, took a stainless steel 9 mm Beretta from his backpack, and stuffed it inside his waistband.

Rahimi put his foot on the clutch and released the hand brake, allowing the Land Rover to roll down the steep, potholed street silently. They coasted several seconds before he keyed the ignition, put it in gear, and popped the clutch. Its momentum increased as they descended upon their intended victims. The women never saw them until the SUV halted in front of them. Tariq leaped out of the vehicle and walked toward them.

The daughter screamed at the sight of the man, pointed at him, and dropped the empty wicker basket she was carrying. Iqbal hustled around the SUV to the old lady and began pulling her by the arm towards it, shoving her in the back seat, leaving the door open.

Tariq grabbed the young woman around her thin waist. Tariq's powerful arms caused her to scream as he carried her towards the SUV's back door. She planted her feet on the door's frame, refusing to get in.

"Get in!" he commanded. Together, Rahimi and Tariq bent her over and pushed her into the back seat. Her mother sat terrified, bracing her head firmly between her knees with her hands covering it. She was afraid to look up. Rahimi straightened his clothing, slammed the door, and glanced around before getting back in the driver's seat. Iqbal jumped back in the front seat and trained his shiny Beretta on the two women as the car rolled slowly. Tariq hustled to get in the right rear seat.

Rahimi shifted into first gear and stomped on the gas pedal while Iqbal kneeled backwards in the front passenger seat, watching the women. It was not long before he noticed through the rear window the police were approaching. "Trouble behind us," he said.

"Damn," Rahimi said while glancing into the rearview mirror seeing the flashing blue lights on the police vehicle. The daughter's persistent screaming annoyed Rahimi. Turning left into an alley, he made a sharp right onto another street and a quick left into another alley. Rahimi slowed while staring at the side-view mirror to see if he had lost them. Then he saw the police Land Cruiser again. "Shut that woman up, will you?"

"We're trying," Tariq said just before the younger woman grabbed his left wrist with both hands and bit his thumb as hard as she could. The Pakistani cursed and yelled even louder than she was. Iqbal reached over the front seat and grabbed a handful of her hair, eventually forcing her to release his brother's bleeding thumb. Tariq grabbed the mother's dress to wrap around his thumb to stop the bleeding as Rahimi tossed them about while making hairpin turns.

Rahimi drove straight ahead for several blocks and soon came upon a massive traffic circle. He had no chance of maneuvering around it. He glanced over his right shoulder and saw the police were about 150 meters behind them.

When Rahimi completed his mental calculations, he slowed the car to a halt, quickly forced the gearshift into reverse, and drove backward as fast as the transmission would allow.

"What are you doing?" Tariq yelled above the woman's screams while nursing his sore thumb.

"Get ready to take those cops out," Rahimi ordered.

"You're going to take us all out!" Iqbal shouted back while clutching the door handle and the dashboard. The daughter's screams suddenly turned to whimpers. The mother still held her spinning head between her knees and threw up, as if on cue.

Rahimi wound out the reverse gear as he sped backward, causing the Land Rover to slightly serpentine. He grabbed the steering wheel with his left hand at the 3 o'clock position and jerked it counterclockwise as hard as possible. The SUV expertly slid 180 degrees within the same lane and was now facing the police vehicle. He crunched the transmission into first gear and sped towards them on a collision course.

"Shoot them, you fool! Do it now!" Rahimi yelled. In a panic, the driver of the police Land Cruiser locked its brakes, creating a swirling plume of smoke from its tires. At the last possible moment, Rahimi swerved to the left to avoid hitting them head on. Iqbal fired several shots from his Beretta, piercing the windshield and wounding the driver. The passenger police officer attempted to apply the out-of-control SUV's brakes, but the vehicle's momentum hurtled it into several cars stopped in traffic.

Rahimi traveled east out of the city and soon saw the countryside through the windshield. Driving about half an hour, they finally came upon the faint markings of a dirt road and followed it towards the cedar tree-studded hills.

"Who are you men, and where are you taking us?" the daughter demanded to know. She had calmed down. Rahimi grinned at her as he looked in the rearview mirror. Iqbal and Tariq glanced at each other and ignored the question. Rahimi drove twenty more minutes coming upon flat, barren desert terrain where they only occasionally saw inhabitants.

An hour later, they arrived at a white, two-story L-shaped cement structure. It had large picture windows and a huge hand-carved rosewood door. The dwelling was an anomaly in the desert. Palm and cedar trees shaded the ground, and a sizeable kidney-shaped pool graced the rear yard. Two young men dressed in black T-shirts and designer blue jeans, carrying Uzi machine guns, waited for them by an opened black iron gate attached to an enormous stone wall surrounding the compound. They waved them in and shut and locked the gate. After Rahimi parked at the crest of the circular driveway near the front door, two other armed men snatched the women from the car and escorted them into the artificial oasis.

"The young one bites," Tariq cautioned as they led the women away.

Rahimi snickered when he heard the remark and leaned against the fender of the Land Rover, lighting another cigarette, taking a long drag. The plan was in motion. The anticipation put a shiver down one leg.

CHAPTER 2

Robaire Assaly pulled into the carport of his modest west side apartment complex. Holding his groceries, he got out of the car and locked the doors to his new Mercedes S550 sedan. This was Los Angeles, the car theft capital of the world, and he did not want someone stealing his new baby.

He fiddled with his keyring and got the apartment door open, careful not to drop the grocery bag he rested on his protruding belly. Besides the usual microwaveable meals, he bought a new 1.75-liter bottle of Stolichnaya vodka he did not want to drop. As he opened the door his Nokia cell phone rang. He rushed inside and placed his grocery bag on the kitchen table and reached for his phone, answering it on the third ring.

"Hello."

"Is this Mister Assaly? Mister Robaire Assaly?" a woman's voice asked.

"Yes, last time I checked, it was," he replied. "Who is this?"

"My name is June Cohen. I work for the United States government," she said. "It's vital I speak with you as soon as possible."

"Why? What is this about?"

"I can't discuss it on the phone. But it's about your family."

That definitely got Robaire's attention. "My family? What about them?"

"Like I said, Mister Assaly, I'll explain it all to you when we meet. Your residence would be preferrable."

"How did you get this number?" Robaire wanted to know.

"I'll explain everything when I see you," she repeated. She confirmed with him the address she had, which was another surprise for Robaire. "May I come over this afternoon?" Robaire thought hard, trying to remember if there were any pissed-off wives or girlfriends of the many drug dealers he set up over the years for the DEA. Women who may now seek revenge for their significant other's federal incarceration.

"Okay. June is it?"

"Yes. Thank you, Mister Assaly. I can be there within the hour. Will that be all right?"

"Yes, I'll be here."

"Great. See you soon," she said, and hung up.

His thoughts immediately came to his mother and sister in Lebanon. What could be the problem? To be on the safe side, Robaire retrieved his Colt Commander .45 caliber pistol from his bedroom nightstand and placed it on a bookshelf in the living room hidden inside a folded Los Angeles Times he had just purchased at the grocery store.

• • •

Forty minutes later, Robaire heard a knock at the door. He pulled aside the curtain on the front window and peeked out to see who the caller was. An attractive blond in business attire and high heels, with red lipstick, stood on his doorstep carrying a large shoulder bag. He opened the door and invited her in.

"Thank you for seeing me on such short notice," she said.

"Please have a seat," Robaire said, pointing to the couch. "Now tell me what this is all about." She seated herself and reached into her shoulder bag pulling out a two-part credential and displayed it to Robaire before handing it to him. The U.S. government issued credentials had her photograph and other information identifying her as June Cohen, Intelligence Case Officer for the Central Intelligence Agency.

"All right, Ms. Cohen," he said, pacing the living room. "I've never met a CIA agent before. Now, please tell me what this is about."

"I'm afraid I have some bad news about your mother and sister. They were kidnapped last Monday in Beirut."

"Kidnapped? By whom?"

"We're working on it, but we have a good idea who's behind this," she said. "Let me show you something." She pulled out a folder from her bag which held an eight by ten photograph. Robaire sat on the couch next to her.

"The kidnappers have taken this photograph and mailed it to the U.S. Embassy in Beirut." The photo showed Robaire's mother and sister seated on a bench inside a building in front of a white sheet, both in handcuffs and leg irons. They looked terrified.

"The bastards!" Robaire said. "What would kidnappers want with two harmless women?"

"We believe the people who took them are members of a Shiite terrorist organization with ties to Iran. Your mother and sister are Christian. Am I right?"

"Yes. What does that have to do with it?"

"We think they were targeted partly because of their faith. They'd never kidnap another Shiite. They also must believe they are dual Lebanese-American citizens. That's why they sent their photograph to the U.S. Embassy."

"What are their demands?" Robaire asked.

"Money, of course. One half-million dollars for each of the women. We know they aren't Americans because the first thing the embassy did was check for registered Americans in the country and they weren't on the list. Even if they were, the U.S. government has a long-standing policy of not negotiating with terrorists. Our assessment is that these kidnappers mistook them for Americans thinking either the U.S. government or a rich relative would pay the ransom."

"The American Embassy isn't interested in helping them?"

"I'm afraid not," June said. "We have notified the Lebanese authorities, but they're inept. The good news is we think we know where they are." She flipped over some pages in her folder to another photograph, this one from a satellite depicting a white L-shaped concrete structure with a pool within a walled compound. She showed it to him.

"Well, if you think you know where they are, why aren't the authorities raiding the place to free them?" Robaire used his handkerchief to wipe a tear away and blow his nose.

"It's complicated, Mister Assaly. May I call you Robaire?"

"Yes, of course, Ms. Cohen. Should I call you Special Agent Cohen?"

"No, no. The CIA calls its operatives agents. I'm a case officer. Please, Robaire, just call me June."

"All right."

"We have a plan of action, but it will require your help."

"I'm listening."

"We believe these terrorists are in the market for a Stinger missile. However, we do not know what they intend to do with it if they had one. That's where you come in."

"I don't see how I could possibly help you with that."

She noticed an ashtray on the coffee table with a snuffed-out cigar. "I see you smoke. Mind if I light up a cigarette?"

"Please do," he replied, wiping his eyes again.

She took out her pack and lit one. "We know you have a long working relationship with the DEA and an agent named Gary Lowery."

"How did you know that?"

"Whenever a federal law enforcement agency creates an informant file, the CIA gets a copy in case we ever need someone with their particular knowledge, skills and abilities," she said.

"That's funny. Gary never mentioned that to me when he signed me up."

"How did you become an informant for the DEA?"

Robaire blew his nose again, and sat down in his worn recliner. "After graduating from the American University in Beirut, I was promptly hired as a purser by Pan Am for its international flights, mostly because of my foreign language skills. I moved to Los Angeles, got my green-card, and became a citizen. I flew every foreign route Pan Am offered. It wasn't long before drug traffickers approached me in Bangkok, Mexico City, Karachi, La Paz, Bogota. You name it. They all wanted me to smuggle drugs for them to the United States. The money was quite good, by the way."

"So, what happened?"

"One day, about ten years ago, Gary Lowery paid me a visit. He said one of my contacts in Bangkok got caught with fifty units of heroin, and the bastard told the police and DEA he used me to smuggle his drugs to Los Angeles. Gary said if I pleaded guilty to conspiracy and agreed to cooperate as an informant, he'd see to it I did no prison time. How could I refuse? I would do *anything* to stay out of federal prison, just like I will do *anything* to help my mother and sister."

"I'm glad to hear that, Robaire," June said.

"Pan Am immediately fired me, so I had little choice but to work with Gary."

"How much did the DEA pay you for your services?" she asked.

"A lot. The first deal I did for Gary, he only reimbursed my expenses. But once my case was over, I made tens of thousands of dollars. Sometimes more than Gary did as an agent. And the DEA doesn't send a 1099 to the IRS at the end of the year."

"Interesting," June said.

"No member of my family know how I earn a living. They suspect I use my wit and charm engaging in various business enterprises. They would never believe for a moment I was a drug smuggler, or worse yet, an informant."

"No matter," June said. "The CIA now finds itself in need of your services."

"How so, June?"

"We'd like you to help us get a Stinger," she said matter-of-factly.

"Just how in the world am I supposed to come up with one of those?"

"We're aware of an Iranian asylum seeker here in L.A. who is searching for one, most likely for these kidnappers. We believe he's a free-lance arms dealer trying to make a quick buck. I'd like you to meet him at one of his favorite watering holes tomorrow, strike up a conversation, and use your 'wit and charm' to convince him you have a contact who can provide him a Stinger." She produced another eight by ten photograph, this time of Amir Rahimi who was lighting a cigarette. The photo looked as though someone conducting surveillance on him had taken it. "That's him."

Robaire stared at the photo. "So, who's supposed to be my Stinger missile contact?"

"That would be Gary Lowery," she said, while brushing the hair out of her face.

"Gary?"

"After your meeting, I want you to tell Lowery you met Rahimi, who is looking for a Stinger missile. He seems like a competent agent, so he'll jump right on it. We need you to convince him to sell a Stinger missile to Rahimi," she said using air quotes when she said 'sell.' "Once Rahimi has the missile, the FBI will most probably follow him to see who he delivers it to. We'll be following the FBI just in case they screw up. But they must never know the CIA is involved." She flicked the ash from her cigarette. "Once we learn who Rahimi's buyer and accomplices are, the CIA will take all of them to a secure location where we will extract their information. At the same time, we'll send in our own special operators to rescue your mother and sister."

"Not until then?" Robaire asked.

"I'm afraid not," June said. "If they're rescued sooner, it would leave Rahimi without a buyer for the Stinger. Spooking him too soon would jeopardize the entire operation."

"I see," Robaire said, pausing in thought. "This sounds complicated, but I think I get it," he said. "So, you'll help me if I help you. Is that about it?

"That's the way it must be, I'm afraid. Say, tell me about Gary Lowery. What's he like?"

"Well, he's in his early forties, an army veteran, and has been on the job about 15 or more years."

"Is he white, black, or what?"

"No, he's actually half Native American."

"Really?" June said. "Go on."

"He once told me his white mother married his full-blooded American Indian father when he was in the army stationed in California. I think he said his father's tribe's name is Lumbee, and I believe it's in North Carolina."

"Does he look like a Native American? You know, long ponytail, turquoise jewelry, things like that"

"No. You might think he's Italian. Black hair, brown eyes, light skin, clean cut."

"I see. Interesting."

Robaire leaned back in his recliner. "Why don't you just arrest Rahimi and be done with it?"

"I haven't told you everything, but I'm afraid it's classified. I wish it was that easy, but believe me, it isn't. The CIA is not a law enforcement agency and Congress passed laws long ago forbidding us from acting domestically. So, we must rely on you and others to do certain things for us."

"I see," Robaire said.

"The FBI and DEA have to follow their legal guidelines," June continued. "We don't. I mean to say we don't have to worry about convicting someone in federal court, and things like that." She watched Robaire for his reaction. "If we could do it any other way we would, Robaire. You must trust me on this."

"So, in the unlikely event I can get Rahimi to talk about Stinger missiles, and somehow convince Gary Lowery to deliver one to him, only then you'll see to it my mother and sister are rescued?"

"I guarantee it, Robaire."

"What if I should fail? Wouldn't that place my family in greater harm?"

"No," she responded. "Like I said, we will send in a team to free them and either capture or kill the terrorists, but first we must try doing this. If you make a sincere effort to help us, we'll rescue your family whether Rahimi gets his Stinger or not."

Robaire leaned forward in his recliner with his elbows on his knees holding his head, thinking. His legs shook. "There's no other way? Are you certain?"

"Yes. And you must not tell Lowery our plans. He needs to be kept in the dark about the CIA's involvement or our entire cover is blown. So, we need to keep him in the dark. He needs to go through his normal investigative routine to make it appear the CIA has nothing to do with this. I hope you understand how important that is," she said. "I know what you must be going through, and I know it's hard, but as of now, it's the only way."

Robaire rose to his feet. "I forgot my manners. Would you like something to drink?"

"No, thank you."

"Hope you don't mind if I do," he said while walking to the kitchen to fetch his virgin bottle of Stoli.

"Not at all," she said.

He found a glass, put plenty of ice in it, poured the vodka to the rim, and returned to his easy chair. "I suppose you're right," Robaire said. "This is a lot to process." He took a long swig of vodka. "Where can I find this Mister Rahimi?"

She asked him to find a piece of paper to write the address down. She also gave him her cell number. "He'll be there Saturday afternoon, around five p.m. Call me after you've had your meeting with him and tell me how it went." She extinguished her cigarette in the tray, leaving red lipstick smeared on its butt.

"How are you so sure he'll be there Saturday?" Robaire asked.

"We have informants, too, you know." She stood and walked to the door. "Good luck tomorrow, Robaire. Don't disappoint me." They shook hands.

"Don't worry, June. I'll take good care of Mister Rahimi."

Robaire watched as June walked out the door to a red Toyota Camry. Her heels clicked against the cement. Robaire waved to her as she got in her car and drove off.

He paced his living room and took out his cell phone. He called his mother's apartment in Beirut where she and his sister lived, hoping for an answer. No answer meant June was probably telling the truth about the kidnapping. It was 2:24 a.m. there. The phone rang at least twenty times before he hung up. He sat back in his recliner and placed his face in his hands and sobbed loudly.

Once he regained his composure, he sat at his small kitchen table that doubled as his desk. He removed a yellow legal pad from a nearby drawer and wrote. In case something went sideways, he wanted to chronicle his dealings with June. He felt terrible about using his long time DEA agent handler, whom he considered a friend. However, he knew he had no choice but to cooperate with June. Once this was over and his family was safe, he hoped Gary would understand his reasoning and forgive him.

Robaire completed his writing and put the notepad back in the drawer. He dropped his head on his folded arms and sobbed again. Robaire felt trapped. He didn't know or trust June, but felt he had no option but to cooperate.

CHAPTER 3

Pasadena, California
Sunday, February 2, 2003

DEA Special Agent Gary Lowery squinted from the bright February sunlight reflecting off the windshield of a parked car. He stood alone in the parking lot. His informant was late as usual.

Finally, Robaire Assaly's new black Mercedes S550 pulled into the lot. He cruised past a prime parking spot and shamelessly parked in a handicap space, only two spaces closer to the restaurant's entrance. He opened the door but did not get out. Gary shook his head in disgust as the fat man dumped the car's overflowing ashtray onto the asphalt. Robaire rolled out of the car and hiked up his pants while smiling at Gary. Gary hoped no one noticed. Being seen with some asshole that would deprive a disabled person of a parking space and then trash it with cigar ash and old stogies made him wince. The man's profile resembled the comedian James Corden, but Robaire Assaly was no James Corden.

Gary had his hands on his hips as Robaire walked up. "I hope you get a ticket."

"If I do, the DEA will take care of it for me, right?" Robaire shrugged.

"In your dreams, partner," Gary scoffed as he held the front door of the restaurant open.

Gary requested the hostess seat them at a corner table. The restaurant was convenient to Gary's townhouse, had a nice food selection for lunch, and the prices were reasonable. Times were tough for a divorced father of two who had to pay for two mortgages and child support.

In a short while, a waitress appeared. "What can I get you gentlemen to drink?"

"Just an iced tea, please," Gary said.

"And you, sir."

"Double Stoli on the rocks, with a twist, my dear."

"Coming right up," she said and headed straight for the bar.

"Don't you ever drink anything else?"

"Gary, there's nothing like Russian vodka. It coats the throat while going down and relieves one's tension. Nothing like it in the world."

Gary shook his head as he opened the menu. "Whatever."

The waitress returned a few minutes later. "Your drinks will come up shortly. Have you decided on your food selection?"

"I'll have the turkey sandwich on sourdough with fries," Gary said.

Robaire Assaly stroked his cheek while thinking. "The filet, medium rare, twice baked potato and a small Caesar salad."

"Excellent choice, sir." She headed for the kitchen.

Within a minute, the server appeared with their drinks. "Thank you, my dear," Robaire said.

Gary thought they must look like quite a pair. He was dressed in a forest green Polo shirt, blue jeans, brown Rockports, and a brown tweed sports coat, while his informant wore a dark blue thousand-dollar silk suit and Gucci loafers. Gary figured Robaire's shirt and tie alone cost more than his entire outfit, and his suit and gold cufflinks were worth more than his entire wardrobe.

"Tell me about the dope-for-guns deal you mentioned on the phone. This better be worth dragging me out here on a Sunday."

Robaire sipped his drink and licked his upper lip. "Can you get your hands on a Stinger missile?"

"A Stinger?" he said, loud enough to attract the attention of everyone seated next to them. Gary leaned forward and, in a soft voice, asked, "You're talking about a shoulder-fired missile?"

"Precisely," he said. "The one used to shoot down aircraft."

"Are you kidding me?" Gary glanced around and looked back at Robaire, who wasn't smiling. "You're serious, aren't you?"

"How long have we known each other, Gary?"

"Nine or ten years."

"Have you ever known me to kid around?"

Gary didn't answer.

"Well, can you get one?"

Gary thought for a second. "Do you know how hard it would be for me to get something like that?"

"No, but I have confidence in you. If you put your mind to it, I'm sure you can come up with one."

Gary sat erect. "Who wants it?"

"A man I met at an exclusive club in Westwood last night."

"This guy you met for the first time just happened to mention he was in the market for a Stinger?"

"No, no, no. A sub-source of mine told me about him. I met him and struck up a conversation. Before I knew it, Stinger missiles came up."

"You got some sub-sources, Robaire."

"You're not the only one with informants, you know," he chuckled. His stomach bounced when he laughed. He didn't dare tell Gary who his sub-source was. At least not now.

"So, what did you tell him?"

Robaire shrugged his shoulders, implying it was no big deal. "I told him I knew someone who may be able to find one."

"What did he say to that?"

"He said he'd be interested in meeting such a person."

"Did he say why he wants a Stinger?"

"No. He claims to be the middleman for the deal."

"For whom? Any idea who the buyer is?"

"No, but you can wager whoever he is must be a Colombian."

"What makes you think so?"

"He said he had just returned from a trip to Bogota. Consequently, I can only surmise the buyer is a Colombian."

Gary leaned back in the booth. He was intrigued since he had read DEA Intelligence reports about the Revolutionary Armed Forces of Colombia, FARC, attempting to get their hands on military armament. The FARC was the last of a dying breed of Marxists who wanted to turn Colombia into a Communist state. It also protected cocaine laboratories.

"And you think this guy will trade drugs for it?"

"I told him my connection preferred cash but would take product, of course." His smile revealed capped teeth.

Gary laughed. "And?"

"He was non-committal, and I didn't want to press him on it this soon."

Gary sipped his iced tea as he thought. "He didn't even hint who the buyer was or why he wanted it?" He produced a notebook from inside his sports coat pocket. "What's this guy's name?"

"I only know him as Amir."

"That's it, just Amir?"

"Yes. It would have been improper of me to ask him to produce his California driver's license, don't you agree?"

"It seems to me you could have learned his entire name from your sub-source, especially since he wants you to find him a Stinger missile," Gary said louder than he wanted. He looked for the reaction of the people around them. A man seated next to them enjoying his lunch appeared interested. Gary leaned forward and whispered, "You know the drill."

"In time, Gary," Robaire whispered back. "I'll get his full name and license plate number for you when I see him tonight. We're having dinner."

"Say, what kind of name is Amir?"

"I believe he is Iranian."

Gary got his pen ready. "Okay, what's this guy look like?"

"What's the name of the British actor who played Gandhi?"

"You mean Ben Kingsley?"

That's the one. He looks like a taller Ben Kingsley with bad teeth. Too much smoking. Thin build. Taller than you. He's suave, and very cosmopolitan."

"How old?"

Robaire adjusted his gold pinkie ring with a one-carat diamond stud before sipping his drink again. "Late forties or early fifties. He dresses exquisitely, carries a Mont Blanc fountain pen, and wears a gold presidential Rolex, the whole works. That's the best I can do at the moment."

"Does he speak English?"

"Yes, excellent. Better than most Americans, I might add."

"I wouldn't doubt it." Gary paused a moment to look at his notes. "Okay, so he's an Iranian Ben Kingsley look-a-like who wears an expensive watch, carries a fancy pen, and lives on the west side. That really narrows it down in this town." Gary tucked his notebook away in his jacket pocket. "Do you know Los Angeles has the largest Iranian population of any city outside Teheran?"

"I do now," Robaire said. "Say, you should be on *Jeopardy!*"

"Maybe I will someday."

"Patience, Gary. Remember, patience is a virtue."

"I lost mine with you long ago," Gary said with a wink.

They laughed, to the annoyance of the man at the table next to them.

• • •

Robaire Assaly listened to the news about President Bush's State of the Union Address while driving back to Los Angeles. The president implied the U.S. intended to attack Iraq. His ringing cell phone interrupted his concentration.

"How did your meeting with Lowery go?"

"Fine. Just fine, Ms. Cohen. I laid out the groundwork just as you ordered."

"Never mention my name on the phone again. Do you understand?"

"Yes, of course. Sorry." Her reaction and tone of voice took him aback.

After composing herself, she asked, "Does he suspect anything?"

Robaire laughed as he merged his Mercedes onto the Golden State Freeway. "No. Nothing, my dear."

"Good."

"Just as you expected, he wants me to proceed. He's intrigued why an Iranian is interested in one of those things."

"Uh, ha," she said.

"To whet his appetite, I told him the man had just returned from Bogota, which you and I know is a total fabrication."

This news caused June to pause a moment before saying, "Don't get too cute, Robaire. You've got to follow my instructions to the letter. He must never know who he's dealing with. Your mother's and sister's lives depend on it."

"You don't have to remind me. That's the only reason I'm getting involved in this sordid affair. Nothing to worry about, my dear. He has no idea the seed has been planted. He doesn't suspect a thing."

CHAPTER 4

Gary Lowery awoke the next day at seven a.m. to the sound of his beeping alarm clock. He reached over to the nightstand, turning it off and fumbled to find the remote to switch on *Good Morning America*.

The lead news story was about military reserve call ups for a potential war with Iraq, and a few tidbits on the war on terrorism, as had been the case ever since September eleven.

He rolled out of bed and shuffled to the bathroom mirror in his one-bedroom condominium. He noticed the bags under his eyes were growing larger. His messy, full head of black hair, slowly turning gray, looked like an exploded mattress after tossing and turning in his sleep. He became accustomed to people thinking he was at least five years older than his actual forty-two years. He realized he'd be forty-three next month and would look fifty by then. That wasn't too bad, was it? Not like having the clap or AIDS.

• • •

When Gary arrived at the office, there was already a message from Robaire in his voice mail. "It's me. I have news."

Gary punched his speed dialer, and Robaire answered the phone on the second ring.

"Hello."

"Well, what happened last night?"

"I met with our new friend, and I have his license plate number for you."

"Good, shoot."

"It's a California plate." He recited it to him. "He drives a white Jaguar S-Type."

"Okay," Gary said, writing the information down.

"And his last name is Rahimi," Robaire said.

"Good. Good."

"He's an accountant and has a business on Wilshire Boulevard."

"What did he say about the item?"

"He's desperate for one of those items we discussed and needs it by the end of the month." Like all people in the drug business, he had developed a habit of talking in generalities over the telephone in case someone else was listening.

"Did he mention why it's needed?"

"No."

"That's something you've got to find out," Gary insisted. "But don't push him too hard."

"When I call him today, I'll say you want to meet him to ensure he isn't an FBI or ATF agent. I'll assure him you aren't and after you have a feel for him, you'll make your decision about selling him the merchandise."

"Good. He shouldn't balk at that."

"No, I don't think he will either. Quite frankly, I think he'll be expecting it," he said. "When do you want me to set up the meeting?"

"Tomorrow afternoon. It's going to take some time to get things rolling, so we need to make it sooner rather than later. Do you have his telephone number?"

"Yes, and his pager number." He gave Gary the numbers.

"All right. Call him and tell him your contact will arrive in town tomorrow afternoon to meet him. Let's make it at the Bonaventure. We'll hook up in the lobby and later go up to a room to talk privately."

"What time?"

"Make it four. Tell him I'm driving down from Barstow and won't arrive until then. We'll meet in the lounge just across from the registration desk. You know the one." Gary opened the bottom drawer to his desk and flipped through one of four different undercover wallets in various stages of wear. "By the way, what did you tell him about me?"

"I used the same cover story you've used in the past. You know, the one where you're a crooked civil servant who works for the army at Fort Irwin and has access to such items, assuming the price was right. I didn't tell him anything else."

"That's a little more detail than he needed to know," Gary said as he picked up another wallet and examined it. "But we can work around it. Did you mention a name?"

"No."

The wallet contained various credit cards and a driver's license in the name of Gary Locklear. "Good. Let's make it Gary Locklear, but don't mention a last name."

"Whatever you say."

"See you tomorrow." Gary hung up and leaned way back in his desk chair and stretched. He felt jazzed about meeting an Iranian arms dealer who may have ties to drug dealers or terrorists. He was experiencing the rush all drug agents get when they hear the makings of a great case. The investigation would be challenging, and he knew it. This operation will make a great war story to add to all his others.

Gary knew it was time to let his supervisor know what he was up to. For a seasoned agent, he suddenly acquired a rookie's bounce in his step as he walked into the boss's office and knocked on the door frame.

"Hey, Bill. Got something for you."

The fifty-something silver haired mustachioed DEA supervisory special agent, who was one bad day away from retiring, kept looking at the report he was reading. "Come in. What's up?"

"I met with my ace, number one CI, yesterday."

Without looking up he said, "Let me guess, Robaire Assaly?"

"The one and only. He's got a guy who wants to trade dope for a, get this . . ." he paused for effect. "A Stinger missile."

Bill Brownlee looked up at Gary for the first time. "No shit! Who?" He took off his reading glasses and dropped them on the desk.

"Don't know yet, but he's an Iranian he met in Westwood. I've got his license plate and phone numbers so far. Robaire's arranging a U-C meeting with him tomorrow at the Bonaventure."

He paused and tugged on his mustache. "What's this guy want with a Stinger? Is he a terrorist?"

"I don't know. I'm working on it. Can you make the group available for tomorrow?"

"Of course. Anything else you need?"

"Nope. I'll keep you posted, boss."

Bill Brownlee followed Gary into the large open space outside his office and started detailing agents to help in tomorrow's surveillance.

Gary picked the Bonaventure as the location of the undercover meeting because the chief of security was a retired Pasadena PD sergeant he knew named Joseph Montoya. Gary called him.

"Security, Montoya." Gary could hear the Rush Limbaugh radio program in the background.

"This is Gary Lowery. How're you doing?

"Fine, Gary. What's up?"

"Need a favor."

"Name it."

"Got any rooms available for tomorrow?"

"I'll check."

"I need two adjacent rooms."

"Why? Got another dope deal you want to do here?"

"Yeah, sort of, and I'd like you to play a minor role in it this time, Joe."

"Fantastic! I'd love to. What's this one about?"

"I can't go into the details right now, I'm swamped."

"Okay, compadre, I'll get right back to you about the rooms."

Gary hung up, confident his friend would come through with the rooms even if it meant canceling someone's reservation.

Salvador Reyes, a 30-year-old eight-year veteran agent, walked up to Gary's desk. "I've got the license plate info you wanted." His hair was combed back and was always neat looking. In college, he played baseball well enough to interest a few MLB scouts. His father abandoned any hope of his son becoming a professional baseball player when Sal hired on with the DEA. "It comes back to a 2001 Jag registered to an Amir Ra-he-me, spelled R-A-H-I-M-I. What kinda name's that?"

"Iranian. Where does he live?" Gary asked.

"He's got a West L.A. address. I checked the *Thomas Guide*. It's near UCLA."

"Did you run him through our system?"

"Someone else is doing that."

"Thanks, Sal." He dropped the computer printouts on Gary's desk before leaving.

Another agent yelled from across the room, "Call for you on line three, Gary."

He punched the button. "Gary Lowery."

"It's Joe. I've got two rooms reserved for you tomorrow."

"Great. I'll need to gain access to the rooms in the morning, is that okay?"

"No problema, amigo. I'll have housekeeping do them first thing. What do you intend to do?"

"Like last time, I'll have a guy from my tech group meet you early tomorrow to explain everything. He'll be bringing some equipment to place in the rooms."

"I'll be here. Tell him to have me paged if I'm not in my office. I might have something real important to do, like chase off some homeless Democrats." Joe called anyone he didn't like a Democrat because they couldn't possibly be Republican.

"Sure will, Joe. Thanks a lot." Gary hung up, called his technical surveillance agents, and explained to them what he needed.

CHAPTER 5

'Good. Let's make it Gary Locklear, but don't mention a last name.'

'Whatever you say.'

'See you tomorrow.' Robaire pressed the stop button on the cassette recorder and looked over at June. He thought if Jennifer Aniston had a better-looking sister in her early thirties with larger breasts, this was her. He exhaled a large plume of smoke from his Montecristo cigar. "That was our conversation this morning, my dear."

"And Rahimi still thinks he's dealing with some army civilian employee who has larceny in his heart?"

"Absolutely. He thinks Gary's an arms dealer on the side. Rahimi will never think he's a DEA agent."

"He'd better not," she said while rewinding the tape.

"I'm curious, June. How did a nice girl like you get involved with the likes of Rahimi?"

"I'm CIA, remember? We know many people."

"So, it seems."

"A little birdie told me he's in the market for a Stinger and he would be at that club the other night. That's all you needed to know."

"Is that so?"

"Yessir, it is," she said. "Just remember, your mission is to get Lowery to deliver a Stinger to the man so we can find out what he intends to do with it. Keep recording your conversations with Lowery. I want to know everything he says."

"If you insist."

"I do! We can leave nothing to chance." She pushed the eject button, removed the cassette tape, and replaced it with a fresh one. "Don't be surprised if you see me at the Bonaventure tomorrow."

"At this point, ma'am, nothing will surprise me," Robaire said.

"Of course, you know enough to ignore me if you see me. We can't allow Lowery or the Iranian to make the connection between us."

"You are hard to ignore, June," he said with one eyebrow raised. "But as you wish."

She walked to the door of his small, sparsely furnished apartment. The furniture looked like there had been a sale at Good Will. "Call me on my cell if there are any changes. Otherwise, I'll see you at the Bonaventure."

"Goodbye, my dear," he said with an irritating smirk.

"Get this straight, Robaire. I'm not your dear," she said. "This is strictly business. Always remember that. This is a stressful job, Robaire. Just keep your end of the bargain, and your family's troubles are over." She walked down the few steps to the sidewalk. Her heels clicked as she walked to the street and got into a fire engine red Acura.

Robaire muttered an unmentionable under his breath as he slammed and locked the front door. He was anxious about his mother and sister and found it hard not to show any emotion in front of Gary. Not doing so was the most challenging part of his dilemma.

Robaire took out his cell phone and dialed his mother's number again with the same results: no answer.

· · ·

As June drove, she brushed her shoulder-length blond hair away from her light blue eyes and sighed. She was believing she could pull it off, and the DEA would provide a Stinger missile for the Iranian. June wrinkled her brow as she thought of what could go wrong, what snafus might happen.

She had sharp north European facial features, modeled for a while during her college years, and was now in her early thirties. June usually wore conservative business attire complete with high heels. Her jacket concealed a small Sig-Sauer 9 mm pistol in a shoulder holster. Three weeks prior, she received her ten-year service pin from the CIA.

• • •

By 3:45 p.m., the next day, surveillance was established in the lobby of the Bonaventure Hotel in downtown Los Angeles. Some DEA agents were posing as happy hour customers in the lobby lounge, while others rolled around empty suitcases as if they were hotel guests. Gary had given out the driver's license photo of Amir Rahimi he received from the Department of Motor Vehicles. They all knew what Gary's informant, Robaire Assaly, looked like from working with him many times in the past. Same place, different crook.

• • •

Sal Reyes checked his Seiko and saw it was 4:10 p.m. Typical for an informant to be late. He suddenly noticed Robaire and another much thinner man coming up the escalator to the lobby level. Visions of Laurel and Hardy came to his mind. Amir Rahimi *did* look like a taller Ben Kingsley, as Gary said Robaire described him, with his olive complexion and prominent nose. Both men were dressed in expensive suits and Italian loafers, except Robaire was not wearing socks.

Sal saw them walk to the lounge and find an empty booth. Lucky find, Sal thought, since the early Friday afternoon crowd was arriving. Sal removed his cell phone from his belt and dialed Gary.

• • •

Gary answered while driving around the block. "They're here," Sal said, and flipped the cover down on the Nextel, hanging up. Gary didn't want to be in the bar waiting for them to create the illusion he wasn't too anxious. He drove into the underground parking lot of the forty-story hotel, which stood out as a jewel among the downtown buildings. The valet gave him a ticket stub for his government-seized BMW. He ascended the escalators to the lobby, seeing the decorative pools of water and the glass elevators resembling spaceships from a Jules Verne novel. His eye caught just a glimpse of an attractive blond with long, athletic legs, and high heels. It was June, playing with a swizzle stick in her drink, seated alone a few tables away from Robaire and Rahimi.

Robaire saw Gary and motioned him over. Gary walked up and shook hands with Robaire.

"Gary, this is Amir, the man I told you about."

"Pleased to meet you," Gary said, placing his prop overnight bag on the floor before sitting down next to Robaire.

"The feeling is mutual," Amir Rahimi said with a combination of Middle Eastern and Oxford accent.

"How was your drive?" Robaire inquired for the sake of the cover story.

"Not too bad, considering it's a Friday. I got out of Barstow about one o'clock, so I made good time."

A cocktail waitress appeared and inquired about drinks.

"A double Stoli on the rocks with a twist for me," Robaire ordered. "What will you have, Amir?"

"A tall Schweppes tonic."

"And you, sir?" she asked Gary.

"Just a Miller Genuine Draft, please," he said. She smiled and scurried off.

"How have you been?" Gary asked his informant.

"Fine. I'm always looking for business opportunities, you know."

"Speaking of which, what is your business, Amir?" Gary asked.

"I'm a CPA. I do taxes and handle business matters for members of the Iranian community in Los Angeles, and also offer immigration advice and counseling."

"Are you an attorney?"

"No," he said with a smile," revealing his nicotine-stained teeth, "but I have many lawyer friends. How about you, Gary? What line of work are you in?"

"I'm a supervisory logistician at Fort Irwin. That makes me in charge of all the army equipment running through the National Training Center. Everything from beans, blankets, and bullets." Fort Irwin is a massive training center in the middle of the Mojave Desert where tank brigades train before deploying to the Middle East.

"Interesting. Robaire tells me you may have some excess inventory?"

"Occasionally," Gary smiled, glancing away for a moment as if to see who might be watching.

"I'm glad to hear that," Rahimi said.

The server returned with the drinks and placed them on napkins. She left the bill on the table near Robaire, who shoved it toward Gary. "Thank you, my dear," Robaire said.

"How's the weather been here?" Gary asked.

"Pleasant," Robaire said. "About right for February."

"It's been cool in the desert. The rain cooled things off yesterday." Gary was glad he had studied the weather section of the *Pasadena Star News* that morning.

"How long have you been in this country?" Gary asked, sensing Rahimi didn't mind talking about it.

"Since 1983."

"Tell him how you got here," Robaire suggested, having heard the story the other night.

"He would not be interested," Rahimi replied.

"Sure, I would," Gary said.

Rahimi interlaced his fingers and placed his hands on the table. He looked down for a moment and then straight into Gary's eyes. "I was a Foreign Service National employee at the American Embassy in Teheran when the Iranians overran it in 1979."

"No kidding?" Gary said. "That must have been one hell of an experience."

"It was. The so-called students thought I was a traitor and didn't quite know what to do with me. I explained to them I was an accountant in the administrative section of the embassy, but it didn't matter. They took me prisoner with the rest of the staff. They let me go after eighty-nine days of captivity."

Gary whistled, "Damn, eighty-nine days!"

"A few years later, the Swiss Embassy arranged a flight for me out of Iran, and I was later allowed to migrate to the United States, where I sought political asylum. I can never go back there now. Not after what happened."

"That's quite a story," Gary said. "Maybe things will work out over there later."

"I hope so. But I'm not optimistic. The Ayatollahs will allow no one who has tasted freedom to return to the country."

"I see," Gary nodded, wishing the son-of-a-bitch had stayed in Iran.

"We didn't come here to discuss politics," Robaire said. "We're here for business, yes?"

"Of course," Gary agreed.

"Yes, business," Rahimi said finishing his Schweppes.

"Speaking of which, I'll check in and we can talk in my room," Gary suggested while standing up. He was ready to walk to the registration desk when Rahimi placed his hand on Gary's forearm to stop him.

"Yes?"

"Sit down, please. Let me get the room. I'd feel more comfortable that way."

"But I'm the one spending the night here and the one who suggested it."

"I insist, Gary. Let it be my treat. This way, we can all speak freely."

Gary shrugged and sat back down. He expected this from a world-class criminal. "Okay, if you insist."

"I do. Have a pleasant chat with Robaire, and I'll return shortly." Rahimi slid out of the booth, buttoned the middle button of his suit coat, and walked to the registration desk under the watchful eyes of Sal and June.

"He doesn't trust us," Robaire said. "He wants to make sure the room isn't wired."

"I wouldn't make a bet on it," Gary replied, winking.

• • •

When Rahimi arrived at the registration desk, a male hotel employee greeted him wearing a nametag that read: J. Montoya.

"Yes, sir, how may I help you?" the distinguished registration clerk asked.

"I need a room for one night."

"Yes, sir. We have a room with a queen-size bed available. Do you prefer smoking or non-smoking?"

"Uh . . .smoking." He didn't care if his new friend Gary smoked or not, but he intended to.

"What credit card will you be using?"

"This will be cash."

"Very well," Joe said, handing him the registration card as he glanced at the lobby bar. "That will be two hundred and thirty-five dollars, including tax, in advance."

"Of course." He removed a small wad of one-hundred-dollar bills from his left front pants pocket and peeled off three, placing them on the counter. Joe Montoya took the bills, put them in a cash drawer, and removed the change as Rahimi filled out the registration card.

"Here's your change, Mister . . ."

"Cangor," Rahimi said.

"Mister Cangor. Check out time is eleven o'clock. You'll be in room 1704. Take the yellow tower elevator over there," Joe said while pointing. "Here's your key."

Rahimi remained silent, and smiled back.

"Thank you, sir." While Rahimi walked back to the lounge, Joe couldn't help but grin about his successful undercover role. He had performed it flawlessly.

•   •   •

Gary asked his informant, who had almost finished his double, "Do you think he's comfortable now?"

"Yes, or otherwise he'd be gone. We'll find out in a minute."

After a momentary pause, Gary asked, "Do you think he really was an employee at the U.S. Embassy in Iran?"

"It wouldn't surprise me. It seems to fit," Robaire said, glancing over to June who was glaring back at him as she nibbled on goldfish crackers.

•   •   •

Rahimi returned to the booth and showed them the key card. "Are you gentlemen ready?" he asked, gulping his tonic water in preparation to leave.

"Lead the way," Robaire said.

Gary picked up his shoulder bag after leaving a wad of cash for the drinks, followed Rahimi and Robaire into the elevator, and glanced around for Sal and his crew. One of the surveillance agents passed by while they waited for the doors to close, and another one followed behind.

Rahimi pushed number 17. It elevated them through the lobby's ceiling and skimmed along the outside of one of the four circular towers of rooms. The ride provided them a magnificent view of downtown Los Angeles and the busy Harbor freeway.

•   •   •

Sal went to a house phone and called room 1706. A man answered, "Yeah?"

"They're on their way up."

"Okay." The agent hung up and started the video equipment. Four agents and Bill Brownlee hovered around the television monitor to watch the upcoming undercover meeting. Within a minute, they heard the door to room 1704 open through the speaker on the monitor.

Gary and Robaire walked in, followed by Amir Rahimi, who locked the door behind them. He walked to the far glass wall and shut the curtains as Robaire took off his suit jacket and hung it up in the closet, leaving the folding closet doors open. Being conscious of the camera hidden in the lamp on the end table to the bed, Gary turned on all the lights in the room and plopped on the mattress and leaned his back against the headboard. The wide-angled lens of the concealed camera captured Rahimi when he sat in one of the two available chairs.

Rahimi crossed his legs European style, knee over knee, and lit a cigarette. "Gary, in our business, you can never be too careful. Do you agree?"

"I couldn't agree more," Gary said.

"I'm glad to hear you say that. Then you won't take offense if I search you for a wire."

"A wire? You think I'm wearing a fucking wire?"

Robaire's asshole puckered. His jacket in the closet contained a digital recorder June had provided him. Please, Lord. Don't let him search me, or I'm dead, and so is my mother and sister, he thought.

"I don't know what to think. That's why I must make sure," he said. "We have to remove any doubt from one another if we are to become business partners."

"I thought you only agreed to this meeting because you trusted us?"

"Don't misunderstand, Gary. Robaire speaks highly of you, but I must be sure. I've only known him for a few days, and we've only just met. I must be able to tell my client you are beyond reproach."

Without another word, Gary stood up and raised his hands above his shoulders. Rahimi walked behind him, touched the outside of his clothing, and used both hands to run down his legs. He reached between Gary's legs and felt around for any concealed objects, making Gary uncomfortable, even though he did not have a wire or weapon on him. Gary did not need to be wired since the room already was, thank

God. Robaire checked the contents of the overnight bag. He only found a change of clothes and a shaving kit. Nothing unusual.

"Empty your pockets, please."

Gary let out a groan. "Is this necessary?"

"You will only have to do this once," Rahimi assured him.

Gary removed his keys, change, wallet, and handkerchief from his pants pockets and tossed them on the bed. He pulled the pockets to his navy-blue wool slacks inside out. Rahimi picked up the wallet and examined it. He counted forty-six dollars in currency. He pulled out four cards in Gary Locklear's name: American Express Gold card, Visa, Mastercard and a Department of Defense Civilian Identification card. The wallet contained Gary's undercover California Driver's license, which listed a Barstow Post Office Box as his address. Rahimi placed everything back into the wallet and handed it to Gary.

"I'm satisfied," Rahimi said. "Thank you for being so understanding."

Robaire let out a heavy sigh.

"Not so fast," Gary said, faking insult. "Let's see what you're carrying."

Robaire froze again, hoping Gary would leave well enough alone.

"If you insist," Rahimi said. He emptied the contents of his pockets on the bed and removed his suit coat, revealing a blue steel Walther PPK .380 caliber semi-automatic pistol inside his waistband. His belt had a cell phone attached to it. Gary saw the gun, as did the surveillance agents, but they didn't react.

"Why do you need that? I thought we were all gentlemen here." Gary said.

The sight of the gun further disturbed Robaire, who didn't expect Rahimi to be armed.

"One can never be too careful in our business," Rahimi said.

• • •

The agents in the surveillance room, who were suited up in their bulletproof vests and raid jackets, stood up and hovered near the door leading to Gary's adjoining room, guns drawn, waiting for any signal from Brownlee that Gary was in trouble.

Gary tried to ignore the weapon. He ran his hands down Rahimi's pant legs and made a cursory check of his crotch, which made them both cringe. He took Rahimi's wallet from the bed and saw Amir Rahimi's California driver's license with the same photo DMV had provided. Everything seemed in order, but he went through the motions anyway by looking through each compartment of the wallet the same as Rahimi had.

"Well, I guess you're not the FBI," Gary said with a smile as he handed the wallet back to him. Rahimi smiled back. Gary thought Rahimi's smile illustrated why parents insist their children brush their teeth.

"I hope I wasn't too rough on you, my friend, but I had to be sure," Rahimi said as they put their property back into their pockets. "You understand the necessity, I hope. If not, I will be going as we have nothing to discuss."

"I understand, Amir. Have a seat. My feathers will be smoothed when we reach an agreement," Gary said as he crawled back onto the bed. "That's why we're here, isn't it? To reach an agreement about a certain piece of equipment?"

Robaire relaxed, but only a little as it wasn't over yet. He stood to walk to the room's mini bar.

"Indeed. Assuming you can deliver," Rahimi said.

"He can deliver, all right," Robaire intervened while observing the mini-bar's contents, disappointed to see the hotel only offered Absolut vodka and not Stoli. "I have complete confidence in him."

"And I'm having confidence myself," Rahimi remarked.

Robaire thought he had dodged a major bullet with that remark.

Amir Rahimi took out another cigarette and lit it with his gold-plated S.T. Dupont lighter. He took a long drag while holding the cigarette between his right index finger and thumb. "Gary, I need something, and I'm told you can supply me with it."

"Go on," Gary said.

"I know people willing to pay top dollar for an American piece of equipment. A Stinger missile, to be precise. What do you say to that?"

"I don't think your buyer knows what he's getting himself into," Gary said.

Rahimi hesitated a moment at that remark and asked, "Oh? Why do you say that?"

"It's because a Stinger requires training and practice to master. The army's Stinger school is eight weeks long."

Rahimi shrugged his shoulders. "So?"

"So, your buyer needs to know he can't just pick one of these things out of the box and expect to hit a moving target at Mach one. It takes training and practice, which means they'll need more than one, and that's going to get awfully expensive," Gary said.

Rahimi tried to reassure Gary. "These things have already been considered. There's no need for you to worry about such details."

"I just don't want any misunderstanding with your buyer. I don't want any strangers knocking on my door in the middle of the night looking for a refund when it's their damn fault for not knowing how to operate the thing to begin with."

"This will not happen. I assure you," Rahimi said while exposing his palms in a gesture of sincerity. "The buyer assures me he has trained personnel available to operate the weapon. He merely requires the device."

"How does your buyer intend to pay for it?" Robaire asked, cracking open his second small bottle of Absolut vodka and pouring it into a glass. "And don't forget about my finder's fee."

"You'll receive fair compensation, my friend. No need to worry." He looked at Gary. "What is your price, Mister Locklear? Let me hear your offer."

Robaire thought that was a clever move because the first one to mention a price loses in a negotiation like this.

"What are you willing to pay?" Gary countered.

Rahimi sat holding the cigarette. "My buyer will pay one hundred thousand dollars."

"Ha. You must be joking!" Gary said and turned to Robaire with a look of mock surprise and then back to Rahimi. "Keep in mind I'm the one taking all the risk. It's my ass on the line, not yours. I don't want to spend the rest of my life being somebody's butt boy in a federal pen somewhere. These things are tough to come by, especially since a lot of them are being shipped out to the Gulf."

"I don't want to see you go to prison either, my friend." Rahimi took another drag from his cigarette and said, "Tell me what you consider a fair price, Gary? What is your counteroffer?"

"That baby's gonna cost you a minimum of one million dollars, U.S.," Gary said. "Cash. And that doesn't count expenses," he added. "That needs to be taken care of up front. And Robaire's finder fee is on you, not me," he said poking his own chest with his index finger. "There may be palms to grease and inventory sheets to fudge. The whole thing will cost your people around one point two."

"That's a substantial amount of money," Rahimi said without blinking.

"That's because there's a war against terror going on in case you haven't heard. And it looks like we're about to invade Iraq. Security's so tight you can't fart without the Army CID smelling it."

"If your people can't come up with the money, tell them to go find a Stinger elsewhere," Robaire said.

"No need for that," Gary said. "My shop just got audited and inventoried. Those bean counters won't be back until the war is over. By then, there'll be so much ash and trash from all the training going on, they won't be able to discern what was expended, lost in transit, or sent in for reloading."

"Good to hear, Gary," Rahimi said.

"If that's too much cash, I'll consider something in trade," Gary suggested, thinking about drugs.

"What do you have in mind?" Rahimi inquired.

GREGORY D. LEE 39

"Coke, and lots of it. I figured at least eighty kilos for the weapon, and another twenty for my risk of turning it into cash. And I still need the two hundred thousand for expense money upfront. Plus, I'd want a couple of kilos up front to make sure I will not get stiffed."

"That's impossible," Rahimi said. "What makes you think I can acquire that amount of cocaine?"

Gary was surprised. "Well, I assumed from talking to Robaire you were buying the Stinger for people in South America."

Rahimi waved an index finger at Gary, "Assume nothing, my friend. Those people are murdering thieves, and I want nothing to do with them."

Gary shot a glance at Robaire, who was unusually quiet while nursing his drink. "Well, I just thought . . ."

"You thought wrong, Mister Locklear. Cash is the only term of this agreement. Getting it is my problem. Getting the missile is yours."

"Then cash it is," Gary said, trying to recover from his surprise.

"What do I receive for one point two million dollars?" Rahimi asked.

Gary sat on the edge of the bed. "I guarantee delivery and authenticity. You'll get exactly what you ordered - no last-minute surprises. No bullshit. You'll be able to examine it to make sure it's the real deal before any money changes hands. Once you're satisfied, I expect payment on the spot. I don't want to dick around holding the goods while the feds figure out what's going on."

"That's reasonable," Rahimi replied, and stared at Gary. "Keep in mind my buyer will become extremely agitated if I enter an agreement on his behalf and the other party does not live up to his commitment. Retribution is a terrible thing."

"Why do you bring that up?" Robaire whined.

Rahimi narrowed his eyes narrowed as he stared at Robaire. "I don't want any misunderstanding about what will happen if Gary commits to delivering the missile and later reneges. Things are in motion which demand the item be delivered on time."

"What things?" Gary asked.

"That's not your concern," Rahimi replied.

"When do you need it?" Robaire slurred.

"By the end of the month. I must take delivery by then. Tell me now if you cannot deliver so I can search for another supplier."

"I can do it," Gary said, "provided the expense money's up front. Is that going to be a problem?"

Rahimi laughed. "Hardly, my friend. I think we can entertain your proposition." He stood and adjusted the gun in his waistband. "Stay here please while I go to the lobby and make a private phone call. I'll be right back." Rahimi retrieved his suit coat and left without another word, shutting the door behind him.

•   •   •

Robaire looked at Gary and in a low volume asked, "Who do you think the buyer is?"

Gary shrugged. "I don't know. If he's not a drug dealer, he's got to be a terrorist. Maybe the buyer's bin Laden himself. That's why money is no object. He's probably calling Osama right now telling him the Stinger will cost two million dollars and pocket the difference. That's nothing for him."

•   •   •

An agent in the adjoining room called Sal's cell phone to alert him and the other surveillance team members stationed in the lobby, Rahimi was heading in their direction. Another agent spotted Rahimi at a bank of pay telephones and walked up and faked using the phone next to him. All he could overhear was Rahimi speaking what he believed was Farsi or Arabic, but he couldn't be sure which one.

The agent watched Rahimi finish his phone conversation and returned to the elevator. As he waited for the car to pick him up, he noticed June still seated at the table in the lounge, applying a fresh coat of bright red lipstick.

• • •

To Robaire's relief, two quick knocks came on the door. Robaire looked through the fisheye peephole and saw it was Rahimi.

Robaire opened the door, and Rahimi strutted in, rubbing his palms together. "I have good news, gentlemen. The buyer has accepted your terms. We will all be celebrating in a couple of weeks."

"If the money's right." Gary emphasized.

"It will be my friend. I can promise you that," Rahimi said as he lit another cigarette.

Suddenly three sharp knocks came from the door. "Are we expecting someone?" Gary asked.

"That should be my people," Amir Rahimi said, springing out of his chair.

"What the hell?" Gary said. "You didn't mention we were gonna have company."

Rahimi peered through the peephole before opening the door. Tariq and Iqbal Khan entered, each dressed in a new pair of Calvin Klein jeans. Tariq wore a black Guess tee shirt while carrying a large, prominent leather lawyer's briefcase. Iqbal sported a Polo oxford shirt half un-tucked and was holding a cell phone. A bandage was visible on Tariq's right thumb. They both looked as out of place as two rodeo clowns at an opera.

Rahimi commanded something to the men in Urdu. Tariq swung the heavy case on the bed and took a couple of steps back. Rahimi manipulated the combination locks and flipped open the flaps, dumping the contents of the case onto the bed. Robaire's eyes widened when he saw ten bundles of what turned out to be one-hundred-dollar bills. Each bundle contained one hundred thousand dollars.

Rahimi pointed to the money. "There it is gentlemen. One million dollars. I'm showing you the money now as a sign of my good faith. I wanted to prove to you we have the funds and are serious about doing business."

"You've convinced me," Robaire said fanning the bills of one bundle.

"I had it nearby just in case," Rahimi said. "Go ahead and count it. Fan through each bundle to satisfy yourselves they are, as you American's say, all Benjamins."

Gary picked a bundle at random and saw it was comprised of ten smaller bundles, each secured with its own rubber band. He walked up to the lamp as if to get better light, fanned the edges of each smaller bundle, and saw they were indeed all one-hundred-dollar bills. After his examination, Tariq gathered the bundles and neatly stacked them back in the briefcase.

"Impressive," Gary said. "When do I get my expense money?"

Rahimi reached into the case and tossed two bundles to Gary. He took another stack and handed it to Robaire. "Here's your finder's fee, my friend. Refundable if Gary doesn't deliver," he said.

Rahimi snapped his fingers and rattled off something causing Tariq to shut the briefcase and spin the numbers on the combination locks. Rahimi spouted off some other commands in Urdu, and the two men obediently left the room with the briefcase without a word. "There's your expense money," Rahimi said.

"Perfect," Gary answered. "I like your no-bullshit style, Amir."

"Then it's agreed, yes? Deliver the missile to me by the end of the month," he ordered.

Gary looked at his watch for the date: the fourth. Twenty-four days to get his hands on a Stinger. "I'm sure I can manage it."

Rahimi buttoned his suit coat. "I hope for your sake you can, Mister Locklear, now that you've accepted the expense money. I'll be in touch with you through Robaire on how the delivery will take place. Good day to you both," he said. He shut the door on the way out behind his two accomplices.

Robaire exhaled a sigh of relief.

Gary locked the door and looked at Robaire, who was holding his stack of money. "See Gary, what did I tell you? I knew he was good for it."

Gary put his forefinger to his lips. "Shush! The recorder might still be on."

"What recorder?"

"This entire room is wired for audio and video."

"You clever devil!" Robaire said, now feeling relaxed, thanks to the vodka. "I should have known. You've thought of everything!"

Gary hesitated before saying, "I hope so."

CHAPTER 6

Bill Brownlee was elated when Rahimi gave one of his undercover agents three-hundred-thousand dollars with one million more to come. Too bad the other seven hundred grand had to walk, he thought. Or should he be elated? Questions surfaced the next day from the agents in the group about Rahimi, especially from Sal.

"What happened to the Colombians?" Sal asked.

"How should I know?" Gary replied.

"And where did those other two clowns come from? They must be Iranians because they sure weren't Colombians."

"It seems your new friend is shopping for a Middle Eastern terrorist," Sal said. "That entire story about Colombians was bullshit."

"Hey, Gary," Brownlee yelled from his office. "Get yourself in here."

Gary hurried to his boss' office and asked, "What's up, Bill?"

"That cable you sent out got everyone's attention at headquarters. The Special Agent in Charge is getting phone calls from all the pencil pushers at headquarters wanting more information," Bill said. "The Chief of Operations called her, wanting to know why an Iranian wants a Stinger missile."

"So do I, Bill."

"And, the Chief said he notified the FBI because terrorism is their baby, not ours."

"Well, I guess that was inevitable," Gary said, not too happy to have his case turned over to the FBI.

• • •

The next day after lunch, two FBI agents arrived at the DEA office and the receptionist asked them to wait in the lobby. After Gary walked into the crowded reception area, he immediately picked out the two FBI agents. It was obvious. They were dressed in dark suits, white shirts, and conservative ties. One, a black man, was carrying a leather portfolio. His partner, a Caucasian, wore wing-tipped shoes. Gary walked toward them with his hand outstretched. "Hi, I'm Gary Lowery."

"Hello," the white agent said as they both stood up. "I'm Special Agent Mark Olson and this is my partner, Special Agent Calvin Rowe."

"Glad to meet you both. You didn't have to dress up for the occasion."

"Being assigned to the JTTF, we normally wear Levi's and tennis shoes because we're constantly conducting surveillances, but we had a grand jury appearance this morning," Rowe said. "We just indicted some idiot who wanted to join al-Qaeda and was ready to fly to Afghanistan. We snatched him up at LAX yesterday."

"That's great," Gary said. "Follow me back to my office."

They walked down the stairs and the long hallways of the nineteenth floor of the federal building in the civic center of Los Angeles. The three entered a large open bay area where a dozen desks sat in no particular pattern. Bill Brownlee was the only one with his own office. Gary's seniority entitled him to a desk near a corner window affording a commanding view of downtown. On a clear day, he could see the famous Hollywood sign and the television transmitters on top of Mount Wilson.

"Nice view," Olson said. "This beats the hell out of our office in Westwood."

"Have a seat," Gary said. "Sometimes you can almost see Catalina," he joked.

"Yeah, right," Rowe responded.

They pulled up chairs, and Rowe unzipped his portfolio and took out a legal pad preparing to take notes.

Gary told them about how Robaire Assaly had met Amir Rahimi, and what led to the meeting at the Bonaventure hotel, forgetting a "sub-source" of Robaire's had introduced him to Rahimi.

"Here's a copy of the tape of our meeting," Gary said. He pressed the play button on a small combination VHS tape player and monitor placed on a two-drawer filing cabinet next to his desk. They studied the conversation, and when it was over, Olson asked, "Any idea who the buyer is?"

"That's the million-dollar question," Gary said. "Initially, Rahimi insinuated to my CI Colombian cocaine traffickers may be involved and might trade dope for the Stinger, but he denied that, as you heard."

"That's because he's a terrorist," Olson opined. "Forget the Colombians. This has al-Qaeda written all over it."

"Rahimi never brought up drugs during the meeting," Rowe observed.

Gary leaned back in his chair. "In fact, he got a little pissed off when I brought it up. But it doesn't mean he was telling the truth, either. You saw how small a package a million dollars is. He knew it would fit in that briefcase. Everything he did mimicked a dope deal. They divided the money with rubber bands into ten-thousand-dollar stacks, and banded them into one hundred-thousand-dollar bundles. Classic drug deal."

"If he had agreed to exchange coke for it," Rowe interjected, "that would have been over two hundred pounds of weight to move around. That's a lot of trouble when a million bucks is so much easier."

"Good point," Gary said.

"We've learned a million dollars is no trouble for bin Laden," Olson said. "Is Rahimi in your databases?"

Rowe scribbled notes as Gary ran his fingers through his hair. "Unfortunately, no. I'm hoping he turns up in yours. But we've confirmed his address, and surveillance has been with him all day today. I've ordered up six months' worth of toll records to see who he's been talking to. Hopefully, we'll have some answers soon."

"Who's the informant?" Olson inquired.

"Robaire Assaly. He's someone I've worked with for a long time."

"You trust him?" Rowe asked.

"Yeah, I sure do."

Rowe spoke up. "So, he's been proven reliable?"

"Very. He's world-class. A little cocky at times, but that's because he's so confident."

Mark Olson followed up. "He's never gone sideways on you?"

Reaching over his desk to a wooden penholder, Gary rapped his knuckles on it. "Not yet. His information has always been solid."

"How long has he been an informant?" Rowe inquired.

"Almost ten years," Gary said. "I told him he was about to be indicted on a smuggling case I was working with Customs. The next day he walked into the office and offered his services. I told him we wouldn't indict him if he continued to cooperate. He didn't realize I never had enough evidence on him to satisfy the U.S. Attorney. He was never in jeopardy of being indicted, but I never had the heart to tell him."

"What's his background?" Olson asked.

"He's a Lebanese Christian who graduated from the American University in Lebanon and speaks at least three languages: English, Arabic, and I think a little French, or maybe German, I forget which. He worked as a purser for Pan Am and made big-time drug connections around the world making big bucks as a commercial air smuggler until he got wind he was being investigated." Gary pondered for a second. "Come to think of it, I believe he still has family in Beirut."

"We're going to need a Stinger if we're going to pull this off," Mark said. "Any ideas where we can get one?"

Gary said, "I have an old army buddy who may be able to help. He's a CID agent at the National Training Center at Fort Irwin. That's how I came up with my cover story, saying I worked in logistics there."

"If he can't come through, somebody at the Hoover Building will make some phone calls to The Pentagon," Olson said.

• • •

Robaire Assaly drove to the Griffith Park Observatory as instructed. June was waiting inside, looking over an exhibit where a heavy sphere with a six-inch rod protruding at its bottom slowly swung back and forth from a long cable in the ceiling. The Earth's rotation propelled it as it gently knocked over another domino forming a circle with others. Some school children ran amuck while others studied the exhibits.

Robaire thought June looked stunning in her crimson silk dress and matching high-heeled shoes that flexed her calves. She seemed calm, in charge, a risk-taker. He admired those qualities in a woman. They were qualities he took for granted in most men. And now, his family's safety depended on her.

"Follow me," she said, bending her right forefinger. They walked through the building to a balcony with a view of the Golden State freeway. She glared at him. "Tell me what happened yesterday inside that hotel room?"

"Amir called his people. They brought a million dollars over to the room to show us they meant business. Rahimi left two hundred thousand dollars with Gary for expenses," he said gesturing air quotes. "Can you imagine, two-hundred-thousand dollars? I tell you; this is going to happen." He didn't mention Rahimi also handed him one-hundred-thousand dollars as his finder's fee.

"When?"

"By the end of the month. He wants delivery no later than the 28th."

"Where?"

"That hasn't been decided."

June appeared surprised. "Surely Lowery has discussed this with you?"

"Not at all. I don't think he's given it much thought. He said he's got a lot of paperwork to catch up on before he does anything else."

"Typical Justice Department weenies," she muttered to herself.

He reached for a Montecristo inside his sports coat. "What did you say?"

"Nothing." She jerked her head back to remove her hair from her eyes. "We're coming to a crucial point, and I must make sure it goes as planned. Make damn sure Lowery understands he must show Rahimi the Stinger before he delivers the money. We don't want to spook him. Lowery knows Rahimi's good for it, but we must make him think his people are insisting on seeing the Stinger before a million bucks are brought out again. Understand?"

"Yes, of course, my dear. But I don't think that will happen until we get closer to the end of the month."

"Why?"

"He'll want to buy time to identify Amir's accomplices, especially the two men who came to the hotel room with the money," he said as he snipped the end of the cigar with his I. M. Corona cutter. "I know the way he operates. He's very methodical and leaves nothing to chance. He'll want to identify as many people as possible before he delivers the missile."

"Make sure Lowery delivers. I'll have things ready at this end whenever he makes his move." She folded her arms while looking at the traffic on the freeway below, deep in thought about the situation. A slight smile came to her face. "I've got to admit he's good."

"Who?"

"Lowery. He convinced Rahimi he can deliver the Stinger and got him to fork over two-hundred grand. Not bad."

Robaire placed his hand to his chest. "I'd like to think I had something to do with it."

She turned and faced him. "Just keep up the good work and your family's problems are over." She made an about face and walked away, until she thought of something. She turned around and walked back to him, snapping her fingers.

"The recorder, Robaire. Where is it?"

"Right here, my dear." He reached into his inside jacket pocket and produced a small Sony digital recorder, handing it to her. He dipped into his left outer jacket pocket and removed a gold Dunhill lighter.

"Did you remember to turn it on?"

"Ma'am," he said in between puffs while lighting his cigar, "do I look like some rank amateur?"

She smiled as she dropped the recorder in her handbag. "Keep me advised, Robaire. And return my calls. Things can change rapidly. I hate not knowing what's going on." When she turned to walk away, she mentioned to him, "By the way, there's no smoking on the balcony." She waved goodbye to him over her shoulder as he heard her heels clicking away.

CHAPTER 7

David Page was the Special Agent in Charge of the Army's Criminal Investigation Division field office at Fort Irwin. Gary knew him from his active-duty army days as a CID agent before transferring to the Reserves.

Page, a Chief Warrant Officer, was one of the most senior agents in the Command. Gary explained to him he wanted to "borrow" the weapon from the army and assured him it would be safe. "I'm sorry, Dave, but I can't be more specific on the phone about why I need it."

"I don't know, Gary. We don't get phone calls like this every day; you know. But since September 11th, nothing surprises me anymore. I'll have to get back to you on this."

"All right, but in the meantime, please keep the number of people privy to this at an absolute minimum, Dave. If I've got to brief someone up the food chain, I'll be glad to do it."

"I'm sure that'll be necessary. Can you drive up on a moment's notice?"

"I'll make sure of it. Call me when you find out something."

"I sure will, Gary."

"Thanks." Gary hung up. Could it be that simple? He couldn't imagine the army operating with that kind of efficiency. At least, that was his experience from eight years of active duty and sixteen in the Reserves.

An agent shouted his name from across the room. Gary looked over and saw he had two fingers in the air and punched line two on the phone. "Lowery."

"This is Joe. How's it goin'?"

"Great, Joe. I was going to call you later to thank you for your help the other day. You did a great job."

"That's why I'm callin'. I was wondering how your case was goin' and if I can help anymore?"

"The case is cruising right along, but I don't think we'll be using the hotel again. At least not for a while."

Gary thought Joe sounded disappointed. He knew Joe must have enjoyed his fifteen minutes of undercover work, even if it was only pretending to be a hotel registration clerk. "Well, if you do, be sure to call me. I'm your man."

"I sure will," Gary said.

"Oh, by the way, Gary. My compliments to your surveillance crew. It was interesting watching them work. They looked real natural, especially the good-looking blond. She was smooth."

Puzzled, Gary asked, "What good-looking blond?"

"You know, the younger blond babe seated several tables behind you. She was there the whole time you were at the hotel."

Gary paused a moment to think. "Joe, I don't know who you're talking about."

"Sure, you do, the blond! You'd know her if you saw her. She's got a hard body all the way, man. Nice rack, too, and they weren't bolt-ons!" Gary fell silent, wondering who the hell Joe was talking about. "Gary, you there?"

"Yeah, Joe. Sorry. I'm just trying to think of whom you mean. We didn't have any women working surveillance that day. She was obviously a customer."

Now Joe was confused. "That's funny. I've been in police work long enough to know a surveillance when I see one, and she was definitely working surveillance. She had all the moves and body language surveillance people do. She was furtive yet innocent lookin'. You know what I mean?"

"Yeah, I know what you mean," Gary replied.

"Well, pass on my compliments if you ever see her. When you do, tell her I'd like to meet her. She's a babe. I can't believe you didn't notice her."

"Well, I must have had other things on my mind."

"You musta. I'll let you go. Take 'er easy, Gary."

"Talk to you later, Joe. Thanks again," Gary said and hung up.

Gary spun around in his chair to take in the view, wondering all the while about whom the woman could be. Was she counter-surveillance for Rahimi? Was she a hooker? No, Joe would have known that. Who was she?

The phone rang, which interrupted his thought process. Gary reached over and answered it.

"Hi again, it's Dave."

"Wow, that was quick!"

"I got lucky. I made an appointment for you to brief the Commanding General tomorrow at thirteen hundred, right after lunch. Can you make it?"

"I sure can. What did you tell him?"

"Only there was an urgent matter a Justice Department official needed to discuss with him and they could only do it in person. The curiosity's killing him," Dave explained.

"Terrific, Dave. See you tomorrow at one." Gary felt charged. He was on a roll. Things were jelling. He was confident he could convince the general to see things his way, or he'd be forced to have the FBI or Main Justice call The Pentagon. He didn't want it to come to that. Too many people to deal with.

Gary picked up the phone and punched the speed dial for Sal's cell number. He was overseeing today's surveillance.

"It's your dime," Sal said.

"Sal? How are things going?"

"We're in the sixteen thousand block of Wilshire Boulevard. He went into a business called "*Overseas Financial Services*," which sure sounds like a money-laundering front to me."

"It sure does," Gary agreed.

"It's hard to tell what visitors he's gettin' since we can't position ourselves in the building to see what's happening. It's in one of those fifteen story office buildings with a hundred different fricking businesses in it."

"Any sign of those other two guys?"

"No, we haven't seen them yet."

"Hang in there, Sal. The FBI will take over surveillance soon."

"Yeah, they can smell a headline a mile away. That's the only reason they're interested, ya know. They'll wait until we pop these guys and then call a press conference while we're booking them."

"You're right, but that's how it's got to be. God knows we could use the help."

"Yeah, damn straight. You know the office is down thirty agents who got called to active duty as reservists."

"Yeah, I know, Sal."

"And about another ten guys who are pulling Sky Marshal duties," Sal added. "I'll call you if something comes up."

"Thanks, Sal. Oh, just so you know, I'll be out of the office most of tomorrow."

"Where you goin'?"

"Out to Fort Irwin to see a General about you know what."

"Yep," Sal acknowledged.

"Oh, I meant to ask you . . . Were there any female agents on the surveillance the other day at the Bonaventure?"

"No. We only had the hand full of guys you saw. Why?"

"Just wondering. No big deal."

CHAPTER 8

The next morning, Gary took advantage of not having to go into the office by sleeping in late. When he got up, he drove to Fort Irwin, which was outside the city of Barstow. Barstow is the halfway point between Los Angeles and Las Vegas, and boasts of having the world's largest McDonald's restaurant.

An MP at Fort Irwin's main gate saluted Gary when he showed him his Retired Army Reserve ID card identifying him as a Chief Warrant Officer 4. Since September 11th, the base had gone from threat condition Delta, the highest state of alert, to Charlie, which still required everyone entering to show proper identification. He followed the MP's directions to the CID office. Upon walking in, Dave Page greeted him in the lobby of the office.

"Good to see you, Gary. It's been a long time," Dave said, shaking hands.

"Sure has, Dave. How are you? Nice suit, by the way." CID agents almost always wore civilian clothing.

"I'm fine, and thanks. How was the drive?"

"Very pleasant. No fighting traffic in the morning getting out of town."

It surprised Gary to see Dave had changed little over the past ten years. He was a little heavier, one pound per year, he figured, and he was developing a double chin. He wondered how much he had changed in Dave's mind.

"Let's go," Dave said. "We can take my car."

• • •

Dave pulled his CID sedan into a visitor's space at the headquarters of the National Training Center. Carved into a wooden sign outside the building was: MAJOR GENERAL JOHN T. HARRIS, COMMANDING.

A pleasant secretary greeted them when they walked into the modest foyer of the newer stucco building. She reminded Gary of his high school English teacher.

"May I help you, gentlemen?"

"I'm Special Agent David Page from the CID Office," he said while displaying his badge and credentials. "We have an appointment with General Harris."

"One moment please." She picked up the phone and dialed a two-digit number. "There are two gentlemen from the CID office to see you, sir."

She hung up. "You may step in."

"Thank you, ma'am." Page said. Gary was glad she assumed he was also an army criminal investigator, not a DEA agent. Fewer questions that way.

When Gary entered, the number of plaques, certificates, framed letters of commendation, and photos on the wall of the general shaking hands with Presidents, Secretaries of Defense, and Chairmen of the Joint Chiefs of Staff overwhelmed him.

The General was in his early-fifties, Gary estimated. He had a part in his hair just above his left ear to cover his balding head. His tapered desert Battle Dress Uniform was neatly pressed and starched. He looked to be in good shape for his age and had a firm handshake.

"Sir, this is Gary Lowery from the Department of Justice. He'd like to speak with you about the matter I mentioned."

"Please have a seat," the General ordered, pointing to two leather upholstered armchairs in front of his desk. Gary and Page did what they were told as the General sat down in his executive leather chair and crossed his legs. "Who exactly do you work for, Mister Lowery?"

Gary took out a leather case containing his credentials along with a heavy gold badge and handed it to him. "I'm a Special Agent with the Drug Enforcement Administration working out of Los Angeles. I appreciate you taking time from your busy schedule to see me."

"I'm glad to," he said, examining the photo, glancing up at Gary, and handing the identification back. "But I didn't know this concerned a drug matter."

"I was vague on the phone, sir, because of the sensitive nature of this case," Dave was quick to say.

"I see. Tell me, Mister Lowery, how can I help you?"

Gary sighed before saying, "I'm conducting a joint investigation with the FBI concerning an Iranian who is attempting to purchase a Stinger missile."

The general raised his eyebrows. "An Iranian?"

"Yes, sir. We don't know why he wants a Stinger. He claims to only be the middleman for someone else, but no one involved in the investigation believes that."

"The bastard!" the general blurted. "How much is a Stinger going for these days?"

"About a million dollars on the black market, sir," Gary said.

The General shook his head in disgust. "How did the DEA get mixed up in this?"

"It was my informant who provided us with the information about the Iranian. At first, we thought he wanted to trade drugs for the missile, but he denies that. The FBI came on board because of the possible nexus with terrorists."

"I would say so!" the General puffed. "Those rat bastards could be anywhere in the United States."

"Yes, sir," Gary agreed.

"Any connection between this Iranian and al-Qaeda?"

"Not that we can tell at the moment, sir."

The General leaned back in his leather chair. "How does this matter concern the army?"

Gary leaned forward and said, "We need a Stinger to use as a prop in a, forgive the pun, sting operation. We hope to convince him he has found someone who can deliver a missile. The only way we can do that is to show him one. Once he sees it, he'll be obliged to show us the buy money again, and we can arrest him. It's about as simple as that. But he won't bring the money out again until he sees a Stinger."

"Again?" the General asked.

"Yes. We've already had one undercover meeting with him, and he surprised us by showing us the million dollars. He won't do it again unless we prove to him we have a Stinger," Gary said.

"I see. You show me yours, and I'll show you mine kind of deal?"

"Exactly," Gary said. "Once he shows us the money, we intend to arrest him and seize it to deprive him the opportunity to purchase one elsewhere."

"Well, all that sounds ambitious, doesn't it, Mister Lowery?"

"Yes, sir, I imagine it does, especially since he said he needed it by the end of the month, so we're under a time crunch."

The General didn't seem convinced. "Are you certain it's necessary to show him a Stinger? What if he steals it? Christ, a terrorist could create havoc with the thing. Is taking the risk of a Stinger falling into the hands of a bunch of goddamn Iranians worth it?"

The General had a point. "General Harris, I've done cases like this many times before, but never with a Stinger missile involved. The Attorney General and the NSC are all monitoring this investigation. We reached a consensus that displaying the Stinger missile strengthens our case. We think it's worth the risk to identify as many members of the Iranian's criminal organization as possible."

"Yes, of course," the General conceded. He reached for the phone on his desk. "Dorothy, call the Commander of the five-oh third ADA and have him send somebody over here on the double. Tell him to bring a Stinger MANPAD field manual with him." The General looked back at Gary as he hung up. "I thought you might want to know something about what you're supposed to be selling," the General grunted.

"Good idea," Gary said. He looked over the walls again. "You have a lot of impressive memorabilia."

"Well, I've been around a few years. I'm considering making a career out of the army." He laughed. "I go all the way back to the Vietnam war."

Dave said, "Sir, Gary's a retired Army Reserve Chief Warrant Officer and was with a CID detachment in Los Angeles that was deployed during the Gulf War."

"You don't say?" The General lit up. "How much time did you spend over there?"

"From October ninety to February ninety-one," he said, feeling uncomfortable talking about it.

"Why only five months?"

"That's when my unit was medevacked back to the states."

"The entire unit? Why?"

"A SCUD missile hit our barracks in Dhahran, Saudi Arabia, killing the commander and causing casualties to the entire unit, except for me and another soldier."

"How'd you manage that?"

"My partner and I were in Iraq recovering a stolen Hummer, if you can imagine."

"Damn, what fate!" the General said. He leaned forward, resting elbows on the desk, enjoying the war story. "Did you see any Iraqi soldiers while you were there?"

"I sure did. As my partner and I were recovering the Hummer, an Iraqi battalion came upon us."

"What happened?"

"They surrendered."

"Fantastic!" the General said. "What was the official count?"

"Eight hundred eighty-three. We marched them ourselves back to Saudi until an MP Company met us. The Iraqis were very cooperative."

"I bet they were after we kicked the crap out of them! Damn, how I envy you. I wish I had been there." The phone buzzed, and the general answered. "Send him right in."

A major in his early thirties, walked into the office. He was dressed in a desert battle dress uniform and timidly walked into the office. He looked like he had just dropped everything to get there. He was disheveled, perspiring, and panting. His jog to the General's office was faster than waiting for a driver to take him.

He carried an unclassified field manual on the Stinger. He walked to within ten feet in front of the General, snapped to attention, and saluted smartly. "Major Schmidt reporting as ordered, sir."

"At ease, major," the General replied, returning the salute. "Gentlemen, this is Major Tom Schmidt, the executive officer of the five-oh third Air Defense Artillery. Major, this is Mister Page of the CID Office, and this is Mister Lowery from the Drug Enforcement Agency."

"Good afternoon," the major said.

"Major, pull up a chair and have a seat." the General ordered.

"Yes, sir," he said, complying.

"Major, Misters Page and Lowery need a quick briefing on the Stinger missile weapon system. Nothing too technical, just a general overview of its capabilities and how it operates. Keep it unclassified, but this discussion will not leave this room, understand?"

"Roger that, sir," he said, having caught his breath. "The FIM 92A is a MANPAD, or man-portable air defense, shoulder-fired missile for low altitude air defense of forward area troops. The Stinger, as it is called, is used only by the United States and allied forces. Infantry soldiers use this weapon system for air defense. Air Force personnel use it to protect airfields. Stingers are also used on ships by the Navy. It has a reusable, self-contained firing system."

"Go on," the General ordered.

Without having to consult the manual, the major said, "The weapon is an infrared shoulder-fired surface-to-air missile that has an effective range of about five klicks, or three miles, weighs fifteen kilos or thirty-three pounds or so. It is one point forty-seven meters, or about four and three quarters feet long. It's an accurate heat-seeker that strikes the engines of an aircraft rather than the fuselage. Stingers were successfully against Soviet aircraft during its war in Afghanistan."

"I saw news reports about that," Gary remarked.

"The United States supplied the weapon to the Afghan rebels, and Special Forces operators trained them in its use against Soviet aircraft. It worked well against their helicopters," the major added.

"Hmm," Gary pinched his lower lip. "How long did it take the average Afghan to learn how to work one of these babies?"

"I can only speculate, but I would guess it wouldn't take very long."

"How long would that be?" Dave asked.

"Probably three hours."

"What?" Gary found that hard to believe. "I read somewhere the Stinger school was about eight weeks long."

"It is, but they taught the Afghans while on the run from the Soviets. They needed to use the weapons immediately, so they only got the bare basics. Sight acquisition, target engagement, pull the trigger, wham," he said, slamming his fist into the palm of his other hand. "A whole lot of Afghans got this version of the training on their home turf."

"So, Major," Gary replied, "just about anyone with average intelligence can fire one of these things and probably hit the target?"

"Not probably, sir. It *will* hit the target," the confident major responded.

"How can you be so sure?" Dave asked.

"It can read where the aircraft is, lock on it, and when fired, seek that target until it either hits it or runs out of propellant trying. It's so quick most targets, especially helicopters, don't stand a chance. The pilots only have a few seconds to react with countermeasures once the thing takes off."

"Is it good on all aircraft?" Gary asked.

"That's classified, sir."

"Okay, can it be used on most aircraft?"

"I can only tell you it will work on aircraft prevalent in the old eastern bloc, Cuba, and all former Soviet airplanes and helicopters. The ones that count."

"Oh, you mean our planes can outrun this thing?" Gary asked.

"No," Major Schmidt said. "That's not it at all. The Stinger will only work against enemy aircraft."

"Come again, Major?" Gary asked, confused by the last statement. "How can that be?"

"I-F-F," Major Schmidt said.

"Whoa, what's that?" Gary asked again.

"Identification Friend-or-Foe. The Stinger transmits a beam to the targeted aircraft and reads its radar signature. If the signature matches a United States or allied aircraft, it will not fire. This prevents friendly fire from shooting down their own aircraft, which is easy to do without it. It's difficult to identify aircraft from the ground traveling at Mach speeds when you're dealing with dust, smoke, and other battlefield conditions where it's easy to become disoriented."

Gary looked at the General and turned back to the major. "So, if a terrorist got hold of one of these, he couldn't use it against a U.S. aircraft. Is that right?"

"Yes, sir. That's right. It would be useless against any of our aircraft or that of our allies," he added.

"Are the people trained in the Stinger's use aware of this IFF device?" Dave Page asked.

"Of course," the major was quick to respond.

"Even Afghan rebels?" Gary asked.

"I can't say for sure, but I can't imagine them not knowing that. What's this about, anyway?"

"Thank you for your time, Major," the General said. Schmidt got the hint. He jumped from his chair and pulled it back to its original place against the wall. "If I can answer any more of your questions, Mister Lowery, please don't hesitate to call me. Good day, gentlemen."

"Thank you very much, Major," Gary said. The major left and quietly shut the door behind him.

"Interesting," Gary said.

"I know what you were thinking," General Harris said. "What in the world does an Iranian want with a Stinger he can't use on American aircraft?" He rubbed his hands together. "By the way, Mister Lowery, I know for a fact the IFF prevents the Stingers from being used against commercial aircraft, too."

"I'm sure going to rethink this," Gary said. "I've got a lot of questions that need answering."

"While you're thinking, I'll call the Army Operations Center at The Pentagon and see about having a Stinger released to you."

The General stood, prompting Gary and Dave Page to do likewise. "Thank you, sir," Gary said. "If The Pentagon has questions, I'll be glad to answer them." He handed him his business card. "Please let us know when you get an answer, sir."

"I'll let Mister Page know when I get word," the General said. Gary shook General Harris' hand. "Thanks again for your cooperation, sir."

"Glad to help," the General said. While Gary and Dave opened the door to the office to leave, he said, "Find out what that son-of-a-bitch intends to do with it."

CHAPTER 9

On his way back to his office, Gary's wondered why a terrorist would want a Stinger if it couldn't be used against a U.S. aircraft. Either the buyer did not know about the internal safety device, or the target was obviously a non-U.S. aircraft. If that was the case, who is the intended target?

He mulled over what Amir Rahimi said during the meeting at the Bonaventure Hotel. He stated the buyer had someone who knew how to operate the weapon. Then he must know the weapon cannot be used against U.S. aircraft, right? Or did Rahimi conceal this information from him? Take the money and run? Yet another distinct possibility. Stung by a Stinger, how ironic.

•   •   •

The next morning Gary entered the fourteenth-floor offices of the FBI at the Westwood federal building.

After a few minutes, Olson arrived at the reception area. "Hi, Gary. Come with me."

They walked to a windowless interview room where Calvin Rowe was waiting. "Hello," he said. "Welcome to the puzzle palace."

"*The New York Times* city desk comes to mind," Gary said. "That's about how busy this place looks."

"You're not exaggerating," Rowe said. "We've been overloaded ever since nine-eleven."

Gary took a seat in a straight-back gray steel chair. "I wanted to get you up to speed on what I've come up with."

"Good. We've got stuff to run past you, too," Olson said.

How refreshing, Gary thought. The FBI had a well-deserved reputation within law enforcement for taking information but providing none.

"I went to Fort Irwin yesterday and talked to the Commanding General about borrowing a Stinger missile. He said he'd do what's necessary to get us one."

"Perfect," Rowe said. "When's he going to let you know?"

"Could be soon. He has to call The Pentagon, and God only knows how long it will take before he hears something. But he understands our time restraints."

"Does he think The Pentagon will cooperate?" Olson inquired.

"He seemed pretty optimistic. If not, you guys and the Attorney General have enough juice to make it happen."

"For sure," Olson said. "We'll get a Stinger if we have to go to the White House for permission. Considering all the warnings the CIA is putting out about future terrorist attacks, it shouldn't be a problem."

"What else is going on?" Rowe asked.

"All the agents surveilling Rahimi can come up with is he has a normal routine, you know, goes from home to work, and back again. They can't get a good look inside his office. By the way, it's only about six blocks east of here. He's in one of those high-rises on Wilshire."

"So, we found out," Olson said. "We sent a couple of our guys over there to scope it out."

Olson put his feet on the steel desk. "Our tech people have gone by his home and business and figure it'll be easy to set up pole-cams, especially at the home. We'll have wires up and running in the next few days."

Gary was astonished. "A few days? How can you get authorization to do a wiretap in such a short time?"

Olson shrugged as if to say, "What's the big deal," and said, "National Security. We've already filed Foreign Intelligence Surveillance Act applications."

Rowe unzipped his portfolio and refreshed his memory from his notes. "We verified through the State Department and INS that Rahimi was a government employee for the American Embassy in Teheran in 1979. He was among those taken hostage by the Iranians. Later, after they released him, the Swiss smuggled him out of the country, and he was given the opportunity to apply for asylum in the United States. Because there are no diplomatic relations with Iran, a final outcome of his asylum hearing is still pending."

"After all these years?" Gary asked.

"Yep," Rowe said.

Olson added, "He can't be deported while his asylum application is pending."

Rowe continued. "U.S. Citizenship and Immigration Services can't take any action on his application, so we're stuck with the asshole. Even if we indict him for conspiracy to illegally acquire the Stinger, we can't ship him back to Iran after he serves his sentence."

"Well, shit." Gary muttered.

Olson looked at Gary and lowered his voice. "We also found out Rahimi helped the CIA establish ties with the Afghan rebels during the war with the Soviet Union. He helped funnel arms to them."

Gary nodded his head. Rahimi's connection with Afghan rebels made his request for the Stinger even more intriguing. "Anything else?"

Rowe flipped through the papers in the file in front of him. "He's not married. He doesn't own any property in California or elsewhere we can find, and he drives a leased vehicle."

"No other Intel on this guy?" Gary asked.

"Nope." Olson replied.

"Well guess what?" Gary said.

"Yeah?" Rowe said.

"I found out the Stinger can't be used against United States aircraft."

"It can't?" Olson gulped.

"No, nor against our allies. Commercial airliners included. Soviet-era aircraft are about the only exception."

"No shit?" Rowe exclaimed.

"That's the beauty of the thing," Gary explained. "It can tell if the target is friend or foe. It has a fail-safe to keep GIs from shooting down their own aircraft. That kinda changes things, doesn't it?"

"It sure does," Olson agreed.

"I wonder if Rahimi's buyer knows that." Rowe asked.

"I wonder if Rahimi knows," Gary said. "But he must." He paused for a few seconds. "You know, he could be pulling a scam on his buyer by selling them something they can't use."

"Wouldn't that prove unhealthy?" Rowe asked.

Gary laughed. "It sure would. The al-Qaeda would use him for target practice at one of their training camps for ripping them off."

"I wonder if there really is a buyer," Olson interjected. "We haven't connected him to any terrorist organizations."

"Good question," Rowe said. "But who's the intended target?"

"Beats me," Olson said, shrugging his shoulders.

The room was silent as they pondered the question. "I guess we'll just have to ask him when we arrest him," a confident Gary Lowery said.

Olson had a strange look on his face. He jumped up from behind the desk. "Wait, a minute! I think I've got it."

"What?" Rowe asked.

"If the Stinger is useless to Rahimi against the U.S., he's got to be selling it to a foreign government for the technology. They'll reverse-engineer it to make their own version and put in their own fail-safe system."

"That makes sense," Rowe said.

"It sure does," Gary agreed. "Otherwise, it would be useless, wouldn't it?"

"That's the way it seems," Olson commented.

"Then why the time limit?" Gary asked. "Why was he so adamant about getting the thing by the end of the month?"

No one could answer the question. Gary paused to think. "The CIA funneled hundreds of Stingers into Afghanistan during the war, and they knocked the hell out of Russian helicopters. That was the first time the Stinger was battlefield tested. After that, their accuracy became legendary. There must be a lot of foreign governments that would love to have their own version."

"A lotta countries already have their own version," Rowe said.

"Yeah, but they're crap compared to our Stinger. Remember when al-Qaeda fired two Russian SA-7s at that Israeli charter jet in Africa and couldn't hit it? What pieces of shit those things must be?"

"Well, until we get some answers, we've got a lot of follow up to do," Olson reminded them.

"I've got tolls from AT and T yesterday," Gary said.

"We did too," Olson said. "The phone numbers are being analyzed as we speak."

"Any interesting calls come up?" Gary asked.

"Not that I know of," responded Olson. "But it's still too early to tell. We'll have to give it more time."

"What's your next move?" Gary inquired.

Rowe zipped up his portfolio. "A black bag crew is going to his office building tomorrow to set up a camera and transmitter in the hallway to his office."

"What phones are you going to go up on?" Gary asked.

"His home, cell, and business lines. We've also ordered a clone pager. We have Farsi speakers coming in from around the country to help with the monitoring, and a couple more surveillance teams will join in to be on him around the clock," Olson said. "Hopefully, he'll lead us to other actors."

"Especially the two guys who delivered the money," Gary added. "Any idea who they are?"

Olson shook his head. "Not a clue."

Rowe stood up. "You need to stall Rahimi as long as you can before delivering the Stinger. Our guys need an opportunity to do their jobs."

"No argument there," Gary agreed. "It'll be interesting to see who visits Rahimi over the next few days."

CHAPTER 10

Robaire Assaly parked in the driveway of The Ritz-Carlton Huntington Hotel in Pasadena, where June told him to meet her. After squeezing out of his Mercedes and taking a stub from the waiting valet, he easily found the hotel's restaurant.

He scanned the dining room and spied June waving. She looked business-like, dressed in a white skirt, a crimson silk blouse, and an orange and black plaid jacket. Of course, she wore her trademark high heels and red lipstick. "I'm meeting the lady over there," he told the hostess and made his way to her booth.

"You're late," she puffed.

"You're always so serious, June. Why don't you take life a little easier and relax occasionally?" He placed the linen napkin on his lap.

"We have work to do. There's a lot to be done."

"Any word on how my mother and sister are doing?"

"No. Their status remains the same."

A waitress appeared at the table to take their order. "Have you decided yet?"

"No, just a few more minutes, please," June said, flashing a brilliant smile.

"Then can I take your drink order?"

"Yes, please" Robaire said. "I'll have a Stoli bloody Mary."

"And you, Madame?"

"Just black decaf coffee, please," June said sweetly. The waitress left.

"Why can't you be that sweet towards me, June?" he asked when the waitress walked away.

She looked him straight in the eye. "The only reason I'm with you is because I get paid to. The minute this assignment's over, that's the end of our relationship. I'm looking forward to that day."

"But tell me how you *really* feel. Please don't sugarcoat it."

"Decide what you want. Here comes the waitress again."

The woman walked up and smiled at June, who by now had her pearly whites showing again. Robaire wasn't as skilled at hiding his feelings and looked somewhat perturbed.

"The fruit plate, orange juice, a glass of skim milk, and some more decaf later," June ordered, batting her eyelids.

"Eggs Benedict, orange juice, home fries, and a side of blueberry pancakes with coffee when the meal is ready," he said.

When the server left, June interlaced her fingers as her elbows rested on the table. "Have you heard from Lowery yet?"

"No. Not since I talked to him on the phone a couple of days ago."

"You need to call him and find out what he's up to. I need to know what he intends to do. We've got to get him to show the package to Rahimi."

"I'm sure he will, especially since he already showed us the money. Gary's handling this just like a drug deal."

"But this isn't a drug deal," she reminded him.

"I realize that. But you must humor him if you want him to do certain things."

"All right. But it's imperative he does it *my* way. The objective is for him to expose the Stinger, and don't forget that."

"How could I ever forget, June? You're on my back about it all the time," he said while adjusting his napkin. "Calm down and let me do my work. I've got a lot more at stake in this than you do. I know Gary better than you, and I'm telling you he'll do it. So quit worrying about it."

The waitress came up and served their coffee and juice on a silver tray. "Your breakfast will be right up," she said. June flashed another perfect smile at her. She left.

"Gary's a lot like you, you know."

When the waitress was out of earshot, June demanded, "What do you mean he's a lot like me?"

Robaire add cream and four lumps of sugar to his coffee. "Cunning, decisive, confident, *very* confident. He never entertains the possibility of failure . . . But there is one thing he's isn't."

"What's that?"

"He's not as good looking as you."

"Now stop that!" she said, gently slapping his forearm.

"Just a little levity to keep my mind off my family's predicament, even for a short while."

"I get it," she said, before drinking her orange juice. "You might want to know you're not my type."

"And who would be your type?"

"Good-looking women," she said before sipping her decaf, looking him straight in the eyes.

"Women?"

"Do I have to spell it out for you?"

"I see," he said. "I would have never guessed."

"Get used to it, Robaire. It's a changing world."

"The world may be changing, but I haven't," he said. "I'd like to find a woman who can put up with me. Maybe someday, I hope."

"I think that day will come," June said.

"I certainly hope so." Robaire took a long swig of his Bloody Mary.

Silence for thirty-seconds, until June spoke up. "Since you know Lowery so well, how do you think he'll handle the delivery?"

Robaire slurped his coffee. "Let me give you an example. About five years ago Gary and I did a reverse."

"A reverse?"

"Something like he's doing now. That's when he poses as a drug dealer instead of someone looking to buy drugs. When the unsuspecting buyer shows him his money to make the purchase, he gets busted, and they take the money as drug proceeds."

"I see. So, what happened?"

"Gary posed as an ecstasy dealer who was supposedly going to sell a thousand tabs of it. Gary selected the Arcadia Fashion Center parking lot to meet the crook and show him the phony drugs. The place was swarming with shoppers who never suspected for a second a big drug deal was going down right in front of them. Gary parked his car next to the buyer's. They both got out of their cars and Gary made a cell call. About thirty seconds later, another agent drove up. The agent popped the trunk of his car and Gary showed the buyer the sham drugs in a transparent plastic bag. The packaging was perfect! He slammed the trunk and the agent drove away."

"Then what happened?"

"The buyer made a call to his partner, who arrived a short while later with the money. When he showed the money to Gary, they were both arrested. There was never a chance of Gary getting ripped off."

"So, he's careful."

"Extremely. But he has a cut-off point. He'll shut the deal down when he feels it's too dangerous, or unmanageable. He's learned from the mistakes of others. He's greedy but not stupid."

"Interesting." She appeared unconcerned as she inspected her manicured nails. "I have a plan of my own."

"What is that?"

"You'll know soon enough. But I can tell you this . . ."

"Yes?"

"My plan is a lot better than Mister Lowery's. I can guarantee you that."

CHAPTER 11

A white Ford cargo van with two men parked in front of the office building on Wilshire Boulevard, where *Overseas Financial Services* was located. The two FBI tech agents, in dingy white coveralls took their tool boxes and a stepladder from the van and went into lobby. A security guard behind a counter glanced up from his Stuart Woods paperback novel just as they entered. "Can I help you?" he asked.

"We're here to repair the air conditioner on the eighth floor," one agent said. "We've got a work order from the building manager."

"Let me see that," the sixty-year-old retired military man requested.

The FBI agent handed the paper to him. His partner looked around the lobby and found the business directory listing Rahimi's business on the fifth floor.

The guard handed the agent back the paper. "I guess it's okay. Why doesn't anyone tell me what's happening around here?"

"Can't help you there, mister," an agent said.

The guard went back to reading as the two men took the elevator to the eighth floor. The security guard glanced at the elevator indicator lights as they lit up, one by one, until the number eight stayed on. After getting off the elevator, the two agents walked to one corner of the building and found the stairwell. They hurried down the three flights of stairs to the fifth floor, where they casually walked to the door of Amir Rahimi's office and began their work.

One agent removed a false ceiling panel near the door and cut a hole in it. He covered it with a metal speaker grill, securing it with tiny bolts and wing nuts. He mounted a small video camera affixed to a custom frame onto the backside of the ceiling panel and replaced it. At the same time, his partner removed another panel and located a power source for the camera. They placed a small microwave transmitter next to the camera and hooked it up.

They completed their job in less than fifteen minutes. One of them pushed the transmission button to a concealed radio he carried and asked how things looked. The reply he received through an earpiece nicely concealed by his hair was: "A little to the left." The agent climbed back on the ladder and made the adjustment.

A second radio transmission came. "Perfect."

They gathered their ladder and tools, walked up the three flights to the eighth floor, and waited patiently for the elevator to take them back to the lobby. Both strolled past the security guard, who was engrossed with his reading. Together they put their equipment back into the van and drove around the block. The passenger agent got on the radio. "Still looks good?"

"Come see for yourself."

"Ten-four, we're headed back to the office."

The van pulled into the enormous fully enclosed FBI garage in the massive parking lot to the federal building. They got out of the van, removed their coveralls, stowed their equipment, and walked to the main building to meet with agents Rowe and Olson.

The two tech agents knocked on the door of a large room on the FBI's main floor. An agent answered the door and led them to where a large rack of eighteen monitors were situated. Most displayed images of the outside of homes, trailers, parking lots and businesses, all being observed as part of other investigations throughout Los Angeles. A casual observer might think these were still photographs until an occasional bird flew by or a vehicle drove past the location. Etched on the bottom left of each screen were the time and date, and each monitor was connected to a time-lapse video recorder. Rowe and Olson were watching the monitors with their arms folded. The agent pointed to the third monitor from the left of the middle row. "Just what the doctor ordered," Olson complimented.

The agents focused on the monitor as a customer walked down the hall to the door of Rahimi's business.

· · ·

"Gary," Bill Brownlee shouted from the doorway to his office.

"Yeah."

"Line three."

Gary picked up the phone. It was Dave Page.

"Hi, Dave. Whaddayagot?"

"General Harris just called and said you can have the item."

"That's great news, Dave."

"There's one condition, though."

Gary sighed loudly. "Yeah, what is it?"

"He wants you to sign for it after Major Schmidt and I personally deliver it to you.

Gary perked up. "Hey, are you kidding? That's okay with me."

"The Pentagon wants us to stay close to it, monitor your case, and bring it back to Fort Irwin as soon as you're done."

"That's doable. We may need it later for court or something, but we'll worry about that later."

"When do you want it?"

"As soon as possible. I need my tech guys to take a look at it."

"Oh, that's another thing. There can't be any modifications made to it. That could prove dangerous."

"Don't worry. I don't want to take it apart. I only want to show it off."

"Major Schmidt and I will drive it over tomorrow. Got any ideas where to stay."

"You bet. I can fix you up at the Bonaventure. They've got a government rate."

"We'll leave tomorrow morning and see you right after lunch."

Gary gave him directions to the federal building where his office was located. Things would be happening rapidly from now on. He called Joe Montoya, who set aside two rooms for Dave Page and Major Schmidt.

Gary called Rowe to tell him the Stinger would arrive by special delivery early tomorrow afternoon.

"Aw, right! Can we come by and see it then?"

"Yeah, sure," Gary said. "I've got something in mind."

"What's that?"

"An added security measure. I'll tell you and Mark when I see you tomorrow."

"See you then."

"Hey, wait. How's the wire coming?"

"We'll be up on it tomorrow," Rowe said. "Our tech guys installed a camera in the hallway to his office this morning."

"What phone lines will be up tomorrow?"

"All three."

"That's a lot to monitor."

"Yeah, but we've got agents coming from all over to help us."

"That's what I like about the FBI," Gary said. "When you have a situation, you just throw manpower at it."

"Of course! Otherwise, we wouldn't be the FBI," Rowe agreed.

"See ya." Gary hung up, jumped out of his chair, and trotted into his boss's office.

• • •

"We got it. The Stinger'll be here tomorrow afternoon. The army's delivering it."

"Good," Brownlee said from behind his desk. "Get a hold of your informant and set up a meeting with Rahimi. Find out how he wants it delivered, then tell him *how* it's gonna be delivered."

"Gotcha."

"The final decision on how it's delivered will rest with you," Brownlee reminded him.

"Right," Gary said.

"You've got a lot of planning to do between now and then. I think it's about time you coordinated with the U.S. Attorney's Office."

"Okay. Oh, I've got the two Fee Bees coming over tomorrow to look at the thing."Brownlee grunted. "Be careful with those two," he warned. "They may appear helpful and all that, but those guys have burned us in the past."

"Rowe and Olson?"

"No, I'm talking about the FBI as a whole."

"Who hasn't? Don't worry, Bill, I'll be careful."

"Also, keep in mind these Iranians play for keeps. Don't forget Rahimi carries a gun and is going to be one highly pissed off son-of-a-bitch when he realizes he got screwed on this deal."

Gary shrugged his shoulders to disguise his concern. "Hey boss, shit happens."

CHAPTER 12

Gary lay awake in bed in his cramped condominium thinking about the case, while his green-eyed tabby, *Cannabis*, lay on top the of covers next to him sound asleep. He had called Robaire before leaving work but got no answer. Strange. He didn't return his page either. He intended to call Robaire first thing in the morning to arrange a second meeting with Amir Rahimi.

Gary went over every conceivable response to questions Rahimi may pose, and he refused to consider the possibility of the Stinger getting stolen. He erased that possibility from his mind. The plan had to be sound, had to be safe, and had to be effective.

• • •

The next morning, as Gary drove to his office, the upcoming day's events preoccupied him. He dialed the U.S. Attorney's office from his cell phone.

"U.S. Attorney," a woman said.

"May I speak with Assistant U.S. Attorney Joyce McCarthy?'

"One moment, please."

After a long pause, the phone was finally answered. "Joyce McCarthy."

"Hi, Joyce."

She immediately recognized his voice. "Special Agent Cochise how are you?"

"You can knock off that 'Cochise' business, pale face."

"All right, I get it. I'm just trying to be funny."

"I know," he said. "Hey, I've got a hot one for you."

"That's what you said about that Bolivian case I almost lost my job over."

"That's ancient history, Joyce. Anyway, we won, didn't we?"

"No thanks to you. You left me to fend for myself against seven of the best dope attorneys money can buy. They made O.J.'s 'dream team' look like a bunch of law school dropouts."

"I knew you could handle it. With my guts and your brains, I knew justice would prevail."

"We did get convictions," she conceded.

"Of course. Was there ever a doubt?"

"You really want me to answer that?"

"No, I guess not."

"Okay, Gary, what do you have for me this time?"

"This is too hot to talk about on the phone."

"You're in luck. My calendar's clear this morning. Can you come right over?"

"Sure can. I'll be there in thirty minutes."

•   •   •

Gary flashed his credentials to the security guards as he made his way around the metal detectors on his way to the elevators of the old federal courthouse. TV producers had used the building as the offices of the *Daily Planet* during the original *Superman* television series in the fifties. After a seven-minute wait for an elevator car, it stopped on every floor on his way up to the eleventh. After signing in, the receptionist buzzed him through the door, and he walked down the long hallway leading him to Joyce McCarthy's office.

"Top of the morning to you, Ms. McCarthy," he said with heavy emphasis on the 'Ms.'

He admired how her thirty-five-year-old body filled out her plum-colored dress.

"Top of the morning to you, Special Agent Lowery," she said right back. She stood up from behind her desk, walked to the door, and shut it. She spun around, and wrapped her arms around Gary's neck, and kissed him, slipping her tongue artfully into his mouth.

"Counselor, please," Gary said. "Haven't you ever heard of sexual harassment?"

"I sure have," she said and kissed him again. "When are you going to let me harass your ass again?"

"Soon, I hope."

"What have you been up to? I've been calling but never seem to rate getting a call back," she protested.

"I've been busy. That's why I'm here."

"Not because you wanted to see me?" she frowned.

"That too," he quickly added. He could see he wouldn't get off easily for not having called her for the last several days. "Am I forgiven?"

"I'll tell you after you explain what dope deal has been keeping you away from me."Gary moved to a chair in front of her desk. "Well, for starters, it's not a dope deal."

"Oh? Then what is it?" She opened the door to the office and sat at her desk, taking out a yellow legal pad. She took copious notes as Gary explained what had happened. "Damn, this sounds like a great case! You're forgiven."

"Why'd you wait so long before telling me? Management will ask."

"Tell them I've been busy. Jesus. This case is still ongoing, and I wanted to be sure Rahimi would go for it before I burdened you with only a possible case. I figured Main Justice would have notified your U.S. Attorney by now."

She stood up and sat on the corner of her desk, swinging a crossed leg. "Let me know what happens after your meeting with Rahimi. In the meantime, I'll brief management before the deputy AG calls."

"We should have Rahimi and his two friends in custody in a couple of days. He's not going anywhere with that Stinger. We're gonna shut this down the minute he coughs up the wampum." He got up to leave.

"Gary."

"Yeah?"

"Please be careful."

"Don't worry about me, Joyce. I'm dedicated, but I'm not *that* dedicated." He winked at her and smiled as he left.

When Gary arrived at his office two blocks away, Bill Brownlee confronted him. He looked as though he was having a bad day, and it was only ten-thirty. "Call domestic ops at headquarters. They want another update. I told them what you told me, but of course, they want to hear it from you."

"Big cases, big problems, little cases, little problems," Gary reminded him.

"Yeah, I know," Brownlee said. "No cases, no problems."

"Exactly," Gary replied.

"Where the hell did I put my glasses?" Brownlee asked.

"They're on your forehead, boss."

"Shit."

• • •

After lunch, Gary checked his voice mail again and heard a bunch of phone messages, mostly from DEA headquarters and one from his mother. He had been neglecting her lately and made a mental note to call her.

Exactly at one-thirty, he received a call from the receptionist who said Dave Page was in the lobby. He rushed over there to find him alone.

"Where's the major?"

"He's in the car with the item."

GREGORY D. LEE 83

"We'd better get down there before he gets mugged. Damn, wouldn't that be something if the major got robbed of his Stinger!" Gary laughed.

"Don't even joke about that," Dave said.

They took the elevator to the ground level, exited the building, and trotted to the loading docks where they found an obviously nervous Major Schmidt wearing casual civilian clothing, leaning against an army-marked olive drab green army Chrysler Voyager. "Hey, major. How you doing?" Gary asked.

"I'll be a lot better once we're inside."

Dave slid open the side door and removed an army blanket covering a rectangular, olive drab colored box. A plate on the lower center of the lid read: MISSILE, ANTI-AIRCRAFT (STINGER) MODEL FIM-92A/D. FEDERAL STOCK NUMBER AA2395068. SERIAL NUMBER 29457849657. MANUFACTURED 020623, U.S. ARMY.

"Get in," Gary said. "You can park in the garage."

They drove into the entryway to the underground parking for the federal building. Gary used his gate key card to raise the gate and gave it to Dave. "Keep this while you're here." They parked near the freight elevator used by DEA agents to transport prisoners to their floor. Major Schmidt and Dave Page carried the Stinger's case into Gary's open bay workspace and placed it on his desk. It was about as large as a hard sided golf case golfers use to transport their clubs on commercial airliners. Bill Brownlee and the entire group stopped what they were doing and gathered around Gary's desk. "Major, Dave," Gary said. "This is my supervisor, Bill Brownlee."

They shook hands all around, and Brownlee said, "We sure appreciate the army's cooperation and your help on this."

"Glad to do what we can, sir," the major replied.

"Open that sucker up and let's see whatcha got," Sal said while munching on a Snickers bar.

Schmidt unlatched the rectangular case and lifted the lid, prompting oohs and aahs all around. Inside was a long dark tube with a pistol grip towards the front, a large trigger within a polymer guard, a sighting device on its left side, and a shoulder support. It fit snuggly inside molded OD colored Styrofoam and was loaded, ready to go.

"Man! Look at that thing," an agent said.

"I wouldn't want someone pointing that fricking thing at me," Sal said.

While everyone was gawking at the weapon, Ms. Arminda Garcia, Bill Brownlee's secretary, shouted to tell Gary that Olson and Rowe were in the lobby. Gary immediately went to greet the FBI agents.

Back in the office, Olson gulped when he saw the device. "Man, I didn't realize it was this compact."

"Neither did I," Rowe confessed.

After Gary made the introductions, Major Schmidt shut the case and latched it.

"I want our tech guys to examine it and see what ideas they come up with," Gary informed them.

"What do you mean?" the major asked.

"Before I show it to Rahimi, I want to make sure that if something goes sideways, we can find it."

"You mean if it gets stolen?"

"Wow, calm down, major. No one's gonna steal your precious Stinger. This is just an added precaution to make sure it doesn't happen, that's all."

"I still don't get it," the major muttered.

"Just pay attention," Dave Page said. "You'll see what he means."

Gary helped the major carry the Stinger down the hall, with Dave, Olson, and Rowe in tow. When they entered the Technical Support Unit, Gary placed the carrying case on top of an empty desk. The Tech supervisor walked up with two other agents.

"Hi, Ray," Gary said. He introduced the guests to them. "Well, this is it," he said while opening the case.

"Hmm. Let's take it into the shop and have a good look," Ray, the supervisor, said. The two agents carried the case into what looked like a hobbyist's workshop. The shelves were filled with electronics, screws, nuts, bolts, TVs, VHS tapes, cables, cameras, and monitors. Several work benches sat in the middle of the room with more equipment, tools, and other hardware.

The supervisor made room on a cluttered workbench, placed the case on top of it, and began his examination. "I'm not so much interested in the weapon as I am in the case." He opened it and took a long look. "We can remove the Styrofoam and cut out a space from behind to conceal a transmitter."

"What are you talking about?" Major Schmidt asked.

Gary turned to him. "A transmitter. Ya know, a homing beacon. If the missile gets away from us, we'll be able to track it."

"God, I hope it doesn't come to that," the major whispered.

"Don't worry, sir," Dave interjected. "Gary will take real good care of it. Won't you, Gary?"

"You bet," he said.

Mark Olson tapped Gary on the shoulder and whispered, "We need to discuss our plans."

Gary nodded. "Let's go back to my office and let these guys play with it a while." Dave and the major stayed behind.

Gary said as they walked down the hallway, "The informant's waiting for me to let him know when the next meeting with Rahimi's going to be."

"When do you plan on having it?" Rowe asked.

"It depends on what you guys come up with on the wires," Gary said. "If we can ID the other two bozos, I can go ahead with the delivery right away. If not, I can stall Rahimi to buy you more time."

"That makes sense, but here's the situation," Mark Olson said.

Gary frowned. "Situation?"

"The director called yesterday. He told our Assistant Director in Charge of L.A. quote: 'Arrest Rahimi as soon as you have identified other suspects. You have my permission to release the Stinger to him if necessary,' end quote."

"Just a minute!" Gary said. "We never discussed that. Our goal was to arrest Rahimi and take his money. Not take a chance on losing the Stinger." He paused for a few seconds. "Man, you guys are hanging me out to dry. I promised Schmidt he'd get his Stinger back the minute after we flashed it to Rahimi."

Rowe lowered his voice. "Don't worry about him. The Pentagon's been briefed on this. We can have the Stinger as long as necessary."

"Who have you guys been talking to?"

"FBI headquarters has been in touch with Secretary of Defense Rumsfeld, and it won't be a problem," Olson said reassuringly. "Headquarters has briefed other agencies as well."

"It'll be a problem if the damn thing gets stolen," Gary said. "We don't know why Rahimi wants it or how desperate he is to get it. If that thing gets away from us . . ." He paused again. "I don't even want to *think* about that possibility." They reached Gary's desk and sat down. "What about the wires? Haven't they given you guys any clues?"

"No. He's very cautious about what he discusses on the phone," Olson said. "We doubt we'll be able to identify either his go-fors or the buyer before the delivery. I'm afraid we're going to have to let Rahimi walk with it. It's the only way."

"Jesus Christ. Don't get me wrong, guys," Gary said. "I'm all for finding out who he's getting it for, but this changes things. If that Stinger comes up missing, there really will be a National Security problem. I'm not sure it's worth the risk, even with a transmitter."

"It's out of our hands," Olson said solemnly.

Gary picked up the telephone and paged Robaire. Within just five minutes, the phone rang.

"Yes, Gary. What's happening?"

"Where have you been? I couldn't get a hold of you yesterday."

"Well, Gary, I have a life, you know."

"Anyway, we got the merchandise."

"Fantastic. What now?"

"That's what I'm discussing with the FBI as we speak."

"The FBI? Why?"

"It's a long story I can't get into now. Call Rahimi and say I want to have a meeting to work out some details on the delivery. Tell him I can drive down tomorrow morning and meet with him in the afternoon."

"Okay. I'll call him right now and get back to you." He hung up and immediately called June on her cell phone.

• • •

"Yes?" she answered while window-shopping on Rodeo Drive.

"Well, my dear, now the FBI is involved in this little caper you've orchestrated."

"So? How do you know?"

"I just got off the phone with Lowery. He's talking to them right now, and he's managed to come up with one of the items, just as I predicted. He wants to have another meeting with Amir to work out the details about the delivery."

"Good. Set it up. When does he want to have it?"

"Tomorrow afternoon. He's expecting me to call him back in a few minutes."

"Keep me informed. I *hate* not knowing what's happening."

"Yes, I know."

He hung up and dialed Amir Rahimi's pager number and punched in his cell number to be called back.

• • •

Rahimi was at his office when he got the page. He picked up his desk phone and dialed the number displayed on his pager. The lifting of the telephone receiver from its cradle caused the phone lines to activate the tape recorders attached to the wiretap apparatus. A room full of FBI agents and Farsi translators listened closely as the call was about to be intercepted. Robaire answered his cell phone. "Hello?"

"It's Amir."

"Ah, Amir. I have good news from our mutual friend."

"Good, good. Does he have what I am looking for?"

"Yes, and he would like to meet with you tomorrow afternoon to discuss some details. He said he could drive up tomorrow morning."

"What if I were to drive over there?" Rahimi asked.

"Uh, err . . . I don't think that would be a good idea."

"Why?"

"Gary doesn't want to be seen with strangers so close to home."

Amir Rahimi paused and said, "Very well, I understand. Tell him to come here if he wishes."

"And meet tomorrow afternoon?"

"Just as well. We can meet for a late lunch."

"Where?"

"There is a Mexican restaurant on the northwest corner of Third and Bundy. Do you know the one?" Rahimi asked.

"Yes, I believe so."

"Meet me there at two-thirty."

• • • •

Robaire was thrilled. He was sensing the beginning of the end of his nightmare. He hung up and immediately called Gary at the DEA office to tell him about his conversation.

"Good. That gives me sufficient time," Gary said. "Meet me at Santa Monica Boulevard and Sepulveda at the Texaco station at two-fifteen. We'll drive over together."

Robaire was hungry for details. "Can you tell me what's happening?"

"Not yet. I'm not sure myself. We'll talk about it tomorrow."

"All right, Gary." He disconnected and immediately called June.

• • • •

"Speak to me."

"Gary set the meeting for two-thirty tomorrow afternoon at a Mexican restaurant at the corner of Third and Bundy in Santa Monica. I'm going to meet Gary fifteen minutes beforehand at a gas station several blocks away. We will drive over there together."

"I must see you before that meeting," she insisted. "Where are you now?"

"La Cienega near Third. I'm just passing the Hard Rock Cafe."

"I'll meet you at your apartment. I need to give you something before the meeting."

"Oh? What's that?"

"I'll see you in a half an hour," she said, ignoring the question.

"Yes, my dear," Robaire said sarcastically.

"Oh, and you can knock that 'dear' crap off," she said.

"Yes, ma'am."

"That too."

CHAPTER 13

Bill Brownlee rolled up his shirtsleeves, loosened his tie and unbuttoned his collar. Bill looked like a candidate for a stroke from all the stress he was enduring. He had been running interference for Gary during the case, and the toll was beginning to show. His personal efforts to discourage headquarters from micro-managing the investigation were exemplary, but not always fully appreciated by Gary, who was too busy to notice. He walked out of his office and called over to Gary, Olson, and Rowe. "Let's go to the SAC's conference room and have a little meeting." He saw Reyes at his desk. "Sal, get the tech supervisor and meet us in the conference room. We'll need his input."

"Right, Bill," Sal said.

"Don't forget Dave Page and the major," Gary reminded him.

"Yes, of course," Brownlee said, waving his hand at Sal. "Do it."

• • •

The men walked up the stairs directly into the office of the Special Agent in Charge. Adjacent to it was the conference room with a large rectangular walnut table surrounded by leather swivel chairs. Walnut bookshelves and upgraded carpeting made this government conference room rival any found in the private sector. The floor to ceiling glass wall offered a magnificent view of the civic center.

DEA Special Agent in Charge Michelle Edgington walked into the room, followed by her two Assistant Special Agents in Charge. She looked tired from fielding all the phone calls from headquarters. She was a tall black woman who knew how to take charge.

"Good afternoon, everyone," she said. "I understand there's going to be a meeting."

Before Brownlee could respond, Gary said, "That's correct, ma'am."

The SAC was dressed casually compared to her management team, who looked like models for Brooks Brothers suits rather than federal drug agents.

"Is everyone here?" ASAC Steven Perkins asked.

"Ah, here they are now," Bill Brownlee said as Ray, David Page, and Major Schmidt entered.

After introductions, the group sat at the table, leaving the head position open for the SAC. When they settled, Gary leaned over to Bill and whispered, "You didn't say the SAC's merry men would be here."

"I didn't know they were coming either," he whispered back. "The walls have ears."

"Someone bring me up to speed," the SAC ordered.

Brownlee opened a notebook and referred to his notes. He told her about Gary's upcoming meeting with Rahimi. "We had to wait until we received the Stinger before we could arrange the meeting."

The SAC tugged on her right earlobe. "Any idea why Rahimi wants the missile delivered to him personally and not to someone else?"

"No, ma'am," Brownlee said, and glanced at Gary.

"What's your plan for the delivery?" the SAC asked.

"Ma'am," Gary said. "What I want to do is meet Rahimi in a public place. The more witnesses, the less chance of a rip off."

"I wouldn't bet my life on that one," the taller of the two ASACs, Charles Clark, commented.

Gary continued. "I'm going to ask Rahimi to show me the money again, but I don't think he will. He's already done that once."

Olson jumped in. "Ma'am, we've received specific instructions from our headquarters on how to proceed with the delivery."

"I'm aware of those instructions," she said. "Besides surveillance, what added security measures do you have in mind?"

Ray, the tech supervisor, spoke up. "We're installing a transmitter in the Stinger's carrying case. I've examined the case, and it'll be relatively easy."

"Good, I like that," she said. "Who will be providing the surveillance?"

It was Calvin Rowe's turn. "The FBI has surveillance teams that will work with your agents operating off our radio net, and we'll have a helicopter at our disposal."

"Your boss tells me there's been no luck with the wiretaps," SAC Edgington said. "Any change in the last few hours?"

"No, ma'am," Olson said. "No pertinent calls have been intercepted yet."

"Damn. How long have your wires been up and running?" she asked.

"Only a day," Calvin Rowe said.

"There is one thing we haven't addressed," Olson said. "You know we haven't identified any of Rahimi's accomplices, as we had hoped. We don't know who the money man is behind this, and we don't have any idea who the buyer is or who the two men are who delivered the money to Gary."

"It sounds like we don't know too much about anything," ASAC Perkins said. This prompted a glare from the SAC.

Olson ignored the remark and continued. "Our dilemma is that Rahimi put a time limit for the end of the month on the delivery of the Stinger. We don't know why that's significant, but the short time period makes it difficult to identify anyone else."

"So, what's your point?" SAC Edgington asked.

"If we can't find out from the wire and surveillances who else is mixed up in this, we can only hope Rahimi will roll over and cooperate."

"Fat chance," ASAC Perkins said.

"I agree," Olson said. "That's why we've been instructed by the FBI Director to let the Stinger walk if necessary."

Major Schmidt leaned over to Gary and whispered, "What's he talking about?" Everyone else in the room knew exactly what he meant. Allowing Rahimi to take possession of the missile was in direct contrast to his orders from General Harris.

Olson overheard Schmidt and turned to him. "What I'm talking about, major, is allowing Rahimi to take temporary possession of the Stinger so we can follow him to the buyer. That way, we'll be able to identify them and the other suspects and maybe learn what they intend to do with it."

"Oh, God. I don't know," Schmidt groaned.

Ray added, "Like I said earlier, major, there will be a transponder in the carrying case."

"We've got more than enough surveillance agents," Calvin Rowe added. "He can't possibly get away."

The SAC caught Gary exhaling deeply after hearing that remark.

With her chin resting on her fist, SAC Edgington leaned on the armchair and asked Brownlee his opinion.

"I think if we don't let the Stinger walk, the deal's done. Then all we've accomplished is seizing a lot of money and only putting Rahimi in prison. We still won't know who the main players are."

Calvin Rowe added, "I've worked Iranians before, and they'd rather cut their dicks off than cooperate with the police. Excuse me, ma'am."

"Quite all right," she said.

ASAC Clark slapped the conference table. "Bullshit! We should have taken those two guys off with Rahimi when we had the chance."

"We didn't know they were going to show the money," Bill Brownlee said in defense of his group. "And we wouldn't have a chance of learning who the buyer is."

"We're assuming the money man is the buyer," Rowe said. "And we're assuming Rahimi's only the broker for the deal, as he claims."

"Those are big assumptions," Clark said. "You know what they say about people who assume things?"

Rowe continued. "And we're assuming he intends to use the missile against a foreign aircraft."

"Elaborate," SAC Edgington said.

"The Stinger can't be used against U.S. aircraft, so it's practically useless to terrorists," Gary said.

The look on her face revealed she was confused. "I don't understand. Why can't it be used against U.S. aircraft?"

Major Schmidt explained the safeguards built into the Stinger missile system.

The SAC followed up. "Can the damn thing be used to shoot into a building?"

Good question, Gary thought. "Absolutely not. Aircraft are its only prey," Major Schmidt said.

"There is the possibility Rahimi may be the actual buyer," SAC Edgington opined."He certainly could be," Olson said. "The only way to find out is by letting Rahimi take the Stinger, unless we intercept a phone conversation from someone who identifies himself as the buyer."

"We have few options," Rowe said.

Silence filled the room. All eyes were on the SAC, who mulled over what to do. She looked at Gary. "When are you meeting with this Rahimi again?"

"We're having lunch at two-thirty tomorrow."

"Ask him what he intends to do with the Stinger. Tell him you know it can't be used against U.S. aircraft. See what he says. Offer to deliver it directly to his buyer for an extra fee. Find out exactly how he wants to take delivery and counter with what's best for safety's sake. You know the situation best. I don't need to tell you how to do your job."

"Yes, ma'am."

The SAC turned to Olson and Rowe. "In the meantime, I'll talk over the situation with your boss. I'd like his input."

"All right, ma'am," Olson said.

"No matter what's decided, we're subject to being over-ruled again by Washington," she said. She turned to Brownlee. "Be sure to call me the moment the meeting's over."

"Yes, of course."

The SAC and her two assistants stood up, prompting everyone else to do the same. They walked out without saying another word, and without giving their blessing to give the Stinger to Rahimi. She knew the decision was out of her hands.

CHAPTER 14

Robaire Assaly frequently thought about his family in Lebanon, but refrained from asking June many questions so she could concentrate on doing her job. He prayed for the day he could find the kidnappers and deliver his own form of justice to them. He called his mother's apartment again, hoping to hear of their release, but he only heard endless ringing. He was eager for word from anyone with information about his mother and sister.

While he sat waiting for June at his kitchen table, he wrote in his journal. He hoped he would not regret getting Gary involved, and that June was not hiding something from him. He briefly had the feeling she was setting him up to be a fall guy, but could not point to any specific evidence she was. She'd regret making a fool of Robaire Assaly if that was the case.

He continued writing in longhand on his yellow legal pad, meticulously chronicling his involvement with June from the beginning, and how he was compelled to cooperate. His notes were his legacy, his revenge if necessary, and his apology to Gary Lowery.

After detailing the day's events, he put the pad aside and started to write his will on another. With his future as uncertain as the Russian economy, he was not taking anything for granted.

Here he was, forty-seven years old, and what did he have to show for it? Nothing. A fancy car, nice clothes, but nothing of any lasting value. No wife, no prospects, no children, a rapidly depleting bank account, and worst of all, no future.

After reminiscing about all the wonderful places he had visited as a Pan Am purser, he wished to return to his favorite, Bavaria, Germany. Bavaria was like a setting in a fairy tale. He volunteered for every flight there was into Stuttgart, Heidelberg, or Zurich, if necessary, to be near Germany's magnificent mountains. He could completely relax there, certain the DEA or the German Polizei would not kick down his door to arrest him or seize his property acquired during his drug-dealing days. It offered an escape from the stress his smuggling activities brought. It allowed him to make plans, escape from the business, and enjoy life for a while. He found peace in the mountains that were covered with tall pines and crisp air. Speaking German made it easy for him to assimilate into the culture. Bavaria was a place with such a beautiful and caring nature, God must have mistakenly blessed it twice.

He wanted his family to join him in America when the civil war in Lebanon began. However, the bureaucratic red tape made their migration impossible.

Gary helped in that regard. He had always kept his promises, and if he could not deliver, he'd say so. He didn't like June's attitude toward him after he agreed to cooperate. She came off nice and considerate the day they met, but soon turned bitchy and demanding afterwards as if she had two personalities. He hoped he would not regret betraying Gary.

Her familiar knock came at the door. He quickly put his legal pads in a kitchen drawer before opening the front door to the apartment. She stood there, his savior and nightmare rolled into one.

He turned around and walked away without saying a word. June stepped in, shut the door, and followed him into the kitchen.

"Want a drink?"

"No. I won't be staying long."

"You won't mind if I do."

"No."

"It wouldn't make a difference whether you did or not. I'm going to have one anyway," he said in a snotty tone.

"Suit yourself." After placing her shoulder bag on the floor, she sat at the kitchen table, and crossed her long legs.

He removed a bottle of Stolichnaya from the freezer and placed it on the kitchen counter.

Moving to a cabinet, he removed a tall shot glass, poured in the clear liquid, and joined her at the table.

"What's on your mind, June?"

She reached in her bag and removed the same digital recorder he had worn during the meeting at the Bonaventure Hotel.

"Don't you trust me by now?"

"It's better than relying on your vodka drenched memory," she said. "I want you to be wearing this and something else at your meeting with Lowery and Rahimi tomorrow."

"Oh, is that right?"

June ignored the question.

She removed a small, thin black metal box from her bag and placed it on the table. It was the size of a pack of cigarettes, but only about a third of the thickness. "This is a transmitter, so I can hear in real-time what's happening."

He looked away and slurped his drink. "Why in the world would I want to wear that thing?"

Her tolerance for his insubordination had ended. "Because I said so! That should be a good enough reason for you. This is something that must be done."

"And why the bandage?" he asked, spying something resembling an Ace bandage rolled up in her open bag.

"It's a holster, you idiot, not a bandage." She unrolled it and exposed two small pockets to hold the spy devices. "You put this on like a shoulder holster and place the transmitter and the recorder in the pockets, one under each armpit. But don't turn them on until you're ready to meet Lowery. It'll save the battery life."

"Rahimi already searched Gary for a wire at the first meeting. What if he wants to search me this time?"

"He won't risk it because the meeting's going to be in public. If he does, refuse and storm out as if he insulted you."

"Much like I feel now."

"Don't be so sensitive, Robaire. Your job's almost over." She explained how to operate the devices and told him she would overhear his conversation with Gary and Rahimi on a radio receiver.

"The digital recorder is to keep me honest, is it not? You can compare what you heard with the recorded version?"

She couldn't help but smile. "You might say that."

"That insinuates you don't trust me."

Again, she ignored his question. "When your meeting's over, I'll come by and pick up the equipment."

"I wouldn't want it any other way," he said, heavy on sarcasm.

"Just come right back here after the meeting." She stood up and turned to the door, flashing a stunning profile that was enhanced by her tapered black blouse and tight red skirt. When she reached the door, she slowly turned and glared at him. "I shouldn't have to tell you we're reaching a critical point. Things must go as planned. Don't disappoint me, Robaire."

"See you in my dreams, my dear," he said, and smiled.

"I mean it. A lot is at stake."

"I know that painfully too well," he said. He paused a moment and asked, "Tell me, June, have you heard anything else about my mother and sister? Are they still all right?"

"Yes. We know where they are, and as soon as this is over, my people will rescue them, so stop your worrying," she said.

"I can't help but worry. They're all I've been thinking of. I keep calling mother's apartment, hoping to get an answer from her or my sister saying they either escaped or were released. I haven't slept well since I met you, and I'm losing some weight fretting over this."

"This will all be over soon, Robaire. You must trust me."

Her heels clicked as she walked to her car, this time a rented white Chevrolet Cavalier."Bitch," he uttered under his breath and slammed the door.

He went into the kitchen, retrieved his journal from the cabinet drawer, and wrote the latest episode. He even drew a rough sketch of the transmitter and shoulder rig. "Of course," he said to himself. He hurried into his bedroom, retrieved a 35-millimeter camera, and returned to the kitchen, where he snapped several photographs of the transmitter and the tiny digital recorder. He placed a ruler next to them to use for scale.

Once he completed his writing, he sat in his recliner in his living room and finished his third shot of Stoli. Within seconds, tears flowed as he thought of his mother and sister.

CHAPTER 15

Gary pulled into a driveway off Admiralty way in Marina Del Rey and parked in a visitor spot. He walked through the huge condominium complex overlooking numerous sailboats in slips and passed several bikini-clad women strolling to the pool. He produced a key to an apartment and knocked on the door as he opened it. "Federal agent, search warrant!" he shouted.

"Come and get me, Copper," Joyce McCarthy said from the kitchen. When she saw him, she kissed him and said, "How'd it go today?"

"You know what they say, big cases, big problems."

"Yes, I know the rest. That bad, huh?"

"Today was tough," he said, opening the refrigerator and pouring her a glass of Chardonnay. An expertly made bone-dry Beefeater martini was on the kitchen counter for him. "The FBI's trying their best to run every aspect of the case their way."

"How?"

"They want to let the Iranian walk with the Stinger and follow him to where he delivers it."

"What's wrong with that?"

"Have you ever seen the Famous But Incompetent conduct a surveillance worth a damn? We're not much better, but at least we admit it. I just think the missile's too dangerous to take a chance of losing it to some Iranian."

A small kitchen television set was on, but neither one of them heard a TV news anchor say the Department of Defense had just called up another 150,000 reservists and National Guardsmen in anticipation of an invasion of Iraq. The anchor mentioned Secretary of State Colin Powell's speech to the United Nations where he laid out the evidence Saddam Hussein still possessed chemical and biological weapons.

"But isn't that the only way you guys can find out who the buyer is?" She knew she was exploring a sensitive area. She knew Gary liked things done his way.

"If the wiretaps don't come up with something fast, it may be the only way," he admitted, sipping the Beefeater. He told her about his meeting with Rahimi the next day and the meeting with his SAC.

Joyce leaned against the kitchen counter with her arms crossed while holding the wineglass. "Doesn't the lack of dirty calls on the wires suggest there may not be a buyer? Could Rahimi be the buyer trying to throw you guys off the track?"

"That's what I'm thinking," Gary said. "There may be no one for him to deliver the missile to. Even more reason to hook the son-of-a-bitch up when he delivers the money."

She paused a moment and said, "Let me tell you what the U.S. Attorney thinks."

"Oh, he's the only one so far who hasn't voiced an opinion."

"He does now since he received a call from Washington. He is in favor of giving the Stinger to the Iranian."

"Oh, is that right? Opinions are like assholes, you know. Everybody's got one."

"He thinks it will strengthen the government case against Rahimi." She put her glass on the counter and slipped her arm around his waist, escorting him into the living room. "Come on, big time federal agent. Relax. Try to take your mind off this for a while."

"That'll be tough."

She smiled. "At times like this, don't you wish you had completed law school?"

"What? And be an attorney?"

"Yes. What's wrong with that?"

"Don't you know they rate below Congress and child molesters in public opinion polls?"She frowned. "No, I didn't." They flopped onto a soft, white leather couch.

"Do you know how to tell if an attorney is well hung?" Gary asked, looking serious.She rolled her eyes and smiled. "No, but I'm sure you're going to tell me."

He placed his glass on the coffee table and kissed her just below her left ear, and whispered, "You place your finger between the noose and his neck."

"That's terrible," she said, pushing him away while laughing.

"Ah, but true," he said, and resumed the nibbling on her neck.

"Come on, red skin. I've got a way to relieve your stress." She stood up and held his hand. He readily complied and followed her to the bedroom. "Let's see how well hung you are."

CHAPTER 16

As soon as Gary walked into his office, email, phone messages, and other inquiries about his plans for later that afternoon bombarded him. Thank God for time zones. Maybe that would wear them out in Washington.

"Gary, line one," Sal shouted.

He sighed and picked up the phone. "Gary Lowery."

"Gary, it's Mark. How's it going?"

"Okay, I guess. What's up?"

Olson paused for a moment, puzzled by his tone of voice. "We're ready on this side of town when you are. We've got our surveillance teams ready to follow Rahimi when the meeting's over."

"Okay, fine," Gary said flatly.

"Oh, by the way, is your SAC on board with letting the Stinger walk?"

Is he kidding? Gary thought. "I don't know, Mark. It's not her call, anyway. You guys are going to do what you want to do. Isn't that the way it normally works?"

"I guess so," Mark admitted.

"You wanna make a bet, Mark?"

"Bet? No. I'm not the betting type."

"Well, I'll bet the order to let the Stinger walk stands."

"Oh?" He sounded surprised. "What makes you say that? Have you heard something?"

"No, I haven't heard anything . . . officially. It's just the way these things seem to go, you know," he replied sarcastically.

"Do you think letting the Stinger walk is a problem?"

"Frankly, yes, I do. But it doesn't seem to matter what the original *case agent* thinks." His voice rose slightly.

"You sound like you know something I don't."

"That's just how sure I am it'll turn out the way you guys want it. You guys have a reputation for that, you know?"

"There's something else you need to know, Gary. We got the toll information back on all three of Rahimi's phones. He made over eighteen hundred calls in the last six months to over three hundred different numbers. Not even one number came back to anyone ever connected to a terrorism case. We crunched the numbers through both our system and yours."

"Thanks for filling me in."

"Whatever you say, Gary. We'll meet you on the radio about two-fifteen after you've met with your informant."

Gary hung up the phone hard and began twisting the end of his right eyebrow. No terrorist connections. Damn. It was looking more and more likely the only option was letting Rahimi have the Stinger.

Sal was observing Gary from across the room. "What's the matter, Chief? Your little powwow with the FBI didn't go well? I can always tell when something's bothering you. You always twist your eyebrow."

Gary let his eyebrow go and vented, "The goddamn FBI's trying to run this case by calling Main Justice and telling them what they want. They even called the U.S. Attorney to get him on board, for christsakes."

Bill Brownlee overheard the comment from the doorway of his office and walked toward Gary's desk. "Does that surprise you?"

"Hell no. But you'd think they'd at least have the courtesy to let the undercover agent know what they intended to do before they do it."

"I detect ruffled head feathers," Sal remarked.

"You're damn right," Gary said.

• • •

Gary drove his little beamer to the gas station to meet Robaire. He glanced at his Casio: 2:10 p.m. He still had a ten-minute drive left.

When he bounced over the curb into the gas station lot, Robaire was already leaning against the fender of his Mercedes with his arms crossed, obviously annoyed and ready to proceed. He was promptly on time for a change.

"Where have you been?"

"Busy. What do you think?" Gary blurted.

"Sorry, I shouldn't have asked." With his arms still folded, he reached under his sports coat and turned on both the transmitter and the tape recorder.

"I apologize, Robaire. I've been acting like a dick today. Sorry."

"No apology necessary," Robaire said.

Gary radioed the surveillance team from his car they were about to depart before sliding into Robaire's Mercedes. Sal and his crew were across the street and watched them drive the few blocks to the Mexican restaurant.

Robaire pulled into the restaurant parking lot and began maneuvering the sedan into the nearest handicap spot.

"Hey! What do you think you're doing?"

"Isn't it obvious? I'm about to park."

"Not there you're not." Gary pointed to several vacant spots near the rear of the lot. "There are plenty of spaces over there."

"The policeman in you is coming out. You need to suppress those feelings."

"Stop the car, Robaire," he demanded. He turned toward him and stared directly. "Let me put it in terms you can understand. How would you like it if the three of us came out of the restaurant and saw some cop scratching out a parking ticket because you were too lazy to park in a regular spot? Do you think that might just spook ole' Rahimi? Do you think it might jeopardize everything we've worked so hard for? Don't you think he might get just a little paranoid when he sees the police so close to where we're discussing delivering a fucking Stinger missile to him?"

Robaire was taken aback and didn't know what to say.

Gary continued. "And besides, only an asshole would deprive a handicapped person a place to park!"

Robaire idled forward and pulled into another space. "Yes, I suppose you're right."

"You know damn good and well I'm right! Jesus Christ, man, think," he said while tapping his forehead.

Robaire had seen Gary under stress on many other occasions over the past decade, but never like this. Pangs of guilt were surfacing.

• • •

They walked across the lot and went into the restaurant, heavy on adobe and an abundance of used red brick. A fountain graced the entrance, and an attractive hostess flashed a seductive smile at Gary when she greeted them.

"We're expecting another party," Robaire said.

She pointed to Rahimi, who sat near a window in the corner. He had strategically found a table allowing him to look both out at the street and the parking lot Gary and Robaire had just parked. "Is that the gentleman over there?"

"Yes, thank you," Robaire said.

They walked to the table as Rahimi stood and shook their hands. "How are you, Gary?"

"I'm good, Amir. How's business?"

"Couldn't be better," he said.

"Glad to hear it. Have you been waiting long?"

"No, just got here," he lied. He had arrived thirty minutes earlier, specifically to look for anything he thought might be out of the ordinary.

A waitress appeared and inquired about a drink order.

Gary rubbed his hands. "How about a blended margarita, no salt?"

"Iced tea," Rahimi said.

"Stoli on the rocks, with a twist," Robaire ordered.

"Right away," she said and walked to the bar.

"What has happened since our last conversation, Mister Locklear?"

"I have good news, Amir." Gary glanced left, right, and back at him. He leaned forward and whispered, "The item you've requested is available and ready for immediate delivery."

"That's wonderful news," Rahimi said. "Is it nearby?"

"No. It's still at my warehouse at Fort Irwin." This time Gary lied.

Robaire waved his hand. "Don't worry. It's safe and sound. It can be here on short notice."

Gary took a chip from a basket left by the server and dipped it in a small bowl of salsa. "I take it you have the funds necessary for the purchase?"

"Yes, of course," Rahimi said. "I'm prepared to make payment as soon as you deliver the merchandise."

Gary leaned forward and, in faint voice, said, "I was thinking. Under the circumstances, wouldn't it be appropriate for you to make a deposit before the delivery? You could give the money to Robaire, and when he has it, he can call me up, and I'll deliver."

Rahimi was not happy to hear this. His voice rose slightly. "Surely, you're joking, Mister Locklear. I've already showed my good faith and I expect to take delivery without further delay."

"I know, I know," Gary said. "But I need to know if you still have the money."

"You doubt I have the money?" Rahimi asked, sounding hurt. "I can assure you I do, and I can state unequivocally you won't see it again until I'm shown a measure of *your* good faith."

"Well, you can't blame me for trying?" Gary said.

A waitress returned with a tray of beverages. Gary peeled several bills from a small wad of government money and tossed it on her tray. "Keep it."

"Thank you, sir." Her eyes lit up as she realized he had tipped her five dollars.

"Your point is well taken, Amir," Robaire said. "Don't you agree, Gary?"

"The ball is in your court, as you Americans say," Rahimi said. "When can the exchange take place?"

Gary took a sip of his Margarita. "Day after tomorrow, all right with you?"

Rahimi raised his eyebrows. "Good. Now it's only a matter of selecting where."

"You tell me. I'm not familiar with the city." Gary lied again.

Rahimi leaned back in his chair. "Why not bring it to a hotel room? I'll examine it, and if it's what I ordered, I'll send you the money." He stared at Gary for his reaction.

Gary leaned forward and whispered, "Do I look like I'm on drugs?"

Rahimi smiled broadly and laughed. He reached for his glass of iced tea. "You certainly can't blame me, either, for trying, can you?"

They all laughed loudly as the waitress reappeared to take their food order.

•   •   •

After ordering their meals, Gary gazed out the window to the parking lot. "What do you say we do it right here, in this parking lot? Robaire and I drive in with the merchandise in the trunk. I show it to you. We drive off and don't return until you bring the money."

"Hmm," Rahimi said. "Not bad, but how about this instead? You and I both bring cars. We meet in a parking lot like you suggested. We exchange keys and drive off in each other's car to pick up the items. Me for the money and you for the merchandise. We later return to the same parking lot and swap keys again."

"Obviously, I get to look in the trunk before I drive off for the second time," Gary said.

"Obviously," Rahimi said and grinned.

Gary sensed they were close to an agreement. "And the parking lot must be public. I don't want any deserted garages at midnight or any bullshit like that. I don't like surprises."

"Neither do I, Gary. I understand completely," Rahimi said in a calming voice.

Gary leaned back in his chair and rubbed his forehead. "Let me think about this for a while." He glanced at Robaire, who nodded reassuringly. Gary decided. "I like your idea, Amir. That just might work." He pointed to the lot where he and Robaire had parked. "How about this back parking lot?"

Rahimi glanced toward the almost deserted parking lot and then back at Gary. "Agreed."

• • •

June was one-half block away in a Jeep Cherokee. She was listening intently to the conversation picked up from Robaire's transmitter. She concealed her radio receiver inside a brushed aluminum Zero Halliburton briefcase on the front passenger seat. "Yes!" she exclaimed. She was hoping Gary would agree to the arrangement.

Olson and Rowe listened to Gary's conversation from a distance in their government sedan. Gary was wearing the identical transmitter Robaire was. "All right!" Olson said. Rowe turned up the volume when he heard them speak again.

"I'm so pleased we have reached an agreement," Rahimi said. "At noon the day after tomorrow we will both arrive, exchange keys, and return within, say, thirty minutes?"

"Make it fifteen minutes," Gary said. "I don't want to hang around anymore than I have to."

"Good point," Robaire interjected.

"That's reasonable," Rahimi agreed.

The waitress returned with their food.

"Another round," Rahimi said. "We have much to celebrate."

Robaire seized the opportunity. "This time," he told her. "Make mine a double."

• • •

Half-way through lunch, Gary felt the timing was right. "I'm just curious, Amir. What does your buyer intend to do with his newly purchased item?"

"I have no idea. I'm just procuring it for him," Rahimi replied. "He can do whatever he likes. It's not my concern."

"He must know he can't use it against U.S. aircraft, right?"

Rahimi didn't like the sudden questions. "This does not concern either of us, Gary. My buyer will do whatever he intends to do with it. I'm sure he's aware of its capabilities and limitations."

"How about those Lakers?" Robaire said to change the subject.

CHAPTER 17

Gary drove on the Santa Monica freeway back to his office. His spirits had picked up considerably. The thought of seizing a million of Rahami's dollars pleased him immensely, even if it meant he had to let him take the Stinger. It was on the FBI's shoulders now. He had endured enough brain damage and disruption of his personal life, but it would be well worth it to see Rahimi, his two bag men, and the buyer, whoever he was, in federal prison. Things were looking up, even the traffic didn't seem so bad today.

His cell phone rang. It was Sal, with a progress report.

"We followed him back to his office. That's where he is now."

"Where's Salt and Pepper?" Gary asked.

"Who cares? They're probably on their way back to the FBI office."

"If you can raise them on the air, ask them to call me at the office, will you?"

"Sure. Say, want to meet at the Central City Cafe after work?

Gary liked the sound of that. He hadn't gotten together with the guys for some time. "Yeah, that sounds great. See you there."

Gary arrived at his office just as Ms. Garcia was hanging up the phone. "The SAC wants to see you right away."

Now what? The stress was suddenly returning. He picked up his phone and checked his voicemail. Only one message, this time from his mother.

He hurried to the staff floor and into the SAC's secretary's office and was told to go right in. Gary peeked around the corner and softly knocked on the opened door to get her attention. SAC Edgington spun around in her leather executive chair from her computer desk and motioned for him to come in. She had been reading a cable from Washington that had a red "SECRET" cover sheet attached. "Shut the door."

Gary complied. "Yes, Ma'am. You wanted to see me?"

"What happened today?" she asked, looking up from the document.

"The informant and I met Rahimi. We agreed to do the exchange in the same restaurant parking lot the day after tomorrow on Valentine's Day."

"How appropriate. And that's exactly what will happen," she said with a stern face.

"Ma'am?"

She scanned the paper with her index finger until she found the place. "We've been directed to quote, 'allow the Stinger missile to be temporarily placed in the suspect's possession to facilitate the identification of other members of the Rahimi criminal organization.'" She looked up at Gary over her reading glasses. "What do you think about that?"

"May I see it?" Gary asked. The SAC handed him the cable.

SECRET NOFORNPOST FOR DEA 122144Z FEB 03
ACTION: DEA-1
INFO:
DISTRIBUTION: DEA
CHARGE: DEA
VZCZCILW0724
RR RUEHIL
ZNR UUUU
R 122144Z FEB 03 ZFD
FM DEA HQS WASHINGTON DC
TO RUEHLR//DEA FIELD DIVISION//LOS ANGELES//

RUEHIL//FBI FIELD OFFICE//LOS ANGELES//
INFO RUEABND//WHITE HOUSE SITUATION ROOM//
NATL SECURITY COUNCIL//WASHDC//
DOJ/ATTN DIR INVES POLICY//
FBI HQS//WASHDC//
NSA//FT MEADE MD//
CIA//LANGLEY//
DIA//BOLLING AFB//
HQS BATF//WASH DC//
HQS INS//WASH DC//
HQS US SECRET SERVICE//WASH DC//
HQS US CUSTOMS ENFORCEMENT//WASH DC//
HQS US MARSHALS SERVICE//WASH DC//
JOINT CHIEFS//PENTAGON//
BT
SECRET DEA 22007
POST FOR DEA
ATTN SAC EDGINGTON/SA G. LOWERY
SUBJECT: R1-03-0217/INC1I; RAHIMI, AMIR ET AL
REF: TELECON BETWEEN SAC, LADO AND MAIN JUSTICE, 10 FEB 03.
PAGE 02 RUEABND2007 SECRET
1. (S//NF) AFTER EXTENSIVE CONSULTATION WITH REPRESENTATIVES OF THE FBI, DOD, AND OTHER CONCERNED FEDERAL AGENCIES, THE ADMINISTRATOR OF DRUG ENFORCEMENT CONCURS WITH FBI LEADERSHIP THAT SAC, LADO, ALLOW THE STINGER MISSILE TO BE TEMPORARILY PLACED IN THE POSSESSION OF THE UNKNOWN SUSPECT(S) TO FACILITATE THE IDENTIFICATION OF OTHER MEMBERS OF THE RAHIMI CRIMINAL ORGANIZATION.
2. (S//NF) MAIN JUSTICE HAS DESIGNATED THE FBI AS THE "LEAD AGENCY" IN THE CONTINUANCE OF THIS INVESTIGATION AND WILL BE SOLELY

RESPONSIBLE FOR THE CONTROLLED DELIVERY OF THE WEAPON TO THE INTENDED RECIPIENT(S). THE CIA CONCURS WITH THIS DECISION.

3. (S//NF) THIS INVESTIGATION WILL CONTINUE TO BE CONDUCTED AND COORDINATED WITH THE LOS ANGELES FIELD OFFICE OF THE FBI JOINT TERRORISM TASK FORCE AND WILL BE MONITORED BY HQS DEA.

4. (U) QUESTIONS MAY BE DIRECTED TO THE ADMINISTRATOR.

RONALD T. BOYSEN, CHIEF/OPERATIONS

BT

. . .

Before reading the body of the cable, Gary saw it was not only addressed to DEA in Los Angeles but to the White House and a host of other agencies. He handed it back to the boss.

"Look at everyone involved in this. Every three-letter combination in the alphabet wants to get in the act."

The SAC nodded in agreement.

Gary took a seat in one of the leather armchairs in front of the SAC's desk. "Ma'am, I'm not opposed to letting the Stinger walk, if . . . and this is a big if . . . the feebs can guarantee it won't get stolen."

The SAC laughed. "We both know there are no guarantees in this business, especially if you're talking about the FBI taking responsibility if something goes wrong. Look at what happened at Waco. More blame got laid there than Johns at a Nevada whorehouse."

"That's a fact," Gary agreed.

"What time's the delivery going to be?"

"High noon. Just like in the movies," Gary said, attempting to smile. "Also, I did ask Rahimi what his buyer intended to do with the Stinger. He denied knowing what he planned to do. When I told him he couldn't use it against U.S. aircraft, he didn't seem surprised and implied his buyer knew what it could and couldn't do."

"Interesting," SAC Edgington said. "Think he's telling the truth?"

"I don't know," Gary admitted. "He put on a convincing act."

"Get with those two feebs and coordinate your plans. If you don't like what they're up to, say so. You're the undercover agent on this case, and only you can make the calls. If you don't feel right about it, shut it down. I'll back you up."

"I appreciate that, ma'am."

"Good luck, Gary."

"Thank you, ma'am." Gary stepped lively out of the office, past the SAC's secretary, who waved as he walked back to his office. Suddenly, his pager went off. He checked the number and recognized it as the Los Angeles FBI office.

Gary sat at his desk and dialed the number, after which he put both feet on it and crossed his ankles.

Rowe answered the phone. "I guess you got the word?"

"I sure did."

"Are your tech agents installing the transponder?"

"They probably are as we speak."

"Okay. Mark wants a briefing the day after tomorrow at nine a.m. at our office. Is that all right?"

Gary sighed. He disguised his lack of enthusiasm to drive to the west end of town during the morning rush hour. "Hey, no problem. I'll be there."

"Don't forget to bring the Stinger," he joked.

"I'll try not to, Cal."

"See you later. If anything comes up over the wire overnight changing things, I'll let you know."

"Please do. Has there been any wire activity since our meeting today?"

"Nothing worth mentioning."

"All right. See you later."

GREGORY D. LEE   117

In one flowing motion, he lowered his feet, rose out of the chair, and hung up the phone as he headed for the technical group. While rounding the corner into the hallway, his mind sorted through all the things that could possibly go wrong.

He walked into the tech group and saw Dave Page and Major Schmidt watching a tech agent at work. The molded Styrofoam inside the Stinger's container had been removed, and the tech agent was in the process of cutting away a bottom portion of it to house a hidden transmitter. Page looked impressed.

"How's it going?" Gary asked.

The tech agent spoke up. "I'm breaking down the inside compartment of the carrying case to find a suitable place for the transponder, and I think I've just found one."

"Good, where?"

Ray removed a pen from the pocket of his short sleeve dress shirt and pointed it at the center of the material. "Right there. I'm cutting out an area to slip the transponder in and replace the packaging. Then I'll glue it to the container's frame, which should discourage anyone from poking around."

"Good idea," Gary said.

"How long will the transponder work?" Page inquired.

"Close to a week."

"How far will it transmit?" Dave asked.

"Miles if the receiver is high enough. A helicopter can easily detect the signal five to ten miles away."

"I need it by the close of business tomorrow. Briefing's set for nine a.m. the following day at the FBI office."

"No problem. I'll be done with this before I go home tonight, and the glue will set nicely by then."

Page opened his mouth and was about to say something to Gary when Gary interrupted."Gotta go and get things ready." He whirled around and headed for the door to go back to his office. He didn't want to give Page a chance to question him about a decision made by others.

As he walked, he detected a slight bounce in his step again, like when he was a young, inexperienced DEA agent, hungry for excitement.

He was feeling better about the decision to let the Stinger walk. Thank God he didn't have to make it. The FBI was taking full responsibility. DEA would come out clean no matter what happened, but he didn't want to be around when Major Schmidt found out.

CHAPTER 18

Robaire Assaly was experiencing the initial stages of depression. Everything was going according to June's plan, but the thought of him causing Gary so much grief upset him. He knew June would achieve what she was setting out to do, and had mixed feelings about being a party to it. The time was closer. He would have to prepare. He drove to his apartment faster than usual. When he turned into his driveway to park in the carport, he saw June seated in a black Jaguar parked on the street. He locked his car doors and headed to the front door of his apartment when he heard the familiar sound of high heels coming towards him.

"You did a wonderful job today," June smiled, complementing him. "It sounds as though everything's set."

He unlocked the door and walked in, leaving it open for her without saying a word. She flung her heavy bag on the couch. "You're going to be there for the delivery, aren't you?"

Robaire took his coat off and draped it over a kitchen chair, and finally said, "Gary didn't mention it, but I suspect he wants me there to make Rahimi feel comfortable."

"Good, because I'll need an extra set of eyes and ears." She ran her fingers through her hair and sat on the couch. "Are you all packed and ready to go?"

"Yes, and I'll be glad when this is over!" He removed the elastic holster with the tape recorder and transmitter and held it at arm's length like it was a smelly dead cat. "Here, take it."

She rose from the couch. "Calm yourself, man - just a couple more days. Don't get emotional this close to the end."

"Don't worry about me. I'll do my job. Just make sure you keep your end of the bargain," he said and plopped onto his battered recliner.

Robaire watched as June retrieved a cigarette from her purse and lit it. She inhaled deeply and exhaled a large plume of smoke towards the ceiling. She took another drag and flicked the ashes into a tray on the coffee table next to a copy of *Cigar Aficionado* magazine. "Let me warn you about something, Robaire," she said calmly. "You don't want to piss me off. That wouldn't be smart."

Robaire stared at her and smirked. "That's what I like about you, June. You're always so sensitive to the needs of others."

"My job doesn't allow sensitivity. They picked me because they know I can get the job done, and that's all that matters. It's going to get done, with or without your help."

She stood up with her purse in hand, grabbed the recording equipment, and turned toward the door. "Don't disappoint me," she said, pointing at him with her cigarette between her fingers. "There's a lot riding on this, more than you know." The lingering cigarette smoke looked like it was coming from her ears.

"Under the circumstances, my dear, I couldn't be more cooperative."

She stormed out the door and flicked the cigarette into the street, clicking her way back to the Jag.

Robaire seized the opportunity. When she was almost to the car, he rushed to his bedroom and retrieved his 35-millimeter camera that had a telephoto auto-focus lens. He pointed it at her through the mini-blinds and pressed the shutter release. A series of still photographs whirled off as the motor advanced the film. He was pleased he captured her pissed-off looking face on film before she got into her expensive car.

Robaire hurried to the living room to lock the front door. He went into the kitchen and retrieved his journal. After making himself comfortable at the kitchen table, he scribbled out on the yellow legal pad what had transpired at the restaurant and the plans for the delivery of the Stinger. He removed a separate sheet of stationery from a box he maintained in another kitchen drawer and sat back down at the table. After concentrating for several minutes, as if in a trance, he pondered his words. He penned his thoughts in a letter to his sister, Nadia, in Virginia, his only sibling in the United States.

My dearest Nadia,

I am writing to inform you of something I can only trust with you. Words cannot express my feelings towards you, our mother, and Leila. It pains me to tell you that about three weeks ago, they were kidnapped on the streets of Beirut. A CIA agent, who calls herself June Cohen, informed me of the crime. She claims she is investigating the kidnapping that was perpetrated by terrorists. She showed me a photo the kidnappers took of Mama and Leila. They were in chains! Can you imagine?

June told me she was working to free them but needed my help, and now I need yours. She has devised a plan to get a Stinger missile into the hands of an Iranian living in Los Angeles who she thinks is connected to the kidnappers. This way, she believes, the authorities can follow him to other terrorists so they can kill or capture them. She said if I cooperated with her, she would see to it mother and Leila are freed. Of course, I agreed without hesitation to help her, and we are on the verge of getting a missile delivered to the Iranian bastard. But to achieve our goal, I had to lie to and betray a good friend of mine, Gary Lowery. Hopefully, when this nightmare is over, he'll understand my situation and forgive me.

God willing, I will be in Cairo by the time you receive this letter. Ms. Cohen insists I go there to help her do something as part of our agreement, but I don't have any idea what that will be.

The significance of the contents of this envelope is that it contains information about what I have been doing to secure the release of our loved ones. I've chronicled the events leading to my flight to Egypt in a log I have maintained throughout this ordeal. I also have photographs corroborating my claims.

My dearest, I do not possess the imagination to create such a story. My actions are purely for unselfish reasons. I do not wish to die. However, I believe she will make it impossible for the truth of the matter to be known if something goes wrong. I fear June may try to double-cross me. I do not trust her.

Please reach out to Special Agent Gary Lowery of the Drug Enforcement Administration in Los Angeles about receiving this envelope. His telephone number at his office is 213-555-2650. Please give this envelope and its contents to him. He will know what to do.

God bless you and kiss the children for me.

Your Loving Brother,

Robaire

He signed the letter, wound the film in his camera back in its cannister, and placed it inside a large, padded manila envelope before sealing it. After addressing it to his sister's Alexandria, Virginia post office box, he began to tremble. Perspiration beaded on his forehead. He got up and fixed himself a healthy dose of vodka. He shuffled into the living room and spread out on the couch. The alcohol soon soothed his throat and relieved his tension.

·   ·   ·

"What do you mean, you're going to let the Stinger go?" Major Schmidt demanded to know while he stood in front of Gary's desk. He had just heard about the decision from the tech agents. He dragged Dave Page along for moral support when he confronted Gary. "That was never part of the agreement!"

"This is way above our paygrades, major." Gary said, trying to reassure him. "The decision's been made to let it walk, but only to see where he takes it. The FBI will follow it to find out who the buyer is."

"Has it ever occurred to anyone what might happen if the Stinger falls into the hands of terrorists?"

"Of course, major. Don't you think they have considered all the possibilities? Fortunately, it can't be used against one of our own aircraft, right?" he asked to reconfirm.

"That is, unless they somehow dismantle the IFF system," the major said.

"What! Now you tell me they can dismantle the system?"

"I'm not saying it's possible, or that they will. However, if they screw with it long enough, who knows?"

"Well, that's just great," Gary said.

The major said, "Never mind terrorists. Did anyone think about the Iranian selling it to the Chinese, or the North Koreans? They'd tear it apart and figure out how it works, and reverse engineer it. Or he may try to sell it on the open market to the highest bidder. God only knows what his intentions are." Schmidt was rapidly losing his composure.

"All the more reason to let it walk." Gary suddenly realized he was defending the FBI. "The FBI's going to have surveillance so tight on Rahimi he won't be able to breathe." Gary wished he could believe that, but he wanted to assure the major. "As soon as it becomes apparent what he intends to do with it, they'll swoop in and grab it so you can take it back to Fort Irwin. For Christ's sakes, major, we've got a transponder in the case that'll tell us exactly where it is."

The major wasn't buying it. "*I'm* the one responsible for the weapon," he said, "and I don't want to see anything happen to it."

"We're *all* responsible for it," Gary said reassuringly. "Trust us." He regretted saying that the moment the words left his mouth.

Gary looked at Dave Page, who listened to the exchange without comment. He sighed whenever Gary mentioned anything about the FBI and assurances of safety. He'd seen too many surveillance situations when something unexpected jumped up and bit him in the ass. But he admired Gary's optimism.

"You look like you need a drink, major," Dave said. "Come on, I'm buying. Gary, you coming?"

"I'd love to, but I've made other plans. I'll see you guys tomorrow."

· · ·

Gary walked to the freight elevators that took him straight to the parking garage. He drove to the Central City Cafe. The lot already had Sal's Mustang parked in it.

Gary walked into the rustic drinking and dining establishment, which was an old hangout for the agents since the office moved from downtown to the new federal building in the civic center. Most late afternoons, agents from U.S. Customs, Secret Service, Alcohol, Tobacco and Firearms, and Immigration and Naturalization Service could be found tipping glasses. Federal agent groupies frequented the establishment, giving the agents an added incentive to gather there. Gary found Sal seated at a table in the corner with a bottle of beer and an 'it's about time' look on his face. Gary ordered a beer at the bar and brought it to the table. "You don't look too good, Sal. Sorry I'm late."

"No problem, Gary. I keep thinking about your case."

"It's *our* case, Sal. Remember that." Gary smiled. "It's only my case if all goes well. If it turns to shit, it's *your* case. Isn't that the way it works?"

"Usually."

"So, what have you been thinking about?"

"Ya know, things are goin' awfully smooth. Usually by now there'd be so many frickin' twists and turns you wouldn't recognize what kind of case it was to begin with."

"Well, I'd like to think it's because of the superior performance of the undercover agent," Gary said, trying to be funny.

"No, I'm serious, man. Things are just goin' along too smoothly. There's got to be a kink in this somewhere."

"Well, we don't have long to find out. You know about the briefing at nine a.m. day after tomorrow at the FBI?" Gary asked.

"Yeah, I got the word. And that's another thing," Sal said, suddenly sitting erect. "The FBI's doin' the surveillance? These terrorists aren't stupid, ya know. They'll be really cautious. Remember that time I bought that kilo of heroin from an Iranian in Santa Monica?"

"How can I forget?"

"Remember all the counter-surveillance he had? There were more frickin' Iranians running around that restaurant than at a mosque on Friday in Teheran." He sipped his beer and stared straight ahead. "You can expect to see tons of 'em when you show up with that missile."

"I'll keep that in mind, Sal."

"All I'm saying, Gary, is watch your ass with these guys."

CHAPTER 19

Gary spent the entire next day preparing for what would be the most significant undercover role of his career.

No detail was too small. He had reserved a Ford Explorer in his undercover name at a Pasadena Enterprise for delivery to his home at seven a.m. tomorrow. Gary hoped Rahimi would see the rental car contract in the glove compartment. He reasoned Rahimi would feel better about taking a rental car to deliver his million dollars in.

Gary's office was receiving an extraordinary amount of cable traffic to and from the Washington micro-managers. Main Justice, the FBI and The Pentagon all got their obligatory briefings on the investigation's status and anxiously awaited its outcome. The FBI was now obligated to take full responsibility for conducting the surveillance on Rahimi. Sal and his crew would only have to follow Gary back to the DEA office with the money. After that, the FBI would be on its own and had to rely on their experience and the transmitter. The FBI assigned a helicopter to assist their ground units, and its own tech experts examined the Stinger. They concluded the DEA technical crew had done the most logical thing by placing the transmitter in the case, eliminating any need to modify the missile. Fortunately, the weapon was built to withstand battlefield conditions and could endure arduous trips across varying terrain. Driving on a freeway wouldn't be a problem.

Gary got up at 5:20 a.m. the next day to dress, shower, shave, and make the long haul to the Federal building in Westwood after he received the rented Explorer. He verified on his cell phone the Stinger was on its way to the FBI office, along with his investigative group for the briefing. SAC Edgington and her two assistants intended to monitor the progress of the investigation from the FBI Assistant Director in Charge's office. To his surprise, Gary arrived with twenty minutes to spare.

Everything was in place. Agents were clinging to coffee cups and notebooks as they filed into the briefing room. The FBI and DEA agents, as well as state and local investigators assigned to the task force, wore their traditional surveillance uniform: blue jeans, sweatshirts, athletic socks, and tennis shoes.

Gary's anxiety rose considerably when he entered the briefing room and drew a layout of the parking lot where the delivery was supposed to take place. As the enormity of the event set in, he knew the outcome of the investigation would rest heavily on his performance, and so did everyone else in the room.

Gary made one more call to Robaire at his home to see if anything had changed since their last conversation, which was less than twenty-five minutes ago.

"No, Gary. Believe me, everything's fine. I haven't heard anything from Rahimi, which is good news. I'm waiting for him to return my page, and when he does, I'll tell him you are on your way here."

"If anything changes, *be sure* to page me 9-1-1. Don't assume anything. I must know exactly what's happening. When I'm finished with the briefing, I'll call you before I drive to your place."

"Fine, fine. Relax, Gary. Everything's going to be all right."

"See you soon," Gary said, and hung up.

• • •

The briefing room was almost filled. At least forty agents, mainly FBI, were in the room going over the game plan Olson and Rowe had reduced to paper. It included Rahimi's driver's license photo and surveillance photos of his two accomplices.

Major Schmidt entered the room with Mark Olson, Calvin Rowe, and Dave Page carrying the Stinger missile. Rowe saw Gary and asked, "You all set?"

"Can't wait," Gary lied.

The crowd became silent when the FBI Assistant Director in Charge and the DEA Special Agent in Charge, with their entourages, entered the room. Mark Olson, who was clearly senior to Calvin Rowe, started the briefing from behind a podium in front of a whiteboard. He cleared his throat. "Ladies and gentlemen, may I have your attention, please?"

The noise level lowered significantly except for two DEA agents in the back finishing a joke that brought an icy stare from Bill Brownlee. The joke abruptly ended, and Olson began the briefing.

"This morning we are going to conduct a moving surveillance of an Iranian named Amir Rahimi, spelled R-A-H-I-M-I. I know it's spelled with I's, but it's pronounced Rah-he-me. He'll be exchanging one million dollars for a Stinger missile we're going to be supplying him. Your job today, and possibly for the next few days, will be to follow Rahimi and the missile to its ultimate destination. We do not yet have any solid leads to indicate what Rahimi intends to do with the Stinger or who the moneyman is behind the purchase. As many of you know, the carrying case of the weapon is equipped with a transmitting device our helicopter observer will monitor. Hopefully, Rahimi will lead us right to the other coconspirators."

"Don't hold your breath," Sal whispered to the agent next to him.

"The undercover DEA Agent, Gary Lowery, set the exchange for noon in the parking lot of a Mexican restaurant which is at the northwest corner of Third Street and Bundy in Santa Monica. He'll be driving a Navy blue rented Ford Explorer to the parking lot and meet Rahimi. He gave the license number. There they will exchange keys to their vehicles and drive off to load the money in Gary's Explorer and the Stinger in Rahimi's car. We don't know what he'll be driving since the Stinger won't fit in his Jag. When they return to the parking lot about fifteen minutes later, they will show each other the booty in their vehicles. They will exchange keys back again and drive off. That's when the real heavy surveillance will begin. DEA supervisor Bill Brownlee and his crew will follow Special Agent Lowery back to the DEA office and handle the money count. Our guys will follow Rahimi wherever he goes."

Rowe walked up to the podium. "When we've got Rahimi's car I'll slap another beeper on it for some added insurance."

Olson added, "The helicopter will be operating off channel A-3. Does anyone have questions?"

A young towheaded FBI agent leaning against the rear wall asked, "How long are we prepared to follow this guy?"

"The tracking device will last for close to seven days, but we hope we don't have to wait that long," Rowe remarked, drawing laughter from the audience.

"Hope you packed your toothbrushes," Gary said, getting a few more laughs.

The FBI Assistant Director in Charge, Michael Mason, walked up to the podium. Absolute silence filled the room. "We're not going to risk losing the Stinger under any circumstances. I have assured the Director, the Attorney General, and The Pentagon we can keep track of the weapon to its final destination. We weighed the circumstances carefully and concluded the only way we can identify additional suspects in this organization is to follow the missile to its intended recipient. We feel it is a risk worth taking. It goes without saying there will be enormous problems if we lose the Stinger. I'm sure everyone here appreciates the gravity of the situation." He stepped away from the podium.

Olson stepped up to the microphone again. "Okay. Does everyone have a game plan and photos? Before you leave, take a good look at the Stinger. If anyone sees it being removed from a vehicle, get on the radio immediately."

A procession of agents filed by the open case like a group of mourners viewing a casket at a funeral.

Major Schmidt closed the Stinger's case and picked it up. He walked out the door with Gary and the others.

Gary's pager went off. He looked at the displayed number. "It's Robaire Assaly," he said to Olson. Gary stopped at the nearest desk and dialed Robaire's home number.

"Have you heard something?"

"Amir just called and said everything's on schedule. He'll be in the parking lot at noon."

"How'd he sound on the phone?"

"Optimistic."

"Did he say he had the money?"

"No." He added, "But he didn't say he didn't have it."

"All right. I'll be by to pick you up no later than eleven forty-five. I'll be in a dark blue Explorer."

"See you soon," Robaire said and hung up.

• • •

June crossed her long legs while seated in Robaire's modest recliner in the living room. She hung up the extension phone on which she had been listening.

"What did I tell you?" Robaire said.

June swung her leg, reflecting sunlight off one of her highly polished black high-heeled shoes. Robaire thought she looked especially appealing, dressed in a dark gray double-breasted jacket and matching skirt. He watched her reach into her shoulder bag and pull out a golden tube of red lipstick and expertly glossed her lips. Her eyes narrowed as thoughts raced through her mind. She dragged deeply from her cigarette before reaching into her purse again, pulling out an airline ticket envelope. "Here's your ticket to Cairo. You'll have a four-hour layover in London. And here's your U.S. passport with the necessary visas. Check in under that name. I'll be meeting you at the

Cairo Hyatt in four days." She stood up and faced him. "Don't disappoint me by not being there."

"I still don't understand why you need my help in Cairo. I thought you were going to follow the FBI while they follow Rahimi. Isn't that your plan?"

"It is."

"Then why do you need me in Cairo and why the phony passport?"

"I'll explain it all to you when I see you in Cairo. I'm a spy, Robaire. Remember? This is spy tradecraft. I don't want Lowery and the FBI to know you've left the country. You'll be back soon enough."

"And when do you intend to send in your team to rescue my mother and sister?"

"Soon, Robaire. Very soon." She smiled and took one last drag from her cigarette before crushing it in the cigar ashtray on the coffee table. "I'd wish you luck, but I don't think you'll need it," she said while leaving. "See you in Egypt." She swung her bag over her shoulder and opened the door. She hurried to her car, clicking all the way.

CHAPTER 20

At eleven forty-five sharp, Gary parked his rented Explorer to the curb where June's Range Rover had once been.

Robaire watched him from his kitchen window facing the street. He placed the suitcase he was packing in the closet and shut the door. He answered the doorbell when it rang.

"Ready?" Gary asked.

"As I'll ever be," Robaire replied. He buttoned the middle button of his suit coat out of habit and followed Gary to the SUV.

During the short drive to the restaurant, neither one spoke, as there was too much to contemplate. Gary passed the parking lot once and didn't see Rahimi standing near any parked vehicles. He circled the block. It was only two minutes after noon. "Where the hell is he?"

Don't worry, Gary. No crook worth a damn is ever on time." Gary grunted something and continued to drive.

Gary's cell phone suddenly rang. He removed the tiny cell phone and answered it. "This is Gary." He recognized Sal's voice. He was in the DEA surveillance van, parked in the lot at the restaurant with Bill Brownlee and others.

"The feebs are following Rahimi over to the parking lot right now. They're less than two minutes out."

"Good." Gary was relieved. "Tell Olson I'll wait three minutes before pulling in."

"Right." Sal hung up.

Gary drove two blocks over, two blocks down, and two more blocks to the restaurant to time it to arrive about a minute after Rahimi. When he pulled into the lot, he found Rahimi standing near a gold-colored Chrysler minivan with moderately tinted windows to the sides and rear. Amir Rahimi smiled broadly when he recognized them parking next to him.

• • •

"He just pulled into the lot," Bill Brownlee whispered over the radio from his vantage point in the surveillance van that had a carpet cleaning business logo magnetically adhered to its sides. They were parked only three spaces away from Rahimi. Brownlee sat in the back with three other agents, all suited up in bulletproof vests, gun belts, and raid jackets. Sal carried a Colt 9-mm sub-machine gun, and another agent had a shotgun with a pistol grip resting on his lap. Bill was looking through a periscope concealed in an open vent window on the roof of the van. He was particularly interested in any counter-surveillance that might be present. No signs of it, yet. They were ready for the worst, while hoping for the best. "They're out of their cars now, shaking hands."

• • •

The parking lot was only half-full when Gary and Robaire pulled in and parked. Gary looked, but it didn't appear to him there were any other Iranians providing counter-surveillance for Rahimi. Gary glanced a second time around the parking lot just to make sure.

"Good day, Gary. Everything's in order, I presume?"

"It is. I'm ready to do business if you are."

"I am, and so is my buyer." He looked around as if to see if they were being watched, and asked, "Is it far from here?"

"Let me put it this way," Gary said. "I can drive away, get it, and be back here in fifteen minutes. How about you?"

"About the same. No more than thirty minutes."

"Make it twenty," Gary snapped.

"As you wish."

"You have all the cash?" Robaire asked.

Rahimi looked slightly irritated. "But of course, my friend. I'm a man of my word, and I hope you are as well."

"Then let's do it," Gary said. He handed the keys to the Explorer to Rahimi, who handed Gary the keys to the minivan. "Twenty minutes," Gary reminded Rahimi as he and Robaire got into the vehicle.

"Twenty minutes it will be," Rahimi said, exposing his nicotine-stained teeth.

• • • •

Gary drove out of the lot and around the block.

"Robaire, look behind us for a tail," Gary ordered.

"Do you seriously believe he would have someone follow us?"

"Goddamn it, don't argue with me," he blurted, while looking into the rear-view mirror.

"Tell me if anyone is following us!"

"All right, all right." Robaire went through the motions, knowing full-well no one was following, but forgetting Gary didn't. "Looks good to me. Why are you so uptight?"

"The last thing I want is someone to rip us off."

"You're right. I apologize. I wasn't thinking." He let a few seconds lapse before he had the courage to ask, "How much further?"

"Right down the street," Gary said. He drove down an empty alley where Olson, Rowe, Page, and Major Schmidt were waiting for them with the Stinger.

Gary got out of the minivan and slid open the sliding side door. Page and Rowe folded down the second-row seat and placed the Stinger case on it. They covered the case with an old army blanket Schmidt had. Olson held a radio near his ear, listening to the progress of the surveillance on Rahimi. "It sounds like he's returning to his office . . .

wait," he said with his hand outstretched like a traffic cop, "Yes, he did just pull into his building."

"We better get going," Gary said. Robaire didn't say a word but was impressed with the agents' efficiency.

"Just a minute," Rowe said. He ran to his car and retrieved a small black metal box with a black antenna sticking out of one end. Two magnetic strips the size of popsicle sticks, only thicker, were attached to it. Rowe ran back to the minivan and dropped to his knees. He rolled onto his back and reached way under until he found a suitable spot for the magnets. "There, it's on."

"What's that?" Major Schmidt asked.

"That's another bird dog," Rowe said. "It's our added insurance policy."

"Good idea," Schmidt said. He began feeling a little better.

Olson stuffed his portable radio into his rear pocket. "I just checked with the helicopter crew and they're getting strong signals from both transmitters."

"Wonderful." Rowe said.

"Rahimi's still at his office?" Gary asked.

"Yep." He glanced at his watch. "You guys better get going," Rowe suggested.

Gary and Robaire got back into the minivan. "Adios," Gary said as they drove off. He dialed Sal's cell. He and the other agents were still in the parking lot.

"What's going on, Sal?"

"Nothin' right now. The guy took off, and I heard on the radio he went into his business's underground parking lot. Where are you?"

"We're on Santa Monica Boulevard heading west, waiting for you to tell us he's heading back. Any sign of counter-surveillance?"

"No. But hang on a second, Gary. Something's happening."

Gary fell silent for a few seconds, and Sal got back on the phone. "Surveillance has Rahimi comin' out of the building and headed back towards us."

Gary's heart was pounding. "I'll stay on the phone until you put him down in the lot." He checked his watch. Only fourteen minutes had elapsed. He could overhear the radio transmissions of the surveillance agents through Sal's phone.

"He just pulled back in."

"We'll be right there, Sal. Does he have any company?"

"No. He's alone."

"I'm a minute away." Gary hung up and looked at Robaire. "This is it, partner. He's back at the lot. Are you ready?"

"Yes, I'm ready." Robaire removed a clean, folded handkerchief from his suitcoat's breast pocket and wiped his forehead. "I'll sure be glad when this is over."

"So will I, partner. So will I."

•   •   •

Gary pulled into the lot and backed in next to Rahimi to give the agents in the surveillance van a better view. They stepped out of the minivan after Rahimi opened his door.

"Do you have it?" Rahimi asked.

"Yes. It's in the back." Rahimi stuck his hand out for the key.

"Not so fast, friend. Let's see the money," Gary insisted.

"Certainly." They walked to the back of the Explorer, and Rahimi opened the rear hatch. In the back was the same briefcase they had seen earlier at the Bonaventure Hotel. Rahimi thumbed the combination to both locks and opened the case, exposing the neatly stacked one-hundred-dollar bills. "The combination is 1-2-3."

"How original," Gary said. "May I take a closer look?"

"But of course," Rahimi said. "I insist."

Gary counted the bundles, ten in all.

"Is it all there?" Robaire asked.

Rahimi looked over to Robaire, "I'm hurt you would think I would cheat you. Go ahead, Mister Locklear. Fan through each bundle to make sure the bills are all hundreds if it will make you feel better."

Gary rubbed his thumb over the end of a bundle he selected at random and saw it consisted entirely of one-hundred-dollar bills. He did the same to a second bundle with identical results. A man and woman walked by on their way to the Mexican restaurant, causing Gary to stop for a moment. Once they passed, Gary continued counting and saw there were ten one-hundred-thousand-dollar bundles.

Gary handed the minivan keys to Rahimi. "Looks good to me."

"Now, may I see it?" Rahimi asked.

"Definitely," Gary said. He shut the case and closed the rear hatch. He and Robaire followed Rahimi to the side of the minivan, where Gary opened the automatic sliding door with the remote key pod. Rahimi quickly removed the army blanket covering the box and saw it was indeed a case for a Stinger. He manipulated the latches, opening the lid and began visually examining the missile. He gently lifted the missile only a few inches to feel its weight, making sure the warhead was still in it, and slowly placed it back in its resting place.

"I'm satisfied," Rahimi said as he closed the lid, latched it, and placed the blanket over the carrying case. He slammed the sliding door shut and extended his right hand to Gary, who shook it. Gary returned the keys to the minivan to Rahimi with his free hand. Rahimi handed Gary the keys to the Explorer. "Have a safe drive back to Barstow, my friend." He shook Robaire's hand. "Thank you, Robaire."

Gary couldn't resist asking. "Oh, Amir. What happens now you have it?"

Rahimi smiled slyly while getting into the driver's seat and starting the minivan. "Don't worry, my friend. Curiosity killed the cat, you know."

"Enough said," Gary remarked while holding his hands up. "Nice doing business with you." Gary motioned Robaire to get into the Explorer.

Rahimi drove out of the lot, turning toward his business. Gary walked back to the Explorer, making sure he had shut the rear hatch tight. He climbed into the driver's seat, and drove the vehicle out of the parking space, and headed to the driveway, making it a point to turn the opposite way Rahimi did. "Let's get the hell out of here," Gary said.

The surveillance van backed up and drove out of the lot, following Gary and Robaire, who was now feeling a little cocky. "Well, was there ever any doubt?" Robaire asked.

"I gotta hand it to you. It went off without a hitch." Gary suddenly thought about Sal's observation. "Too smooth, in fact."

"What do you mean?"

Gary hesitated and said, "I think Sal, my partner, is right. Something's missing. Something's not right."

Robaire turned in his seat and studied Gary as he drove. "Please explain."

"This deal. It's just gone . . . too smooth, you know? I can't quite put my finger on it. He even came back in twenty minutes like he said he would. Usually nothing goes the way it's supposed to, but everything did this time. I expected those two guys who were with Rahimi at the Bonaventure to show up as security, but they were a no-show."

Robaire managed a faint smile. "Quit complaining. You've taken a million dollars from a terrorist, and the FBI will get their man. What more do you want?"

"Some answers. Deals don't go down this easy, particularly with Iranians."

Gary thought aloud as he headed for Robaire's apartment. "Something's not right."

CHAPTER 21

Bill Brownlee and his crew followed Gary and Robaire straight to Robaire's apartment. Gary drove around the block twice to assure himself they weren't being followed and then quickly pulled to the curb. He leaped out of the SUV and opened the rear hatch as everyone got out of the surveillance van. Gary removed the large briefcase filled with money and handed it to his boss. "This'll be a lot safer with you."

Brownlee took the case that weighed about twenty-two pounds and handed it to Sal, who placed it inside the surveillance van. An agent with a shotgun slammed the door shut from the inside.

Gary smiled as he stepped onto the sidewalk and bear hugged Robaire. "Well, buddy, it looks like we pulled this one off. So far, at least. I'll call you in a couple of days to let you know what's going on."

"Please do that," Robaire said. "I'll be dying to find out. I'll call you if I hear anything from Rahimi."

Gary got back into the SUV and started the engine. He was about to leave when Robaire trotted up to his door. Gary rolled down the window, and Robaire placed his clammy hand gently on his left arm resting on the door window frame. "You take good care of yourself," he said, meaning it. He shook Gary's hand and walked up the few steps to his apartment. The sincerity of his statement and the tone of his voice struck Gary as being very odd. Almost like there was closure to it.

Robaire waved to Gary as he drove off, with the surveillance van following close behind.

Once they were out of sight, he lit a Montecristo and entered the apartment.

• • •

Amir Rahimi drove like an experienced drug dealer. He changed directions to throw off the surveillance agents. He made abrupt U-turns for no apparent reason and drove onto residential streets he knew were cul-de-sacs, just to see if anyone would follow him. When he didn't detect surveillance, he drove directly to the nearby I-405.

The FBI agents kept up with him, thanks to the helicopter and the *two* transponders, which nullified Rahimi's tactics.

The helicopter observer reminded the ground agents, "Keep off him. We'll tell you which way he goes. It looks like he may get on the San Diego freeway."

"Roger," Mark Olson said on the radio.

"He's obviously not going back to his office," Calvin Rowe commented to Olson.

"He's committed to the southbound 405," the helicopter observer said. Rahimi entered the transition lanes of the 405 and drove like a California Highway Patrol car was hooked to his rear bumper. He did not exceed sixty miles per hour despite the flow of traffic going closer to seventy.

• • •

The helicopter continued monitoring Rahimi's progress. The ground units were far enough behind him to not to be noticed. Rahimi drove five miles per hour below the speed limit, so the surveillance units had to go the same speed or slower, infuriating drivers on the freeway's southbound lanes.

After a few minutes, the pilot radioed the ground units. "If we continue towards LAX, we will have to break off. We're only a couple of minutes from the air traffic control space."

"Damn it!" Mark Olson, who was driving, said to Calvin Rowe. "Did you hear that? Where's that guy going? The airport?"

"Beats me." Rowe shrugged. He picked up the microphone to the radio and warned, "We can't lose him by the airport. Tighten it up a little."

The FBI agents drew cautiously closer to the Chrysler Town and Country minivan, blending in well with the moderate afternoon traffic. It did not seem to them Rahimi had detected their presence.

Rahimi passed Manchester Boulevard and was coming up to the Century Boulevard off ramp, one of the primary exits for the airport. Rahimi had been driving in the far-left lane since he entered the freeway, which made everyone assume he was not turning off soon. Suddenly, he darted across the four other lanes of traffic at a 45-degree angle, cutting off a black man driving a pickup truck. The man laid on his horn and flipped Rahimi off as he passed in front of him. Rahimi sped towards the Century off-ramp, and at the last moment, exited the freeway, narrowly avoiding crashing into a guardrail. The maneuver immediately lost two-thirds of the cursing ground surveillance agents, who had no option but to continue on to the next exit.

"Son-of-a-bitch!" Olson yelled when he observed the minivan. Fortunately, they were far enough behind the evasive maneuver did not affect them. He merged to the right as he slowed just in time to catch the Century Boulevard exit.

"There he goes," Rowe said. "We got him. We got him." He keyed the microphone. "We've got the eye." When Olson and Rowe came upon a stop sign at a T-intersection, Rowe glanced to his left and pointed. "There he is."

Rahimi had made a left turn and quickly proceeded to the first intersection on Century Boulevard. He veered into the right lane and caught a green arrow to turn right. Other FBI units followed the directions given by Rowe, and the agents who had to go to the next exit rushed to catch up with them.

"We're out of here," the pilot said. "We're taking heat from the Air Traffic Controllers. Tell us when he leaves the area. We'll be standing by at the Santa Monica airport."

"Shit!" Olson yelled. "We've got to get on his ass now!"

Rahimi turned right several blocks down and made an immediate left. He maneuvered the minivan past acres of long-term airport parking lots and passed an occasional rental car lot. His speed had slowed, and he was being cautious as he approached another busy intersection.

"He's real hinky," an agent in another vehicle told his partners on the radio. "He's looking really hard."

Olson and Rowe were rapidly catching up to Rahimi. "I'm going to have to pass him. Who's got the eye?" Rowe asked as they drove straight through the intersection, as Rahimi turned right. "Who's got the eye?"

Silence. No one did. Precious seconds elapsed as agents drove around city blocks and made U-turns to find him. "Goddamnit!" Olson yelled. "He's around here somewhere." Olson pulled his sedan to the curb and grabbed the radio microphone from Rowe's hand. "Let's comb the area four square blocks from where we last saw him and work our way to the center."

"Where did you last see him?" an agent asked over the air.

"He turned north on Aviation Boulevard towards Century," Olson replied, and hung the microphone on the dashboard. "Son-of-a-bitch!"

"I got him. I got him," an excited agent cried on the radio. "He's west bound on Century coming up on the Delta Airlines billboard." While the agents sped to the area, one busted through a red light, almost colliding with a United Parcel truck. They were relieved when they finally converged on a gold Toyota minivan.

"Oh shit. It's not him, Mark," he announced on the radio. "It's a look-a-like."

Olson felt faint. Rahimi had evaded them in less than twenty minutes despite a helicopter, a dozen cars, twenty-six agents, and two transponders.

"Mark, what's your status?" the observer in the helicopter asked. Silence. "Mark, do you copy?"

Olson and Rowe didn't want to talk. They knew Assistant Director in Charge Mason was monitoring their radio traffic. How could they explain this away?

"Make a decision, Mark," Rowe finally said. Olson pulled into a gas station lot to think. He rubbed the back of his neck, calmly took the microphone, and said, "We've lost him. Set yourselves up on corners around the intersection. There's a chance he pulled into one of these airport parking garages. Pick one out and go through the lots and look for him."

"Ten-four," the agents said.

. . .

Rahimi had done precisely what Olson had suspected. He drove into a self-parking structure at the LAX Hilton Hotel. Rahimi drove up the ramps after taking a ticket, which raised the barrier, and passed hundreds of parked cars until he got to the rooftop. He saw June was in her green Range Rover parked in a section behind the ramp, smoking a filtered cigarette. Only a few other cars were parked on the roof level.

Rahimi pulled into the space next to her, got out of the Town and Country, and slid the side door open. Carrying her shiny metal briefcase, June walked up to the minivan. She dropped her cigarette and crushed it with the toe of her high-heeled shoe. She placed the briefcase on the back seat of the minivan and unlatched it. Inside was a battery-operated device designed to detect hidden transmitters. She flipped several switches and watched the needle of the VU meter suddenly move violently, which brought a smile to her face. The needle settled down and pulsated every second. A green diode flashed when the metering level reached a certain point."Were you followed?" she asked.

"Yes, but I lost them after I exited the freeway. They saw me turn off and must be around here somewhere." He took out a handkerchief and wiped his brow as he watched her work. "What are you doing?"

"Looks like you took on some extra passengers, mister."

"What do you mean?"

"Bugs, Amir. At least one, maybe even two." She opened the Stinger missile case and examined its contents. Nothing was obviously out of place. She walked back to her Range Rover, opened the rear hatch, and removed an empty cello case. She carried it to the minivan and placed it on the ground. "Take the Stinger out of its case and place it in here, quick!" The Stinger barely fit. He latched it shut.

"Put the cello case in the Range Rover and leave the Stinger case in the van," she ordered. He immediately complied. June closed the Stinger case, latched it shut, and placed the army blanket back over it. She hid the minivan's keys under the driver's floor mat and shut the front door, leaving it unlocked. She carried her opened briefcase to her Range Rover and manipulated more dials and switches near the cello case. Nothing. She slowly walked back to the Chrysler and received the initial reading. She manipulated more switches and came to the correct conclusion. "They bugged the case *and* the minivan, Amir. Someone thinks they're very clever."

Rahimi wiped the back of his grimy neck with his handkerchief. "Aren't you afraid of a helicopter spotting us?"

"Not a chance. We're too close to LAX," she said, pointing to a Northwest 747 slowly gliding above a few hundred feet, making its final approach to the airport. She shouted over the noise, "Helicopters aren't allowed this close to the airport. That's why I picked this parking structure."

"Not even the FBI's?"

"Especially theirs. Those boy scouts would never consider violating the FAA rules." She laughed.

Suddenly, a white Toyota 4-runner sped up the ramp with Tariq and Iqbal Khan. They parked on the other side of June's Range Rover and got out.

"You have your tickets and passports?" she asked the two men.

They nodded. Rahimi removed his tickets from his inside jacket pocket and showed them to June.

"Go straight to the international border. You have plenty of time to make your flight from Tijuana tonight."

"Okay, okay," Rahimi said.

"You understand what to do?"

All three men nodded.

Rahimi walked around the 4-Runner and got into the rear seat and laid on his side out of view. The Toyota, with all three, roared off down the ramp. June shut the sliding door to the minivan and the back lid to the Range Rover while chuckling at the thought of the FBI chasing its own tail.

June got behind the wheel and drove slowly down the ramp. When she reached the attendant in his booth, she saw a silver four-door Ford Crown Victoria with two clean-cut white men wearing wind breakers and sunglasses speed up to the same booth. The driver flashed his FBI badge while the passenger frantically gestured for the attendant to raise the gate. When the gate lifted, the agents squealed their tires as they sped inside the structure. June flashed a smile at the attendant, revealing her expensive dental work while she handed him her ticket.

He examined the stub from behind his reading glasses. "That'll be four dollars."

She removed the money from her purse and gave it to the man who she caught staring at her cleavage.

"You have a nice day now, ya hear?" she said, with an exaggerated southern accent.

"Same to you, ma'am," he said.

June drove out of the structure and soon reached the freeway heading north. The thought of Gary and the FBI surveillance agents made her laugh out loud. It was a devious laugh. She considered herself a master of manipulation. A woman who plays the international espionage game flawlessly. Someone not afraid to make decisions and take chances. And she was loving every minute.

CHAPTER 22

Mark Olson could see his promising FBI career evaporating. *Why me, Lord? What have I done to deserve such a fate?* Olson wondered what it would be like to wash the Assistant Director's car for the rest of his career. Calvin Rowe got on the radio and ordered an agent to meet the FBI helicopter pilot at Santa Monica Airport. He instructed him to retrieve the monitors for the bird dog homing beacons and to meet him by LAX. He knew Rahimi had to be in the area, and the beacons would tell him.

Suddenly, welcome news came over the radio. "I've found the minivan!" an excited agent exclaimed. "It's on the top floor of the Hilton parking structure, but I don't see anyone in it. We'll drive by it again."

Radio silence. Dead, agonizing silence. Anticipation mounted. Olson was ready to burst. "Where the hell's Rahimi?"

• • •

The agents on the top floor of the parking structure parked on the opposite side away from the minivan and approached cautiously. One of them drew his Glock and aimed it at the vehicle, fearing the Iranian was lying in wait for them.

They peeked in the windows. "He's gone," was Olson's answer on the radio. "The minivan's here, but the suspect's gone. But I can see what looks like the Stinger case in the back. But I can't be sure. It's all covered up, but the shape fits."

• • •

"Who says there's no God?" Olson asked, breathing a gigantic sigh of relief.

"Hey, wait a minute!" Rowe said. "The motherfucker musta left the minivan there for someone else to pick up."

Olson considered that possibility. "Yeah, that makes sense." He suddenly became more optimistic. "That makes perfect sense!" His spirits rose. He grabbed the microphone. "Set up on the minivan, and we'll wait for whoever picks it up."

"Sounds like a plan, my man," Calvin Rowe said, grinning as he did a high five with Olson. "Thank God Almighty we found the minivan with the Stinger in it."

Olson leaned back in his seat for a moment and exhaled loudly. "I'd sure like to know who's going to pick it up."

"Just be patient, my man, and we should know soon," Rowe said.

"And I'd like to know exactly where Rahimi is," Olson added.

"Hey, don't sweat the small stuff. He's in the bag. We know where he lives and works. He obviously dumped the minivan off for his buyer to pick up. Man, we're going to have this whole thing wrapped up the minute someone gets in that thing."

"You think so?"

"Sure. Why else would he abandon the van? He ain't gonna be walking around town carrying a big ass case that says Stinger missile on it, is he? In any event, we'll know for sure when we run the bird dog monitor past the car. At lease we'll know for sure the Stinger's in there."

"I guess we'll just have to wait for the monitor to find out," Olson said.

• • •

Twenty-five minutes later, an FBI sedan with four antennas attached by magnets on the roof arrived at the gas station where Olson and Rowe were still parked. The driver pulled alongside their car, rolled down the window and said, "The signal's real strong and coming from the west," he said while pointing at the LAX Hilton."

"Perfect," Olson said. Drive over there and find out if the Stinger's still in the minivan."

"Right," the enthusiastic agent said, eager to get up there. He and his partner sped out of the lot and over to the Hilton. Eight minutes later, Olson got his confirmation.

"The monitors indicate two, repeat, two signals coming from the vehicle."

"Glory be," Rowe said.

"Thank God for small favors," Olson said. "Rahimi has to have left his car for someone else to pick up."

"It's got to be the buyer," Rowe hypothesized. "Who else could it be? All we have to do now is sit on it until he shows up. Then we've gotta decide if we want to follow him or just take him down."

"Yeah. We can hook Rahimi up after we arrest whoever picks up the car." Olson started to get his color back. The thought of washing cars had left him, and now the idea of getting promoted crossed his mind. Maybe he'd even get the Attorney General's Award for the most significant case of the year.

Rowe answered his cell phone when it rang. "This is Special Agent Rowe."

"Assistant Director Mason would like to speak with Special Agent Olson," a secretary said. Rowe gladly handed the phone to him.

"It's for you."

"Who is it?"

"Mister Mason."

Olson cleared his throat. "This is Special Agent Olson, sir."

"What the hell's going on out there? Have you located the minivan or not?"

"Yessir, we have."

"It's damn hard to tell from your radio traffic. It sounded like you lost him for a while. Is that what happened?"

"Yessir. We did momentarily lose him."

"Jesus Christ, man, how in the hell did that happen?"

"The helicopter was forced to turn back because of the restricted airspace around the airport."

"Damn! How long was he out of your sight?"

"Just a few minutes."

"Where is he now?"

"I'm not sure."

"You're not sure?"

"Sir, please let me explain. We've located his minivan on the rooftop of a parking structure at the Airport Hilton Hotel."

"What about the missile?"

"We think it's in the car."

"You *think* it's in the car?"

"We retrieved the bird dog monitors from the helicopter and ran them past Rahimi's van. We're getting two readings, which means the Stinger's in the van."

"Thank heavens!"

"Yessir."

"Wait a minute," the Assistant Director said. "Has anyone actually *seen* the missile?"

"Not exactly."

"*Not exactly?*"

"We haven't gone into the minivan."

"Why not?"

"We don't have a warrant, and the minivan must be locked."

"You don't need a warrant. It's a vehicle, for Christ's sake! That's government property in there!"

"Yessir. But do you think it's unwise to search the van since Rahimi's accomplice may be in the hotel and see us from his hotel window? The van's on the roof level."

"Shit!" The Assistant Director calmed down for a moment to think. "What do you intend to do now?"

"We're setting up on the minivan, hoping someone will get in it and drive away."

"And if someone does, then what?"

"For right now, we intend to continue the surveillance to see where he takes the missile. That is, with your permission, sir."

Silence on the line as Mason thought about the consequences, as well as what would happen if the Stinger were to get away from his agents again. He wasn't nearly as optimistic as they were. "Until you hear otherwise directly from me, arrest the first son-of-a-bitch that touches the minivan."

"Yessir. That's what we'll do."

•   •   •

Mason hung up and slumped in his leather executive chair. DEA SAC Edgington and her two assistants heard the conversation from his speakerphone and were not impressed. "You've got a real problem here," SAC Edgington said. "If Rahimi's not with the minivan, where is he? In the hotel? On the street?"

"Good question," the FBI Assistant Director conceded.

SAC Edgington pointed to one of her assistants, Steven Perkins. "Get Lowery on the phone and have him call his informant. Have him call Rahimi at home, at his office, his cell phone, whatever, and find out where the hell he is."

Perkins reached for his cell phone to make the call.

"I don't like the sound of this," SAC Edgington said.

•   •   •

Amir Rahimi and his two companions drove south on the San Diego freeway, passing San Juan Capistrano doing the speed limit, headed for the Mexican border. They were only an hour away.

•   •   •

Gary sat at Bill Brownlee's desk as Sal placed stacks of one-hundred-dollar bills in an electronic money counter next to him. The whirl of

GREGORY D. LEE 151

the notes by the high-speed counter created a subtle breeze as the number of bills the machine counted registered on a red LED display.

The phone on Brownlee's desk rang. Sal answered it, and whatever he heard caused him to stare at Gary, who read his body language that something bad had happened.

"Yes, sir." He listened to the directives of his Assistant SAC and about how the FBI had lost Rahimi. "Jesus Christ! I'll have him do it and get right back with you." He hung up and looked straight at Gary. "The FBI lost Rahimi!"

Gary slapped the arms of the chair with both hands. "That's abso*fucking*lutely incredible!"

CHAPTER 23

Robaire checked the contents of his suitcase. He expected the taxicab he summoned would arrive at his apartment at any moment. After he secured the latches, a car horn sounded twice. After wheeling the large suitcase into the living room, he opened the door and waved to the driver. He bent over and set an on-off timer on a lamp to go on at six p.m. and off at two a.m. Robaire grabbed the manila envelope from the kitchen which had the film, sketching, and letter for his sister in Virginia. He held it firmly under his arm as he struggled with the large Hartman, taking one last glance inside before shutting and locking the door for what he thought might be the last time.

When he reached the cab, the driver, fresh from Nigeria, wrestled with the heavy suitcase, finally getting it in the trunk. Robaire slid into the back seat and said, "Los Angeles International Airport by way of a post office." The driver smiled broadly and drove off. Robaire powered off his cell phone and pager.

Robaire checked his new name was on the U.S. passport June gave him. Anwar Nasir was the name chosen. He committed it to memory before arriving at the post office where he mailed the envelope fourth-class, reasoning it would take about a week to get to Virginia that way. By then, he'd know his fate.

Upon arriving at the Tom Bradley International terminal, the check-in at the Lufthansa first-class ticket counter was uneventful. No third degree by the ticket agent, like he had experienced so many times at other international airports around the world. He merely had to show a photo ID, using the passport for that purpose. Robaire made his way to the gate and observed an army of TSA security. After shuffling through the metal detector, he furtively glanced around, looking for anyone who looked like a federal agent. He had seen enough of them during his career as a confidential informant to know when he saw one. Nothing unusual so far. After lacing his belt back on his pants and slipping into his loafers, he strolled to his departure gate. On the way, he spied a cocktail lounge he found impossible to resist.

After first purchasing a *Time* magazine at a shop nearby, he found a corner table in the cocktail lounge to cover his back. He initially faked reading while glancing around, but after seeing nothing suspicious, became engrossed in an article about terrorism in the United States and the imminent war in Iraq over disarmament. The article highlighted the FBI's efforts to find terrorists. Good luck with that, he thought. It was not until he had finished his second double Stoli the paranoia subsided, and he finally began to relax.

Robaire's Omega informed him it was 5:43 p.m. He spent the next ninety minutes preparing mentally for his journey, if that was possible, with two doubles running through his veins.

After a while, his thoughts drifted to his mother and sister and what they must be experiencing. He wondered how his other sister in Virginia would react to his letter. But thinking about the contents of the envelope brought a smile to his face. He'd have his revenge if June double-crossed him, even from the grave, if it came to that. He knew Gary would someday see to it.

• • •

The agents staked out the minivan in the parking structure while Mark Olson and Calvin Rowe ate hamburgers at a Carl's Jr. across from the Airport Hilton Hotel. They patiently waited for someone, *anyone*, to get in that minivan. Other surveillance agents were set up to block off the exit to the parking garage. They would not lose the minivan again. From their vantage points, the agents could see the only car driving up to the rooftop had an older black gentleman driving. He merely parked his car and took the elevator down.

With three hours passing, Olson's optimism was fading.

"How much longer do you anticipate us being here?" someone asked over the radio.

"Until something happens." Rowe replied, irritated.

"When's that going to be?" another agent asked.

"God only knows," Olson remarked.

"Will someone please ask Mister Hoover when that will be?" a smart-ass agent said on the radio.

"Only God, Mister Hoover and Assistant Director in Charge Mason, know for sure," Calvin Rowe reminded him.

"Maybe he intends to leave the car here for a week," Olson speculated. "This lot is used for long-term airport parking, you know?"

"Yeah," Rowe said. "I know. The hotel provides a shuttle bus to the terminals. I've parked here myself before."

"We could be out here for some time."

No shit, Sherlock, Rowe thought. "Maybe we ought to start thinking about shifts and get some more agents out here to help us."

"Let's give it a couple more hours before we start with that," Olson said. "Damn, I wish someone would show up."

• • •

Gary Lowery dialed Robaire's home phone number and got his answering machine. He dialed his cell phone, and it went straight to voicemail. He paged him and punched in the numbers 9-1-1 after the office phone number. Hopefully, he would recognize this as an emergency. Still no response.

"I'm not getting an answer on any of his numbers, Bill," Gary admitted. "I don't know where he is."

"How about Rahimi's office?"

"I've never called there."

"Try now. Just call and ask for Rahimi and see what they say."

Gary dialed the number for *Overseas Financial Investments*. A woman with a Middle Eastern accent answered the phone after the second ring.

"May I please speak with Mister Rahimi?"

"Oh, I'm sorry, sir. Mister Rahimi is out of the office."

"Can you tell me when he'll be back?"

"No. He didn't leave word when he would be returning."

"Thank you anyway." Gary hung up. He knew the FBI had just monitored his conversation. At least now they could forward that information on to the surveillance teams.Gary looked at Bill Brownlee. "Rahimi's not at the office. They have no idea when he'll return."

"Shoot! Where'd that slick son-of-a-gun go?"

"I don't know, but what bothers me is Robaire's also out of pocket," Gary said.

"Me, too," Sal said after observing what was going on. "I don't like the sound of it. Would he go anywhere without his beeper?"

"I've known him to. Come to think of it, I told him it'd be a few days before I got back to him."

Brownlee ran his hand over his stubble. He hadn't bothered to shave that morning. He picked up the phone and called his assistant SAC's cell phone.

"Lowery can't find the informant. Gary stiffed in a call to Rahimi's office and he's not there according to the person who answered the phone."

"That's just great," the frustrated ASAC Perkins said. "I'll get back to you." He hung up and was ready to inform the others of his findings.

SAC Edgington asked, "Well?"

"Negative. Lowery can't find the informant to ask him to call Rahimi. But he did call Rahimi's office, and he's not there."

The desk telephone rang. Mason answered and listened for a few seconds. "Okay, thanks." He turned to his audience. "That was the wire room. They intercepted the call by Lowery and told me they haven't heard from Rahimi since the deal went down."

"What do you think?" SAC Edgington asked.

The FBI Assistant Director leaned way back in his swivel chair, deep in thought. Every conceivable scenario flashed before him. He finally said, "We already lost the minivan once, and now it's beginning to get dark. I don't think we can risk losing it a second time and try to explain it away."

"*We?*" SAC Edgington asked.

"Yes, we. You're as much a party to this as we are."

"But you're the ones who insisted the Stinger walk. You guys backdoored us at Main Justice to get it done your way," the DEA SAC reminded him.

"We'll talk about it later," he said, looking pissed-off.

"You bet we will. If this turns to shit, DEA's not taking the fall," she said. "Not this time."

"But you'll bask in the glory?"

"You're damn right because it was our informant that started this case. You hijacked the case under the auspices of 'terrorism' and now it's up to you guys to determine how this case ends."

The Assistant Director got a little upset. "Well, I'm satisfied with what we have so far. I don't relish the thought of losing the goddamn missile again because we, yes, we, would never hear the end of it from Congressional committees. I'm not about to throw thirty-two years with the bureau down the shitter. In fact, I'm going to order them to seize the minivan and recover the missile right this minute. We can always grab that asshole Rahimi later."

"It's your call," SAC Edgington said. "I'd feel a lot better knowing the Stinger's back in the army's hands."

The Assistant Director picked up the desk phone and called Olson's cell.

• • •

"Yessir. Yessir. Right away, sir." He hung up.

"Who was that?" Rowe asked.

"Mister Mason."

"And? . . . What did he say?"

"He wants us to tow the minivan and take custody of the Stinger, 'before something else goes wrong.' He didn't sound so happy. In fact, he sounded rather upset."

Rowe had to chuckle. "Wouldn't you be if you told Main Justice your agents could follow Rahimi to the ends of the earth, and twenty minutes later, they lost him?"

"Don't remind me, Cal, okay? Let's drive on up there and see what we've got."

• • •

Rowe ordered the entire surveillance team to converge on the minivan. An agent checked the driver's door and discovered it was unlocked. The keys were under the floor mat. Nothing of any other consequence was visible under the front passenger's seat.

Olson took the keys from the agent, with Rowe by his side, and opened the sliding side door. They both let out an audible sigh of relief when Olson removed the blanket, revealing the Stinger's case. Olson unlatched it, sensing it was lighter than it should be, and slowly lifted the lid. "OH MY GOD!"

Rowe's eyes widened when he saw it was empty. "Oh, sweet Jesus."

The gravity of the situation sank in. Olson placed his face in his hands. "What the hell are we going to do now?"

CHAPTER 24

Three large generators powered floodlights on the top level of the Hilton parking structure. Scores of FBI agents and crime scene technicians carried out their individual tasks searching the crime scene.

"Twenty-three feet, seven inches," a crime scene technician shouted to his partner, who recorded the distance the minivan was parked from the structure's west wall. A photographer shot his third roll of film, exposing every conceivable angle of the vehicle, its trunk, and the empty Stinger carrying case.

No less than fifty FBI special agents thoroughly combed every square inch of the lot and looked for the remotest of clues. They stood double arm interval and slowly paced from one end of the parking lot to the other, looking for anything Amir Rahimi may have discarded. *Anything* that might lead them to him and, more importantly, to the stolen U.S. Government Stinger missile. The one the FBI guaranteed it couldn't lose.

A tow truck driver was standing by for word to move the minivan to the FBI garage. Evidence technicians would thoroughly examine it for DNA, fingerprints, hair, and fibers. Agents were on their way to interview the clerk who had rented the minivan to Rahimi.

An agent used tweezers to pick up a red lipstick smeared cigarette butt. He examined it as he walked over to Olson. "This one looks pretty fresh. The lipstick is still glistening," he told Olson. "It wasn't far from where the minivan is parked."

"Good, good. Bag and tag it. See what else you can come up with."

"We'll send everything we find to Quantico for DNA analysis," the agent said. "Maybe they can tell us whose lipstick this is."

"Assuming we have her DNA in our database," Olson said, rubbing his temples. His head was like a pressure cooker. "Get on it, will you?"

"You bet." The agent scurried off.

Another agent trotted up to Olson. "We're getting a lot of questions from the media. Is either public information or Mister Mason going to make a statement to the press?"

"Hell no!" Olson said. "We don't want anyone talking to the press. Make damn sure everyone here gets the word. Absolutely no statements!"

• • •

Gary and Sal had just completed their money count. It impressed Gary that Rahimi was only two hundred dollars shy of the one million dollars he promised for the Stinger. The count had taken close to two hours to complete, and their hands were black from the ink, despite using a high-speed money counter.

They placed the currency in four large transparent plastic bags and heat-sealed them before logging them in with the evidence custodian.

"Not a bad day's work," Sal said, proud of their accomplishment.

"Can't argue with you there," Gary said as they made their way back to his desk. He was eager to sit down and relax for a few minutes. He placed both feet on the desk, crossing his ankles.

"Lowery! Get your ass in here!" Brownlee shouted. "You too, Reyes." They looked at each other, puzzled, and rushed into their group supervisor's office and found him gnawing on a wooden coffee stirrer. "What's the matter, boss?" Gary asked.

Brownlee looked exhausted and disgusted. His sleeves were rolled up, and he desperately needed a comb for his hair. "I just got off the phone with the FBI. The Stinger's gone."

"WHAT?" Gary yelped while Sal burst out laughing. "What do you mean, gone? I thought everything was under control?"

Brownlee looked at Gary. "What exactly is it about the English word "gone" you don't understand?"

"You mean, as in stolen?" Sal followed up.

"That's exactly what I mean, goddamnit," Brownlee shouted. "They took the missile but left the case behind! And Rahimi's still in the wind."

"Oh, shit!" Gary and Sal said simultaneously.

"And we don't know where your 'ace number one informant' is either, do we?"

"No, we don't," Gary admitted. "But it's been a while since I paged him," he said optimistically.

Brownlee stood up and walked to the large picture window in his office and tugged his mustache. He stared at the city below, not actually seeing anything. Nothing registered. The more he considered the situation, the madder he became. "You don't think there's a correlation between Rahimi being missing and Assaly not returning your pages?" asked the thirty-year DEA veteran.

"I don't think so," Gary said. "At least not yet."

Brownlee suddenly turned to them, "Page that son-of-a-bitch again and punch in your cell number. Both of you get yourselves over to his apartment and see for yourselves what's what. I want to know if he's there, or if he's dead, or just what the hell he's doing."

Gary and Sal left without a word. They walked past their desks, grabbing their jackets as they headed towards the door. Sal whispered, "Let's get the hell outta here."

Sal drove as fast as the traffic allowed, pulling up in front of Robaire's apartment in a record thirty-five minutes. They were relieved to see Robaire's Mercedes parked in the carport. "Maybe he just got home," Gary speculated.

They walked to the door and tried the doorknob. One light on inside. Mail was sticking out of the box next to the door. Not a good sign. They rang the doorbell and knocked on the door. No answer. Sal cupped his hands over his eyes to peer through a window. No signs of life. "Don't see anyone," he said.

They walked to the rear of the apartment complex to check the back door. Locked. They knocked again, and again received no response.

They walked past apartments until they found the manager's and knocked.

The seventy-year-old woman manager peeked behind a sheer curtain. "Yeah? What do you want?"

Sal displayed his badge and credentials. "Ma'am, we're federal agents. We'd like to talk to you for a moment, please."

She opened the front door wide. "Federal agents? What's happened?"

"We're looking for Mister Robaire Assaly, the tenant in the front apartment. Have you seen him today?"

"He in some sort of trouble?" she asked.

"No, ma'am. We're just looking for him," Gary said while taking out his notebook. "May I have your name and telephone number?"

She provided it to him and asked, "Are we in some sort of danger? He's a Middle Easterner, you know."

"No, ma'am. It's a long story we can't get into now," Sal said. "When's the last time you saw him?"

"Oh, I don't know, a few days ago, I guess. He's pretty quiet, and I don't get any problems from him."

"Do you have a key to his apartment?" Sal asked.

"Sure, I do. You want to get in there?"

Sal didn't answer.

"I don't know," she said, looking down. "Not without a warrant. You can never be too careful these days. Liability, you know."

Sal became a little irked. He hated it when people tried to impress him when their knowledge of the law came from watching *Law and Order* and did not know what they were talking about. "Look, ma'am, we don't wanna search his apartment, we just wanna make sure he's all right."

"Well, what makes you think he's *not* all right?" she asked.

"His car's in the driveway. There's a light on inside, but there's no answer at the door," Gary replied.

"Well, maybe he's just out for a walk," she speculated.

"Or maybe he's dead," Sal said.

"Dead?" she exclaimed.

"If he's dead with the heater on, he'll stink up the place so bad you won't be able to rent it for two months, assuming you can ever get that smell out of the curtains and carpeting," Sal said.

"The smell of decaying flesh permeates the drywall and everything," Gary followed up. "You may never rent that place again. The health department may red tag it."

"Oh, my," she said.

"Doesn't it look the least bit suspicious to you that his car's in the carport, a light's on, but he doesn't answer the door, ma'am?" Sal asked.

Gary and Sal could see the manager was thinking about the sight of Robaire's fat carcass wasting away on the living room floor. They thought she must be thinking the owner would can her if she didn't let them in and they ended up kicking the door down. "All right, all right. If you say it's okay."

"It's okay, ma'am," Gary winked. "You can trust us."

The elderly lady went into her kitchen to retrieve the key and returned shortly. She waddled through the complex with Gary and Sal tagging close by. She inserted the key when they reached the front door.

"We'll take it from here," Gary said.

Sal gently took her elbows and led her off the step. "Why don't you go back to your apartment in case it's ugly in there? We wouldn't want you to see anything that might upset you."

"You really think something happened to him?" she squealed.

"No, ma'am, but in this business, you never know," he said.

She was more than happy to comply.

Gary and Sal removed their pistols and slowly entered. Gary rushed to the bedroom while Sal looked through the kitchen. "Clear," Sal shouted. The apartment was neat but not clean. No dead bodies or smells thereof were noticed.

"Same here," Gary replied. He met Sal in the living room, and they holstered their weapons. Gary placed his hands on his hips and looked around. He wasn't sure what he was looking for, but wanted something to reassure him Robaire was all right. The answering machine's light was blinking. Gary pressed the play button and heard his own voice asking Robaire to call. Two other messages were also from him. Then he saw it. The cigarette butt in the ashtray.

"Look at this, Sal."

"Whatchagot?"

Gary sat on the couch and leaned forward, looking intently at it with his hands on his knees. What stood out was the deep red lipstick. He knew Robaire only smoked seven and a half inch cigars. Obviously, a woman brought her own cigarettes. He went into the kitchen, found a mailing envelope, and gently placed the cigarette butt into it. He licked it shut and placed it in his jacket pocket.

They walked out of the apartment and locked the door behind them. The manager didn't go back to her apartment but stayed around the corner. "He ain't there, ma'am," Sal assured her. "Everything appears to be normal."

"What a relief," she said.

Gary handed her one of his business cards. "If you see him, please call me right away."

She lifted her reading glasses that were secured around her neck with a tarnished gold-plated chain. "Drug Enforcement Administration," she gasped, shocked. "Is he into drugs?"

"No, ma'am," Sal said. "Just give us a call, please."

They were walking away when Gary had a sudden thought and turned to her. "And ma'am, please don't tell him we were here looking for him. Okay?"

"Don't worry, I won't," she said while looking over her reading glasses.

Neither one said a word on the way back to the office. Sal finally broke the silence. "It don't look good, partner."

Gary ignored the comment and remained silent, occupied with thought. What could have gone wrong? Where was Robaire? Someone he had worked with for almost ten years. Someone who had helped him initiate at least one large-scale investigation per year during their ten-year professional relationship. An informant who had always provided solid information. Gary was more concerned about Robaire's safety than anything else. He couldn't imagine him being in cahoots with terrorists but knew that possibility existed.

Sal was more pragmatic about the situation than Gary was. "What are you thinking about? You haven't said a word in twenty minutes."

"I can't imagine where he can be. I just hope he's okay."

Sal had a reputation for being as blunt as a ball-peen hammer. "I hate to be the one to break it to you, pal, but did it ever occur to you Robaire has flown the coop? Went sideways. Pissed backwards on you. Jumped over to the dark side?" Gary didn't react. "That he's on his way to Paris or some frickin' place right now, sipping cognac with Rahimi after selling the Stinger to the Iranian government." Gary squirmed in his seat as he continued to stare out the passenger door window.

"You know better than I do these frickin' informants only work for you until they get a better offer. Maybe Rahimi made him a better offer."

That possibility went through Gary's mind like a knife. He finally looked at Sal. "You may be right. Maybe Rahimi *did* make him a better offer. Maybe he even threatened to kill him if he didn't set up this deal."

"Or maybe he offered Robaire a piece of the action," Sal said, always the sensitive type. "It wouldn't be the first time it's happened."

Gary became defensive. "It just isn't something he'd do!" he blurted.

"But it's certainly not unheard of," Sal reminded him. "If it happened, you wouldn't be the first agent to get screwed over by an informant. They're all a bunch of egotistical, money hungry sons-of-bitches. I say good riddance." Gary reverted to staring out the window again.

Sal regretted his last remark almost immediately. He had forgotten how long Gary had been working with Robaire. Longer than he had been on the job. Sal continued driving and didn't mention the possibility of Robaire turning bad again.

CHAPTER 25

It was past midnight when Gary opened the door to Joyce McCarthy's apartment. The place was dark except for a small night light in the hallway. She often left it on when she expected his company. He quietly got undressed and slid under the covers next to her. He laid on his back and placed the back of his hands on his forehead, thinking.

Joyce rolled over and rested her arm over his chiseled chest. She snuggled closer and, without opening her eyes, asked, "How'd it go today, G-man?"

"Not so good."

"Oh?" She sat up and rubbed her eyes. "What happened?"

"We made the exchange, and the feebs lost Rahimi right off the bat. He and the Stinger were gone when they finally found his car."

"You've got to be kidding - aren't you? Tell me you're kidding. Tell me that terrorists don't have a Stinger missile."

"I wish I could, Joyce. This has been the worst day of my professional life."

"Oh, baby," she whispered, hugging him.

"To top it off, I can't find my goddamn informant either."

"What?"

"I don't know where the hell he is. As of a few hours ago, he and Rahimi are both missing."

"Oh, shit." Her hand covered her mouth. The possibility of collusion between Rahimi and the informant seemed strong.

Gary remembered the cigarette butt in Robaire's apartment with red lipstick on it and wondered whose it was. "I've got to get back to the FBI in the morning and find out what they're doing."

"At least Main Justice was the one that decided you should give the Stinger to Rahimi," she said to reassure him. "Thank goodness that can't fall back on you."

"Don't be so sure. Remember, he's my informant. I'm the one supposedly in control of him, not the other way around."

"But maybe he'll show up," she said, trying to encourage him. "It's only been a little while, you know."

"Whether or not he ever shows won't be the issue down the road. These things tend to get twisted around and bite you in the ass. The feebs won't take the fall if they can help it."

"Oh?"

"They've got a reputation for stealing cases, screwing them up beyond all recognition, and giving them back to you. It's hard to unfuck something, you know."

She laughed. "Yes, I know." She probed under the covers with her hand until she found him.

He smiled. "Hey, what's going on down there?"

"You're a candidate for Dr. McCarthy's stress relief treatment," she smiled back. "I'm going to make you forget all your troubles, or at least try to."

"Happy Valentine's Day," Gary said.

"You too, baby." She dove under the sheet and made the day's events melt away.

•   •   •

Gary felt depressed when he arrived at the office the next day. He had paged Robaire again and phoned his residence on his way to work. He even called the apartment manager, who said she had been up most of the night watching for him to return, but he had not.

Gary mentally went over the events of the past week but could not allow himself to believe he had been set-up or double-crossed by Robaire. He justified Robaire's disappearance as his way of avoiding the heat that would surely come from Rahimi's arrest. He may have flown to Las Vegas for a few days. Who knows? Either way, Gary felt he was not Robaire's keeper and knew Robaire wasn't obligated to keep him advised of his whereabouts at all times. He was confident he would contact him when he needed either money or a favor. But Gary knew Robaire's disappearance was highly unusual. The thought brought on a slight pain in his stomach.

Gary checked his messages. Only one, from Joe Montoya at the Bonaventure.

Gary called Montoya's office, not knowing what else to do. "Hi, Joe, it's Gary."

"Hey, buddy. What's up? Remember that good-looking blond that was with you the other day?"

"What blond, Joe? Refresh my memory?"

"The blond. The looker. The one you said wasn't a part of your surveillance team?"

"Now I remember. What about her?"

"Well, I went through the security camera videos we have. We've got video cameras running twenty-four hours a day in the lobby in case of robberies, flim-flam artists, and the usual assortment of assholes we get off the street, ya know."

"Yeah, so what's this got to do with me?"

"Not you, Gary. That good-looking broad I told you about. The one you denied knowin'?"

"I still deny it, Joe. We didn't have any women working that day."

"I was thinking about what you said. About not havin' a woman workin' and all. That's why I got the videotapes for that day. I fast-forwarded to the time you met with the Iranian dude, and just as I suspected . . ."

"Don't tell me she's in the video?"

"That's ri-ight. Your gal was within view of one of the cameras."

Gary was becoming a little irritated. "I'm telling you; we didn't have any woman working the surveillance."

"Well, I know a surveillance when I see one, and I'm here to tell you she was doin' surveillance on you. I made a copy of the tape and thought I'd drop it off at your office if you're interested."

"Sure, Joe but . . ." It suddenly hit him like a Sandy Koufax fastball. The cigarette butt! "You think she was pulling counter-surveillance for Rahimi?"

"If she don't work for you guys, she's got to be with the bad guys. I'm telling you, Gary, I stood there the whole time you were in the hotel, and she sat right there just as nice as pie and watched everything that was going down."

"When can you bring that tape over?"

"I'll be there in half an hour."

`"Thanks, Joe. Later."

As Dave Page and Major Schmidt walked up to Gary's desk, Sal was waiting to see what fireworks Schmidt would launch when Gary announced the Stinger had been stolen."Morning, Gary," Schmidt said. "What's our status?"

"Sit down, major. You too, Dave. Let me explain what happened."

"Explain?" Schmidt said. "What needs explaining?"

Gary told them about how the missile got stolen.

"You mean to tell me the FBI lost Rahimi within twenty minutes of the surveillance?" Schmidt began breathing hard and gripped the arms of the chair tightly.

"I'm afraid so. Apparently, they couldn't help it. The ground units lost him when Rahimi went into an area that was off-limits to helicopters."

"What about all that sophisticated electronic bullshit you guys put in the box? Didn't it work?" the major asked.

"It worked, all right. But Rahimi removed the Stinger from its case, which he left behind."

"Well, that's just great! What the hell am I going to tell General Harris?" Schmidt fumed. "What the hell do you suggest I tell him?"

Now it was Gary's turn to get mad. He didn't need to be hearing this from Schmidt. "Tell him what I told you. Or just tell him we fucked up. No, better yet, tell him *I* fucked up, I don't care! If he wants to call me, I'll be glad to explain it to him myself. In the meantime, everyone and his brother are out there looking for the goddamn thing." He purposely didn't mention the informant was also missing. "The one thing I want to tell the general is we'll find the missile and the bastard who has it."

Page asserted a calming voice. "Does the FBI have any leads?"

"I know they're doing their best, but I don't know," Gary said. "But you can bet they've pulled out all the stops for this one."

"What about the informant? Does he know where Rahimi is?" Dave asked innocently.

"Obviously not. If he did, Rahimi would be in custody." Gary thought Dave looked hurt.

"I'm sorry, Gary. I just thought I'd ask."

"No apology necessary," Gary said. "I can appreciate what you're going through. This has turned into the case from hell."

"We can't do anything more here, major," Dave said. "Come on. Gary needs to get back to work." Dave stood up and pulled Schmidt by the shirtsleeve, prompting him to get up. "We'll be back at the hotel. If anything comes up, please call us."

"You bet." Gary continued as the men walked away, "I'm sorry it turned out this way, major. I'll be in touch with you the minute I hear something." Schmidt nodded, and they sauntered to the door. The major looked like he had just lost his family dog.

The phone rang. Gary answered it. "Send him right in."

Sal walked over to Gary's desk from the other side of the room where he had been observing the conversation. "Did you see the look on the major's face? He looked like he was ready to cry."

"He probably sees his army career going down the tubes," Gary said. "I feel sorry for the poor guy. I'd feel like hell if I were him."

"You don't feel like hell now?"

"Sure, I do. But he's got to feel worse."

"Why?"

"Remember, I'm a retired reservist. I know how the army likes to eat their own. They have to blame someone for what happened, so they'll probably blame him, or maybe the general, even though neither one had anything to do with losing it."

"But the feebs are the ones who lost the missile," Sal reminded him. "And don't forget it."

"I won't."

"It'll be interesting to see how they'll spin this. How they'll explain away giving a Stinger to a probable terrorist who later shoots down an airliner," Sal said.

Gary thought about that for a while. Who in the world was the target? He was ready to tell Sal about what the major said regarding dismantling of the Identification Friend-or-Foe when Joe Montoya was escorted in by an agent. "Come on over Joe."

He was holding a VHS videotape. "Here's the tape I told you about."

"Sal, you'll want to see this," Gary said. Sal walked over to Gary's desk.

Gary inserted the tape into a player on the filing cabinet next to his desk. The snowy screen transformed into a color picture of the Bonaventure lounge angled over Montoya's shoulder from behind the registration desk, capturing the images of the customers. They saw an attractive woman sipping her drink.

Joe placed his finger on the screen. "That's her right there. She's the one I've been telling you about."

Gary and Sal immediately noticed she was wearing bright red lipstick. "Did you see that woman, Sal?" Gary asked.

Sal stood there with his arms folded and shook his head. "Nope."

"Joe thought she was with us doing surveillance," Gary said.

"She sure looked like it to me," Joe said.

"I don't remember seeing her," Sal said. "But we were kinda busy. How long was she there?"

Joe pointed to the date and time on the screen that was generated by the hotel's security camera. "She arrived thirteen minutes before Gary did. That's about six minutes before the other two did. She didn't move from her seat until after your deal was over. I couldn't help noticing her. She was right in my line of sight the whole time."

"Did anyone meet her while she was in the lounge?"

"No, but watch this," Montoya said. He pressed the fast-forward button and held it down for several seconds. When he released it, they could clearly see Amir Rahimi. "I noticed when Cangor, or whatever his name is, walked past her after the meeting, she immediately got up and left," he said as he folded his arms while standing. "Coincidence?"

"I don't believe in coincidences," Gary said.

"Neither do I," Sal added.

"That makes three of us," Joe said.

Sal backed up the tape and freeze-framed a shot of June seated at the table. "She's gotta be pullin' counter-surveillance for the asshole," he said.

"She's definitely hinky," Joe said. "I wish to hell I had followed her to her car."

Gary picked up the telephone. "So do I."

"Who ya callin'?" Sal asked.

"Olson. I want to tell him what we've got."

•   •   •

Gary dialed the number from memory. When Olson answered, Gary told him about Montoya's videotape and the cigarette butt in Robaire's apartment.

Olson scanned a list of items with his finger found at the crime scene. "You know, we found a cigarette butt with red lipstick on it near the minivan."

Gary gulped.

"Can you get it over here as soon as possible? I want to send it off for comparison with the one we found."

"What brand was it?" Gary asked.

Olson looked at the evidence sheet and said, "Marlboro."

"So is this one. I'll get it out to you this afternoon."

"Can you bring me a still photograph of her off the videotape?"

"I'll do one better. You can have the whole tape."

CHAPTER 26

Amir Rahimi and the Khan brothers waited anxiously in line at the British Airways ticket counter in the Mexico City International Airport. They had spent the night after arriving from Tijuana the previous day. Rahimi was paranoid, even though Mexican authorities never questioned or harassed him at San Ysidro or Mexico City.

When he handed his ticket to the agent, she ran his fictitious name through her computer and matched it against the flight's manifest. After only asking the standard security questions, she checked his baggage to Cairo. His two partners did likewise, but stood in other lines and made it a point not to speak to each other to give the impression they didn't know each other. Before long, they were in the air on their way to North Africa. Rahimi thought of what awaited them in the second half of his mission. They made fools of the FBI and the DEA, but now they needed all the luck they could conjure up, and they especially would need June's help.

• • •

Gary loaded the tape into Olson's video machine and pressed play. A few moments later, June appeared at the table in the lounge, sipping her drink.

"Well, I'll be damned!" Olson said.

"What?" Gary asked.

"That woman! She looks like the same woman we have on a surveillance tape entering Rahimi's office a couple of days ago. I just got done reviewing it."

Gary had a tingling sensation. "Are you sure?" He was secretly hoping Olson was mistaken. Her presence all but confirmed she, Rahimi, and probably Robaire were all conspirators.

"Sure looks like her," Rowe said without being asked. "I'll go get the tape and show you, Gary."

A few minutes later, Rowe returned with the videotape. He ejected Joe Montoya's tape, inserted the new one in the machine, and pressed the play button. The color in Gary's face drained when he saw it was indeed the same woman from Joe Montoya's videotape. The camera caught her walking down the hallway towards Rahimi's office, and Gary immediately noticed the red lipstick, as did Olson and Rowe. Before opening the door, she ran her long fingers through her hair several times before stepping in.

"What do you make of this, Gary?" Olson asked.

Gary felt ill. He thought his stomach was developing an ulcer. He knew this was no coincidence, not in his business. Now he was getting mad. Gary accepted the fact Robaire had used him, and he hated to admit to the FBI, of all people, but had to. He also would have to confess he didn't have a clue where Robaire was. "It can only mean one thing. I'm afraid Robaire's been involved with them from the get-go."

"Well, let's talk to your informant and see what he has to say for himself," Olson said. "Let's get him in here right away."

Gary took a deep breath before talking. "We can't do that."

"Why not?" Rowe asked, puzzled.

"He's in the wind, and I have no idea where he is." Gary stood up and tossed a transparent plastic evidence bag containing the cigarette butt on the table. He paced in the small room. "My partner and I drove over to his apartment last night looking for him after he didn't return any of my pages. The landlady let us in. That's when we found this," he said, picking up the envelope and throwing it on the table. "Now we have not one, but *two* Marlboro cigarette butts with what appears to be identical red lipstick on them, and *two* videotapes of this mystery woman wearing red lipstick." Gary sat back in his chair with his arms tightly folded.

"Take it easy, Gary," Rowe consoled. "Quit beating yourself up. He may still show up and have a reasonable explanation." Gary just shook his head. "You really don't believe that. Do you, Cal? The evidence doesn't look good."

"I think it's too early to write the informant off," Olson added, trying to sound optimistic. "Let's see if the DNA and saliva come back the same on the two cigarette butts before we jump to too many conclusions."

Gary shook his head. "I know he's gone," he sighed. "I feel like a used condom."

CHAPTER 27

A smiling Egyptian immigration officer stamped Robaire Assaly's new U.S. passport. "Enjoy your stay, Mister Nasir."

Robaire smiled back. "Thank you." Someone gently herded him with the rest of the passengers into another area. A tall customs officer dressed in a tan uniform with bloused black combat boots asked him for his passport again. "What is the purpose of your stay in Egypt, Mister Nasir?" he asked without smiling.

"Tourism. I'm here to experience your wonderful country."

"I see you're traveling alone."

"Yes. I'm meeting friends here in a day or so." He regretted saying that. What if he wanted to know their names? What should he tell him?

Another Customs officer motioned for him to place his suitcase on the stainless-steel table in front of him. Robaire was fishing for the key in his pocket when the first official placed his hand on the case. "That won't be necessary, Mister Nasir. You may go free."

Robaire was relieved, even though he wasn't carrying any contraband. "Thank you, gentlemen." He didn't complain. A rash of bombings by fundamental Muslim extremists had put a damper on the tourist trade. The government didn't want to risk irritating anyone possessing a virgin U.S. passport. He grabbed the suitcase from the counter and walked directly through the automatic doors to the sidewalk outside the terminal. A dozen taxi drivers immediately accosted him.

He picked one and got in the back seat of the taxi. Robaire pleased the driver when he spoke to him in Arabic to take him to the Hyatt hotel, the long way. He wanted to see the city.

. . .

It was an hour and a half later when the cab stopped at the hotel's driveway. The driver turned around and stretched out his hand. Robaire handed the man a crisp, new U.S. fifty-dollar bill, bringing a toothless grin to the man. "Keep it," Robaire said in English. Every cabdriver in the world is happy to take American greenbacks.

Robaire walked into the lobby and found the registration desk. He identified himself. "You have one message, sir," the clerk said, handing him a folded piece of paper. Robaire read it: *Meet me in room 205, J.*

He hurried to his own room to freshen up first. Maybe she would act more civil to him now that they were both out of the U.S. and things apparently had gone well. He hung up his clothing and retrieved his shaving kit. Within minutes he had shaved, changed his shirt, and put on a healthy dose of Polo cologne. When he arrived at room 205, he stopped before knocking to smooth the wrinkles of his jacket and buttoned the middle button. Within a few seconds, the door opened, and Amir Rahimi stood in front of him holding a glass of Scotch.

"You!" Robaire blinked twice.

Robaire caught a moderate odor of alcohol when Rahimi said, "It is I. Come in, old friend."

"Where's June? What have you done with her?"

"I'm right here," he heard her voice say inside the bathroom. Rahimi gently placed his hand on Robaire's elbow and pulled him into the room. June came out of the bathroom and walked to a table containing an ice bucket and several glasses. Next to the ice was a bottle of Stolichnaya and lemon slices displayed on a white towel. "Double Stoli on the rocks with a twist, right?" she asked.

Robaire couldn't speak.

She finished pouring the vodka and ran a slice of lemon around the rim of the ice filled glass before handing it to Robaire. She kissed her fingertips. "Your performance in Los Angeles was magnifico!"

Rahimi pointed to a chair. "Sit down, please. You must be tired after your long journey." Robaire did what he was told.

"I have to hand it to you. You certainly were convincing," June said.

Robaire took a large gulp and glanced over the rim at June. She raised her eyebrows at him and smiled. She was a little tipsy, something he had never observed before. He finally said, "Would either of you care to tell me what in the hell is going on? I didn't know you two knew each other."

June laughed. "That's why you were so convincing. Lowery and his stupid FBI friends never figured it out." She took a sip from her own glass. "I'd give anything to be a fly on the wall in their office right now." She was laughing again.

"Why didn't you tell me Amir was in on this from the beginning?"

June plopped down on the bed, spilling a little of her drink. "That's because I knew you were tight with Lowery, and also, you didn't have a need to know."

Robaire shook his head and was getting mad, feeling like a fool. "What about my mother and sister? What's become of them?"

"They're fine, Robaire. Don't worry," she said, waving the back of her hand towards him.

"You've rescued them?"

"Not yet, but trust me when I tell you they're all right."

"And where is the Stinger?"

June fluffed her blond locks. "It should be in Iraq by now," she said. "It'll be there waiting for you two when you arrive. Amir's two butt-boys are smuggling it in as we speak."

"Iraq?" He took another swallow. "I don't have any intention of going to that godforsaken place."

"Oh, Robaire, but you will," June said confidently. "It's part of our agreement, remember? You said you'd do *anything* to help your mother and sister."

Robaire squeezed out of the chair and poured himself more vodka after adding more ice from the bucket. "You never mentioned anything about going to Iraq. There's liable to be a war there any day now. Why in the hell do you need me in Iraq?"

"Right now, that's not your concern," June said, suddenly turning serious.

"Don't I have a 'need to know' by now?" Robaire argued. "And what's going on with my family?"

June swung her long legs around and sat on the edge of the bed. "The minute this mission is over, they'll be on a plane to the United States."

"Mission? Is that what I'm on? What other surprises do you have in store for me, June? Like what happened to your Southern accent?"

June smiled ever so slightly and ignored the question. Sounding more like a native Californian than a Southern belle, she said, "I'm sure you can handle whatever comes your way. Your mis . . . er, job is almost completed."

Robaire looked from June to Rahimi, who also was close to half in the bag. "I'm beginning to understand now. This isn't about terrorists at all. You two intend to sell the missile to that crazy Saddam. That's it, isn't it?"

June almost choked on an ice cube she was sucking. "Ha! Nice try, old boy."

"Then what is it? What else could it possibly be?" Robaire demanded.

"You're not going to Iraq to sell missile technology to Saddam Hussein, you idiot. You're going there to *kill* him with it."

"God help us, you've gone mad!" He froze in his chair.

"Calm down," Rahimi said. "You're not going to pull the trigger on the missile or anything like that. But your help is still needed, nonetheless. That's why you're here."

"Look, you two. I agreed to help set up Lowery so June could get the missile, but I didn't plan on being involved in a political assassination!"

June reached for her purse and removed her cigarettes and lighter. "You agreed to do what was necessary to help your family. Killing Saddam has become necessary." She lit a cigarette. "Don't you get it? The U.S. won't have to invade Iraq if he gets taken out. Think of the lives and money that would save." She exhaled a deep drag toward the ceiling.

"Why don't you just shoot the bastard yourself, June? You've certainly got the balls for it."

"Why Robaire, that's the nicest thing you've ever said to me," she said, batting her eyelids. Robaire ignored the sarcasm. "Why go through this elaborate scheme to blame others?" It finally dawned on him. "Now I get it. They'll blame me for the assassination!"

June burped slightly and said, "Calm down and let me explain. There's this pesky presidential decision directive that's been around since Gerald Ford. It forbids political assassination. President Bush hasn't even changed it. So, we had to work around it for the greater good."

"Well, that's not my problem," Robaire said.

"Robaire, it became your problem when your mother and sister got kidnapped," she reminded him.

Robaire wasn't listening. He was in a daze. He was tired, irritated, and frustrated. After a long silence, he finally said, "June, why haven't you identified the kidnappers by now? It's been nearly a month. When are you going to find out who they are?"

June kept quiet. Robaire saw what he thought was a furtive glance by June to Rahimi and back to him again.

Rahimi paced the room. "I may as well tell you. You're going to find out, eventually."

"Find out what?" he demanded. "Out with it!"

Rahimi paused momentarily and looked straight at Robaire. "You're looking at one of the kidnappers."

Even though Robaire felt the effects of the alcohol, he clearly understood Rahimi's last statement. "You?" He blinked hard and asked, "Why?"

Rahimi walked over to the table and poured the last drop from the bottle of Scotch it offered. "Let me tell you a story I'm sure you cannot relate to. You being the rich, single American, without children or commitments."

"I'm Lebanese, remember?"

"You're an American!" he shouted, startling June, who glared at him. "Look at you. Your belly gives you away! You fled this region long before the troubles in Beirut began. You were one of the smart ones to leave that damn place when you had the chance."

"What in the hell are you talking about?" Robaire demanded.

Rahimi continued. "During the war between my country and Iraq, a war I might add started by that madman, Saddam. Hundreds of thousands of my countrymen perished. Saddam had more soldiers, more artillery, more bullets - everything! Iran was only plentiful with people. Our population was much larger than Iraq's. And that equally crazy Khomeini sent waves upon waves of human beings, some of them young children, to face down those Iraqi bastards. Thousands of children died in the fighting. One of those innocent children was my only son. He was only a boy of twelve."

"What does that have to do with my mother and sister?"

"I needed them for the plan to rid the world of Saddam. Don't you see? We anticipated you wouldn't help us otherwise."

Robaire jumped out of the chair with his fists clenched. "So that justifies kidnapping innocent women?"

"The end sometimes justifies the means," June remarked, prompting Robaire to stare at her.

Rahimi drew a pistol and pointed it at Robaire. "Calm yourself, man. I swore I would avenge my son's death, and nothing will stop me now, especially you. None of this would have been necessary if Bush senior had finished him off when he had the chance. I will do *anything* to see Saddam in his grave!"

Robaire fell back down in his chair and wiped his brow with his palm. "This is crazy! All this is ancient history."

"Not to me. It's the only way, Robaire," Rahimi said, walking towards him. "American bombs couldn't kill him. His own people are too afraid to try. However, the Stinger, that's different. He won't be expecting that."

Robaire looked at June. "So, you joined forces with this whack job? Rahimi gets his revenge, and the CIA prevents another war with Iraq. Is that about it?"

"Amir isn't a terrorist, but the DEA and FBI think he is," she said, chuckling. "Think about it, Robaire. With Saddam out of the way, America doesn't have a Gulf War II. We achieve our objectives without even firing one shot or sending one soldier home in a body bag. As an added bonus," June continued, "the agency's ass is covered, thanks to you setting up Lowery and the FBI. The White House can honestly say the U.S. was not involved in the plot. A drug informant goes bad and steals a missile. So, what's new? Built-in plausible deniability, wouldn't you say, old boy?"

Robaire slumped in the chair. "So, I'm the fall guy." He realized she was correct in her assertions. The authorities would blame him for everything. "You people are amazing. Do you know that?"

"Just keep your end of the bargain, and you and your family will go free," June said. "I have their new passports."

"Let me see them," Robaire demanded.

June walked over to her shoulder bag, removed two genuine newly printed United States tourist passports issued in Washington, D.C., and handed them to him for his inspection. He opened them both and stared at their photos. He thought his mother and sister looked distraught.

"I'll personally take them out of Lebanon," she said. June handed Robaire another passport from her purse and collected the other two. "Here's a Jordanian passport for you. You'll need it to enter Iraq. Hide your U.S. passport where the sun doesn't shine."

"When will you release them? When can I see them?" Robaire wanted to know.

Rahimi relaxed a bit and sat back down after putting his pistol back into his waistband.

"When and only when either CNN or Al-Jazeera reports Saddam's death," she said. "The people holding the women have specific instructions not to release them until they see the news reports of Saddam's death. Not before. The news report is the only thing that will trigger their release," she emphasized.

June took her last swallow of her drink. "And as an extra precaution, even I cannot release them beforehand."

"How is that?" Robaire asked.

"Go ahead and tell him, Amir," she said.

Rahimi looked out the window, staring at the pollution-filled city skyline. "I've instructed my people to execute your mother and sister in the event they receive a call from me or June instructing them to release the women before news reports of Saddam's death," he lied. "This way you cannot put a gun to my head to force me to have them released prematurely." Rahimi swirled the ice in his glass and smiled broadly, proud of his thoroughness. "So, you see, Robaire, you have no choice but to continue cooperating." He confidently removed his pistol from his waistband and placed it on the small table next to him. "Those are their instructions. When we finish our business in Baghdad, you and your family will be freed. I give you my word."

Robaire sat motionless, still stunned by the news Rahimi was the leader of the gang of kidnappers and that he and June had duped him in the same way he had duped Gary Lowery. He looked helplessly at the pistol. "I guess you've thought of everything."

"I certainly hope so," June said. "We've been planning this for some time."

"When this is over, where do you suggest I go? I can't go back to the United States. You both made sure of that," Robaire said.

"You've got new passports. Use them," June blurted. She was legally drunk in most states if she was driving. "I'm sure you can find a hiding place, so do it! Until then, quit your whining and get some rest. You and Amir must leave early in the morning."

"How are we going to get to Iraq?" Robaire asked.

"I've arranged for a small plane to take you two to Amman. Once you're in Jordan, you'll drive the rest of the way. Baghdad is only a day's drive from there," she said.

Rahimi smiled and motioned to Robaire. "Go now, Robaire. Get some rest. Everything will turn out all right, you'll see. You should pack and be ready to leave at five a.m." Putting his arm on Robaire's shoulder, Rahimi walked him to the door. "I mean no harm to your family, believe me, but it was the only way we could be certain of your cooperation. We'll be doing the world a favor by killing Saddam." Before opening the door, he turned and faced Robaire. He pointed his right index finger within an inch of Robaire's nose. "Don't lose sight that if anything goes wrong on account of you, terrible things will happen to the two women. Make no mistake about that, my friend." A smile returned to Rahimi's face. "Now go, Robaire." He opened the door and slapped Robaire on the back as he exited, a changed man.

• • •

Rahimi shut the door and turned to June and asked, "Do you think he'll continue cooperating?"

"Of course he will. He has no choice," June said.

"Is he still going to be taken care of?"

"That's a stupid question, Amir. I really didn't expect to hear it from you."

CHAPTER 28

Nadia Evans walked into the Alexandria, Virginia Post Office to check her mailbox. When she opened it, she discovered a large manila envelope. After looking for the return address and finding none, she noticed a Los Angeles postmark. She laid her other mail on a counter, opened the envelope, and pulled out a letter. Nadia flipped through several pages of what appeared to be notes, along with an undeveloped roll of film. Recognizing Robaire's handwriting made her grin as she stuffed the contents back into the envelope to read in private once she returned to her car.

She unlocked the door to her Volvo station wagon and sat down, eager to read about her brother's adventures as he suffered from an incurable case of wanderlust. It was not often he wrote. An occasional postcard, but rarely a letter. She received no emails since he did not own a computer. Even at Christmas time, there was no guarantee he would enclose a note with a card. That was when he thought about mailing a card. He often forgot to send a card or claimed the one he had sent got lost in the mail.

The first paragraph immediately got her attention. She read it again and cried. After reading the entire letter twice, she drove to her Duke Street townhouse. Her arms began shaking during the short drive home and she almost had to pull off the road to recover before continuing.

Nadia wondered who Gary Lowery was, and how her brother got mixed up with a federal drug agent. And why did he trust Lowery but not June, the other agent her brother mentioned?

Had he gotten himself into trouble, and if so, when? He always held a job and had the respect of the family for the leadership role he took when their father died. Robaire was now a successful record producer in Hollywood, right? Could he have gotten mixed up somehow in something with those Hollywood types she so often read about?

She thought of her mother and sister in Lebanon. She knew nothing of their abduction. Why would anyone be interested in kidnapping a poor woman and her daughter when neither had anything beyond what it took to survive? They refused to leave Lebanon, despite Robaire and her begging. They insisted on remaining in their homeland and would not even entertain the notion of leaving. She picked up the phone and called her brother's apartment. The answering machine greeted her. "I'm not here. Leave a message, and if you're lucky, I might call you back." It was typical of her brother, who was always the clown.

•   •   •

Gary sat in Bill Brownlee's office when her call came in. Arminda Garcia answered it, walked into the office, and announced, "There's a call for you, Gary."

"Who is it?" he asked.

"Some woman claiming to be Robaire Assaly's sister," she said.

"Jesus Christ! I'll put her on my speaker phone," Brownlee said.

Gary pushed the button and leaned over the phone. "This is Special Agent Lowery."

"Mister Lowery? Mister Gary Lowery?"

"Yes, ma'am."

"My name is Nadia Evans. I am Robaire Assaly's older sister. Do you know my brother?"

"Yes, ma'am, I sure do. Do you know where he is?"

"No, well, maybe. That's why I'm calling. This is so confusing." Her emotions got the better of her as she sobbed, and her voice trailed a bit. "He sent me an envelope with a letter and what looks like a diary and a bunch of handwritten notes. Oh, and there's also a roll of undeveloped film. He instructed me to give them to you. I'm worried about him, Mister Lowery."

"Why couldn't he deliver them himself?"

"He's in Cairo, I think." She paused. "It's complicated. I don't understand what all this entirely means. He wrote you are his friend, so I trust you." She immediately began to sob.

Gary waited a moment for her to compose herself. "Everything's going to be all right, Ms. Evans. You did the right thing by calling."

"I hope so, Mister Lowery. I'm so worried about him."

"What's the postmark on the envelope?" he asked.

"Los Angeles."

"When? What day was it mailed?"

The question further confused her. Why was that important? "The fourteenth. Five days ago."

"What does the letter say, ma'am?"

"It says he's involved with a woman who's investigating the kidnapping of our mother and sister."

"Kidnapping? When did this happen?"

"Three weeks ago, in Beirut. That's where my mother and sister live."

"Would you read the letter to me, please?"

"Certainly." She read it verbatim but had to stop halfway through to sob some more. "I'm calling you because my brother says you are his friend."

"That's right, ma'am. Where are you calling from?"

"Near Washington, D.C. I live in Alexandria, Virginia."

"Will you be at home tomorrow morning?"

"Yes, I should be. Why?"

He glanced at Brownlee while speaking. "I'd like to fly out there and meet with you to go over the letter and to pick up the film and notes you mentioned." Brownlee nodded enthusiastically.

"I suppose that would be all right," she sobbed.

"I can catch a midnight flight and be there about ten o'clock in the morning. Will that be convenient?" Brownlee continued to nod.

"Yes, quite." She gave him her address and phone number.

"I'll see you tomorrow morning."

"Yes, and thank you, Mister Lowery."

"No, ma'am. *Thank you.* Good-bye now. I'll see you shortly and please don't worry. Everything's going to be fine." She hung up.

Bill Brownlee didn't say a word as he rushed to the open door to his office. He spotted Ms. Garcia and shouted, "Make reservations for Lowery and the two feebs on the red eye to Dulles tonight."

CHAPTER 29

The dual prop plane ride from Cairo to Amman was arduous. The Aero-Commander was fast and sleek, but susceptible to turbulence and extremely noisy, in Robaire's opinion. He and Rahimi both felt queasy; however, their pilot didn't exhibit any ill effects. He didn't say much, and appeared to be an American, about thirty-five years old, who wore gold framed tear drop Ray-Bans. Robaire immediately pegged him as CIA.

• • •

While the plane made its way to Jordan, Rahimi could only think about how sweet revenge will be. Saddam Hussein's demise would avenge his only son's death. He felt guilty at times about his role in the kidnapping of Robaire's family, but they usually quickly faded. He felt his actions were justified and speculated Robaire would have done the same if the circumstances were reversed. Robaire shouldn't even question his actions, he thought. After all, he was doing the world, and in particular the United States, a good turn, wasn't he? He knew Robaire would understand his dilemma and remain cooperative. The next few days would be challenging enough without a member of his team bailing out. With or without him, Rahimi intended to follow through with the plan.

The plane landed at a remote airstrip outside Amman. A Jordanian named Mohammed was in a Toyota Land Cruiser, waiting for them.

The pilot shut down only one of the two engines as they removed their luggage.

"I'm Mohammed," he told them, shaking hands with them. "I'll be taking you to your vehicle." Mohammed secured the plane's door and gave a thumbs up to the pilot, who restarted the engine and immediately taxied to the end of the runway. The less time spent on the ground, the better.

Mohammed drove them to the city which looked crowded and cosmopolitan. They even passed a *Hard Rock Café* and many opulent residences, well-paved streets, and archeological sites. Despite its proximity to the world's largest oil reserves, Jordan had none itself. It survived off agriculture and light industry, and a growing tourist trade, thanks in part to the third *Indiana Jones* movie was shot at Petra. It seemed like a playground for the filthy-rich of the Middle East who maintained second homes where alcohol was freely served.

Mohammed had just enough time left for him to get them to their destination before noon prayer. He was a devout Muslim. Muslims in that part of the world regularly pray five times a day. Commerce and industry shut down in places like Saudi Arabia to compel the masses to comply, but not in secular Jordan. They couldn't afford to run the Westerners out like they did. The faithful who prayed did not include Amir Rahimi. He was more interested in other things.

They arrived at a secluded garage in the city's garment district. Mohammed opened the garage door and pointed to a beige 1988 Mercedes 280 SEL sedan with a cracked windshield. The car's paint had oxidized, and the body was nicked and dented. However, the tires were good, and the diesel engine started right up.

Mohammed drove the noisy automobile outside and around the building to a fuel pump. He filled the Mercedes' tank and placed two five-gallon cans with additional diesel fuel in the trunk. He hosed the car down and wiped down the windshield. The vehicle was badly in need of vacuuming, but nobody was complaining.

Robaire placed their suitcases in the back seat as Rahimi palmed Mohammed five American dollars. While driving off, Robaire waved at Mohammed, who just stared at them.

· · ·

The superhighway in the desert was the most boring drive Robaire had ever experienced. He had grown accustomed to the diverse scenery of California. He enjoyed his frequent trips to San Diego and Northern California. The closest he ever came to the desert after leaving Lebanon was on weekend trips to Palm Springs and Las Vegas. However, rural Jordan was no oasis. Before long, they reached the border with Iraq.

The traffic near the border came to a virtual halt. Iraqi soldiers at the crossing carried old British Sterling nine-millimeter submachine guns peered inside vehicles as they walked past them. They could sense the war was near. The United States was negotiating with Turkey to allow sixty-thousand American troops to be based there.

Rahimi and Robaire did not say a word as the young border guards approached them. Rahimi estimated them to both be about twenty-five years old. The sight of the young soldiers made him think about his son, who would have surpassed their age if he had never experienced the terror of war. Robaire avoided eye contact with the guard that waved them through the crossing.

Robaire thought there seemed to be no restrictions between the two countries. Jordan was Saddam's pipeline to the outside world; the pressure release valve that provided him with fruits, dates, vegetables, and satellite dishes. Saddam transported his oil by trucks to the Red Sea, where it was loaded on tankers that would take it to be sold on the black market in open defiance of a long-standing United Nations embargo.

While Rahimi thought about his dead son, Robaire spent his time thinking about his predicament. He realized his dilemma of not being able to do anything until Rahimi's thirst for revenge was quenched. Robaire knew there had to be a way to inflict his own retribution without jeopardizing the lives of his mother and sister. But how? He pondered this as they approached Baghdad. Amir Rahimi struggled with his own inner self. He knew what he had to do, but occasionally felt guilt and shame. His mind recalled verses from the Koran that inspired him to continue unabated. It was a verse he often read to his son. The words to *Al-Lahab*, or *The Flame*, seemed most appropriate.

In the name of Allah, Most Gracious, Most Merciful.
Perish the hands
Of the Father of Flame!
Perish he!
No profit to him
From all his wealth,
And all his gains!
Burnt soon will he be
In a Fire
Of blazing Flame!
His wife shall carry
The crackling wood-
As fuel!
A twisted rope
Of palm-leaf fibre
Round her own neck!

Most appropriate, he thought. Allah would not allow him to fail. For it was His will. Allah's will be done!

CHAPTER 30

The cool weather in Washington, D.C., was in direct contrast to Los Angeles. Gary Lowery, Mark Olson, and Calvin Rowe arrived at the J. Edgar Hoover Building at Tenth and Pennsylvania, N.W., shortly after leaving Nadia Evans' apartment. She had provided them with the envelope and enough information to indict June Cohen for conspiracy and theft of government property. The next step was to take it, along with the other physical evidence they had found, to the FBI laboratory.

After enduring six security checks, they followed Olson, who knew his way around the massive building, which Gary considered quite a feat. Lines where tourists once circled the structure to see "G-men" memorabilia were now gone. Jersey barriers surrounding the building looked like it was under siege. The tour's highlight used to be a live-fire demonstration of a Thompson machine gun. Not anymore. No other federal law enforcement agency had the public relations skills or the 4.5-billion-dollar budget of the FBI. Gary had always heard the Bureau's huge budget was because of the photos and wiretaps they had of members of Congress engaging in various indiscretions. It was all terrorism driven now. America was running scared with an "orange" alert.

Olson went to another office alone to use the phone and talk to the criminalists while Gary and Calvin Rowe waited in a small office. The crime lab photographer had already developed Robaire's canister of film and made three eight by ten prints of each exposure. Besides the photos of June, Robaire had also photographed the transmitter and

mini-digital recorder. The lab techs created still photos from Joe
Montoya's videotape for comparison with Robaire's photos of June.
They created a third set of photographs from the videotape of the
surveillance camera outside Rahimi's office. Nobody doubted the
woman depicted in all three was the same.

Lab techs would later compare DNA from the cigarette butts found
in the parking structure and Robaire's apartment. The scientific
examinations could reveal if the same person were a secreter and had
both cigarettes in their mouth. The agents were confident the
examination would show the cigarettes and lipstick were from the same
person. While waiting for the DNA examination to come back, lab
techs would determine if the two cigarette butts had saliva on them that
matched. It would also reveal the smoker's blood type. Gary studied the
photograph of June taken by Robaire. "Who do you think this woman
is?"

"Good question," Rowe said. "Mark's making an appointment for
us at Langley to talk to one of the head spooks. We'll ask him straight
up if she's on the payroll."

"Do you think he'll tell us the truth?" Gary asked naively.

"Not a chance, but it'll be interesting to hear what he has to say.
He'll also be on notice we're on to their scheme, whatever it is," Rowe
said.

"Why would the CIA want a Stinger missile when they've probably
got a thousand of them stashed in a warehouse somewhere?" Gary
asked.

"Another good question, Sherlock," Rowe said.

A thought hit him. "Elementary, dear Watson," Gary retorted.
"Whoever June Cohen is, she's definitely involved. She might even be a
rogue agent trying to steal a Stinger for herself."

"Ahh, maybe," Rowe said. "But why?"

"Who knows? We'll have a better idea after we talk to them," Gary
said.

Mark Olson returned to the small office they were in and appeared upbeat. "Your hunch about the cigarette butts was right. The lab says the saliva matches. I've ordered DNA comparisons even though it's redundant. The results will be back in about three weeks." Olson continued, "It proves June, or whoever she is, was both inside the informant's apartment and in the parking structure. It corroborates portions of your informant's letter. But it's way too early to tell exactly what her involvement is. Not until we talk to the CIA."

Gary picked up another photograph. "This photo of the transmitter, it's the same type we use."

"So do we," Rowe said. "Seems like everyone in this business uses the same stuff." He picked up the photo of the digital recorder. "This recorder's nothing special. You can get it at Circuit City."

Olson answered his cell phone when it rang. "Okay, we'll be right over."

"Who was that?" Rowe asked.

"The FCI people. They've got something for us."

"FCI?" Gary asked.

"Foreign Counterintelligence," Olson said.

They walked several minutes until they found the FCI offices on the top floor of the building. The unit chief was a twenty-five-year veteran of the Bureau named Ken Gaffney. He was talking to his receptionist when they walked into the office.

"You guys from L.A.?"

"Yes, sir," Mark Olson said, shaking hands with him. "Does it show?"

"Yeah, your lack of an accent gives you away," Gaffney said.

"This is my partner, Calvin Rowe, and this is Gary Lowery from DEA." They all shook hands.

"Glad to meet all of you. Come into my office. I have something interesting to show you."

They walked into his office, plush by government standards, and several other agents greeted them, all experts in the languages, cultures, and activities of Middle Eastern countries. With introductions completed, everyone took a seat and settled down to business at a conference table.

Gaffney turned on a television monitor with a VHS tape player hooked up to it. He inserted a videotape. "We had a look at your undercover tape from the hotel and were quite interested in what we saw."

"Oh?" Gary asked. "Did you recognize someone?"

"Unfortunately, no. However, well ... it would be easier to just play it for you." Gaffney pressed the play button. The picture came on with the time and date of the meeting electronically etched on the bottom of the tape. He fast-forwarded it a few seconds and stopped at a predetermined number on the counter. "Here it goes," he said.

The tape began with the knock at the door and Rahimi letting in his two accomplices, one of which is holding the large briefcase full of money. "There, you hear that?"

"Hear what?" Gary asked.

"What they're saying."

"I hear them, but I don't understand them," Mark Olson said.

"That's because you don't speak Urdu."

"Never heard of it," Calvin Rowe replied.

"In addition to English, it's the official language of Pakistan," Ken Gaffney said.

"You mean they're Pakistanis?" Gary asked.

"The two younger men are. There's no doubt about that," Gaffney said. "They speak it at a level five, or at a native speaker level. Your friend Rahimi is only a level three, which is rather good. Most Iranians speak Farsi. He's good but speaks Urdu with a noticeable Farsi accent."

"How can you tell?" Gary asked.

"Our people played it repeatedly and are convinced the two men with Rahimi are Pakistanis. When you're not familiar with the languages, it's hard to discern one from the other."

"The Pakistanis probably have some experience with Stinger missiles," Gary remarked, remembering his conversations with Dave Page and Major Schmidt.

"Most likely," Gaffney said. "Pakistan is the talent pool for Islamic terrorism. They also have a lot of veterans from the war in Afghanistan when they fought the Soviet Union with their Afghan brothers. That's why we feel if the missile is used, one of those guys will be the trigger man."

"Any guess who the target is?" Rowe asked.

"Not yet," Gaffney said, turning off the machine. "Take your pick. Rahimi could have a hard on for many of people. It's tough to predict, but we're working on it. Quantico's going to run a psychological profile of Rahimi. Maybe they can come up with something that will help."

Olson looked at Gaffney. "Do you know we have an appointment with the CIA tomorrow?"

"No, I didn't."

"Any advice on how to deal with those people?" Rowe asked.

Gaffney scratched his neck and said, "Whatever you do, don't tell them you know the other two men are Pakistanis. That'll be your ace in the hole. Concentrate on the woman. See what he says about her involvement."

"All right," Olson said. "Sounds like good advice."

"Who are you going to see over there?" Gaffney asked.

Olson looked at the name in his notebook. "Wilson, Donald Wilson."

"He's a tough nut to crack," Gaffney warned. "He's a frustrated bureaucrat who thinks he should be the Director but doesn't have the political juice to be nominated. Take *everything* he tells you with a big grain of salt."

"Thanks for the advice," Olson said.

CHAPTER 31

The ten-hour drive to Baghdad was tormenting. The steady stream of dust and windstorms took a toll on Robaire, and the sometimes piss-poor roads added to the agony. He grew tired of hearing all the anti-American speeches on the radio attempting to rally the people and get them ready for war.

Rahimi took the trip in stride and considered the drive to be a minor inconvenience compared to the Herculean effort he had already made in the plot to kill Saddam Hussein.

• • •

During the drive, Robaire had a lot of time to think. Rahimi did not trust Robaire to drive, and that suited Robaire. Robaire had become accustomed to his top-of-the-line Mercedes on smooth American roads. Being the passenger gave him the advantage of sleep over Rahimi, something he needed to carry out his own plan. He was going to make things right.

Robaire thought himself to be as much of a victim of Rahimi as his mother and sister. If he didn't continue to cooperate, undoubtedly Rahimi would kill his family. Should he be captured by the Iraqis, they would surely kill him in retribution. If he cooperated and somehow managed to survive the ordeal, he would remain an American fugitive for the rest of his life. No doubt the FBI and DEA desperately wanted to get their hands on him. He was the only one who could corroborate

June had fooled the FBI into furnishing the Stinger. He questioned if June actually worked for the CIA. If not, then whom did she work for? The Israelis? Perhaps the Russians? The best he could hope for was to remain a fugitive for the rest of his life - some future.

Robaire cursed himself for the problems he caused Gary Lowery, but he considered it necessary. The "mission" he was on was so highly classified no one, including Gary and the FBI, could be told of its existence. He wanted the FBI to understand the reasons for his actions, and why it should set aside any notion of seeking his indictment. He hoped Gary would consider him a hero for helping bring the terrorists to justice. But no! June left out one little detail. She was going to use the Stinger to assassinate Saddam Hussein. He was the fall guy, and she was robbing him of his dignity, friends, and future. She would leave him without a family or even a country.

• • •

They arrived in Baghdad in the late afternoon and easily found their hotel. They carried their luggage into the lobby themselves and checked in, both dusty and exhausted.

Immediately upon entering their hotel room, Rahimi threw his suitcase on one of the two beds, picked up the telephone and dialed a room extension.

"Do you have it?"

"Yes," Tariq said.

Rahimi sighed deeply, relieved to learn his two men had succeeded in smuggling the missile into the country. "We will be up there after we clean up a bit."

"We?" Robaire asked. These were some of the first words he had spoken to Rahimi all day.

"Yes, we, my friend. My men are here, and they have it. I want you to come with me to see them after we wash up."

Robaire frowned at the notion but didn't object. They unpacked, took showers, and changed clothes. They took the elevator to the twelfth floor within an hour and went directly to room 1205.

Rahimi knocked fast three times. An obvious signal, Robaire thought. The taller of the two men, Iqbal, cracked open the door and peeked from behind it. Rahimi pushed it open and barged in. "Let me have a look at it."

Tariq Khan had a pair of Steiner binoculars hung around his neck and pointed to the cello case on a bed. The sight brought a smile to Rahimi's face. "Where's the Presidential Palace?" he asked.

Tariq pushed the curtains aside and walked to the balcony. The curtains fluttered from the breeze through the open sliding door. He pointed in the general direction of the palace as Rahimi joined him. Rahimi took the binoculars and saw the palace was approximately one-half mile away, and a large Russian-made military helicopter was on a concrete pad behind it. What he saw pleased him. They could easily get a shot off at the helicopter once it cleared the surrounding buildings. "What have you learned?"

"Saddam's in the palace now," Tariq said. "That's his personal helicopter on the pad."

"How can you be certain?" Rahimi asked.

"For the past two days, we've seen him get on and off that helicopter. He always uses that one."

"When is he leaving again?"

"The newspapers say he's going to visit a military hospital outside the city tomorrow, and they will surely fly him in."

"Very good," Rahimi said, handing the binoculars back to Tariq. "Well done." They stepped back into the room.

"How are we going to get out of here?" Robaire interrupted.

"That should be easy, my friend," Rahimi said. "When we shoot the bastard down, there will be so much chaos around us by the time anyone figures out what happened, we'll be on the road."

Rahimi moved to the edge of the bed and unlatched the locks to the cello case. Upon opening it, he gazed at the Stinger for a few seconds and gently stroked it. "Make sure everyone packs tonight and is ready to go tomorrow. I don't want anything left behind."

"Or anyone," Robaire added.

Rahimi stood up and faced Robaire. "You must learn to trust us, Robaire. By this time tomorrow, we'll all be safe in Jordan," he said calmly, and put his arm around Robaire's shoulder, leading him to the door. "Come, let's get something to eat and get some rest. We have a busy day ahead of us tomorrow."

CHAPTER 32

After a guard checked their names against the visitor roster for the day, Gary, Olson, and Rowe were allowed into the parking lot of the Langley, Virginia headquarters of the Central Intelligence Agency. Its sheer size dwarfed the headquarters of both their own agencies. They found a parking space and walked into the main entrance, where another security guard greeted them after going through a metal detector. To avoid any problems, they left their weapons locked in the trunk of their rental car. A man in an impeccably tailored suit stood at the security desk. "Mister Olson?" the man asked.

"Yes," Mark said.

"Hi, I'm Donald Wilson."

"Nice to meet you. This is my partner Calvin Rowe, and this is DEA Agent Gary Lowery."

"Nice to meet you all. Come with me."

Wilson escorted them through a maze that had free standing sound absorbing panels near the walls to discourage long-range eavesdropping, and finally came to a bank of elevators. They went up to the fifth floor and, after a long walk, entered Wilson's office, who was the Deputy Assistant Director for Clandestine Operations for the CIA.

They stood by the secretary's desk for a few moments while she handed Wilson a few phone messages. "It's been a madhouse here," he said. "With war in Iraq on the horizon, the country on code orange alert, and receiving three audible recordings from bin Laden, it has been busy."

"I can only imagine," Gary said, impressed so far with what he had seen.

They walked single file into his office, which was large by government standards. They reckoned he must be a member of the Senior Executive Service, one of the highest pay grades available to civilian government employees. It offered a commanding view of Maples, Oaks, and Virginia Pines. His office was gorgeously wood-paneled and had matching shelves and plush carpeting.

Wilson was a man of medium build with a Ross Perot haircut, a close-cropped graying beard, and matching mustache. Dressed in a gray wool pinstriped suit, he reeked of authority. He did not appear to be a standard-issue bureaucrat. He was at the pinnacle of his career, allowing him take part in operations instead of just reading about them.

"Please, come in, gentlemen. Have a seat," Wilson said, gesturing to them to be seated on a leather couch near some handsome leather chairs and a large rectangular coffee table. Wilson took a seat.

Wilson started the conversation by asking, "Gentlemen, how can I be of assistance?"

"You may know, sir," Olson started, "we're investigating the theft of a U.S. Stinger missile that occurred in Los Angeles."

"Oh, yes. I read about it in cable traffic. Too bad. How can I help you with that?" *Mister Sincerity*, Olson thought. "We've come across information which leads us to believe an employee of your agency may have been involved in the theft."

"An employee? Of the CIA? What kind of employee?" he asked.

"That's what we're here to find out, sir," Rowe said.

"You sound pretty sure of yourself," Wilson observed.

"We've spent a lot of time on this, Mister Wilson, and we have good reason to believe someone from your agency is involved," Olson said.

Wilson leaned on the arm of his chair and scratched behind an ear. "What makes you think there's a CIA employee involved?"

"It's a long story," Gary finally said. "We have a photograph and a name we'd like to run by you."

The mention of a photograph got Wilson's attention. "Photograph? You have a photograph of someone you think may be a CIA employee?"

"That's right, sir," Gary said. He was on his best behavior.

"May I see it?"

"Of course," Gary said, while unzipping a soft leather briefcase he carried. He handed an eight by ten glossy made from the videotape at Rahimi's office. Wilson put on a pair of reading glasses as Gary studied his face and body language.

He scoffed after only glancing at it. "This could be anyone. What name do you have?"

"She goes by the name June Cohen," Rowe replied.

"She doesn't look familiar to me, but I don't know every employee of the agency," Wilson said.

"How about this photo?" Gary said, producing a second still, this one taken by Robaire from inside his apartment. The FBI had enlarged it and cropped it to only reveal her head and face.

"Hmm," Wilson said. "Is this supposed to be the same woman?"

"Yes, we're sure of it," Rowe lied. It seemed to them to be the same, but there was no way yet of knowing for sure.

"What name did you say she uses?" he asked again."June Cohen," Gary repeated. "Like the month."

Wilson tossed the photos on the coffee table and removed his glasses, letting them dangle from a cord around his neck. He had seen enough. "We have thousands of employees, Mister Lowery. I doubt whether I can be much help to you."

"Then tell us if you have an operation to acquire a Stinger in such a way it conceals CIA involvement," Olson boldly asked.

Wilson began chuckling. "You have quite an imagination, Agent Olson." Olson thought it odd he remembered his name, especially since he had to ask June's name twice. Most people have a tough time remembering the name of a person they were just introduced to. "Sir, the facts we've uncovered indicate either a CIA employee was involved in the theft, or someone posing as one was."

"Ah ha! See, that could be exactly the case," Wilson retorted. "Someone merely posing as a CIA Officer."

"If this is an imposter, she went through a lot of trouble to be one," Gary said while handing Wilson other photos of the transmitter and digital recorder.

"So, it seems," Wilson said.

"Either way, it's going to cause problems for your agency as well as ours," Olson said. "We don't have anything suggesting she isn't with the CIA."

"What exactly do you have, Mister Olson?" Wilson asked.

After shooting a glance to Calvin and Gary, and back to Wilson, Olson moved to the edge of the seat of the couch and stared at him. "For starters, we've got a woman who claims to be a Central Intelligence Agency Intelligence Case Officer. She convinces a DEA informant that terrorists kidnapped his mother and sister in Beirut. She says she has a plan to locate and free them, but only if he helps her set up his DEA agent handler to get a Stinger missile."

Wilson glanced at Gary. "You're the DEA Agent in question, I presume?"

"Yes, I'm afraid so," Gary hated to admit.

Olson continued. "June Cohen and the informant concocted a story about an Iranian who wanted to purchase a Stinger missile. This Iranian shows Gary a million dollars in cash to prove he can buy it and even gives him a couple hundred grand as good faith money."

"And that's when the FBI gets involved?" Wilson asked.

"Yes," Olson said. "It was decided to let the Iranian take the missile so we could follow him to other actors, but unfortunately, because of a variety of reasons, he eluded surveillance and escaped with the missile."

"Right after that, the informant and June Cohen disappear," Rowe said.

"My God, man! How did they manage to get away?"

"It's a long, painful story," Rowe said. He didn't want to admit they had lost Rahimi only twenty minutes into the surveillance.

"And the kidnapping. I assume that was phony also?" Wilson asked, reaching a bit.

"Most likely," Olson said. "We haven't been able to confirm a kidnapping took place. We were hoping you could tell us about any women being kidnapped in Beirut about a month ago."

"Possibly," Wilson said.

"The informant says he only cooperated with Cohen because of their kidnapping," Gary remarked.

"So, the informant's talking?" Wilson asked.

"Not exactly," Gary said. "He left notes and this second photograph behind with a relative. The instructions were to contact us. That's what he wrote in a letter to her."

"And you believed that?" he asked Gary. "Maybe he's trying to cover his own ass."

"Right now, I don't know what to believe," Gary admitted. "Either there's a rogue CIA Case Officer involved in the theft of a Stinger missile, or someone's posing as one. Either way, you've got a big problem," Gary said.

"How does your problem suddenly become mine?" Wilson asked wryly.

Gary was tired, and not at all happy with Wilson's evasive answers. "It's because the woman is going to be indicted the minute we return to L.A. if we don't start getting some straight answers."

"You're implying I'm not being above board with you, gentlemen," Wilson said, placing one of his palms on his chest.

"Take it any way you want, Mister Wilson," Gary said. "But she's arrestable for conspiracy and theft of government property."

Olson said, "However, if she is a Case Officer involved in a legitimate covert operation that changes things. But if she's not, you've got an out-of-control rogue agent who needs to be found."

"If she's not an employee," Rowe said, "we need to know before someone issues a press release.

That alarmed Wilson. "I certainly hope the media hasn't been called in on this?"

"No, sir," Gary said. "Not yet. But it's just a matter of time before you see June Cohen on *America's Most Wanted*."

"Gentlemen, please. Let's be reasonable," Wilson said. "Before you go jumping to conclusions or do anything foolish, give me the opportunity to verify the information you have."

"Okay," Olson agreed, looking at the others. "That's reasonable. We'll leave the photographs of Ms. Cohen with you. Hopefully, you can find out for sure whether an operation is going on or not. If there's some official connection to this, that should satisfy the U.S. Attorney's office. If there isn't, you've got a major problem on your hands, and we're going to do our damnedest to find her."

"And that could open Pandora's Box," Gary added.

Wilson stared at the photos and said, "I'll tell you what I'll do. I'll check with HR and show these photos around like you suggested, and determine if she either is, or has ever been, a CIA employee, and in what capacity."

"You also need to find out if she's ever been a source of information for the CIA, or a contractor." Gary recommended.

"All right," Wilson agreed. "And I'll also check with our contacts in Lebanon about a kidnapping of a woman and her daughter in Beirut."

"We'd appreciate that very much," Calvin Rowe said.

"Where are you staying?" Wilson asked. "I'll call you the second I have something for you."

"We're at the Washington Hilton," Rowe said. He wrote the telephone and room numbers for him.

"The minute I find out something, I'll call you," Wilson promised.

They all stood up. "Thank you for your cooperation, sir," Olson said, smiling. "We're looking forward to hearing from you."

Wilson smiled back. "Count on it, Agent Olson."

•   •   •

The three federal agents were driving back to the Hilton when it began to snow lightly. The forecasters predicted up to six inches falling over the President's Day weekend. Gary went directly to his room and telephoned Bill Brownlee to update him.

Olson opened the door to his room and noticed the blinking message light on the telephone. He picked up the receiver and dialed the operator, who said he had a message to call Wilson. He dialed the number.

"I just left human resources and the director of operations, Agent Olson," Wilson said.

"Yes?"

"They assured me there is no employee, past or present, by that name and there are no ongoing operations of the kind we discussed."

"So, you're telling me the woman is not affiliated with your organization in any manner, whatsoever?" Olson asked.

"That's correct," Wilson replied.

"Or in any capacity?"

"Yes."

Olson didn't believe Wilson for a second. He thought the whole thing sounded contrived. "When we arrest her, we won't get any interference from your people. Is that correct?"

"Precisely. Why would we interfere?"

"What about the kidnapping of the two women in Beirut?"

"I'm afraid we don't have any information about that either," Wilson said calmly.

"Goddamnit!"

"I'm sorry I couldn't be more help, Agent Olson. You might want to consider the possibility your informant created this whole scenario. And the story about this woman and the kidnapping is complete bullshit to cover his tracks. You know it's happened before and will probably happen again."

"Yes, I know," Olson admitted.

"We've been blamed for everything from the hole in the ozone to the Kennedy assassination, for Christ's sake," Wilson said.

"She isn't the figment of someone's imagination. We have several photographs."

"People are quick to blame us for anything they don't understand or can't easily explain away. We're given credit for a lot of things we had nothing to do with."

"If anything changes, will you please contact me?" Olson gave Wilson his cell number.

"Of course, Agent Olson. I'm just sorry it didn't turn out the way you had hoped it would."

"I am too, Mister Wilson. More than you can imagine."

CHAPTER 33

Late the next morning, Iqbal was observing the Presidential Palace from the hotel room balcony through his binoculars and noticed movement.

"What's happening?" Rahimi demanded.

"A couple of soldiers just got into the helicopter," Iqbal said.

Rahimi experienced an adrenaline rush. "Does it look like they're getting ready to take off?"

"Yes, I think so," Tariq said solemnly. "The rotors are beginning to spin."

"Then get ready!" Rahimi shouted.

"We are ready," Tariq said, annoyed by Rahimi's child-like enthusiasm.

Robaire watched Rahimi savor the moment. He knew the time to decide what he was going to do was near. He had come up with several options and hoped he had made the right choice. "What do you want me to do?"

Rahimi appeared surprised, as if he had forgotten about him. "Err, stay in the hallway, and watch out for security people. Keep them from coming in."

"How am I supposed to do that?"

"Use your imagination, man. Create a diversion. I do not care, but whatever you do, don't let anyone in."

Robaire stood up and walked up to Rahimi. "I would be a lot more effective if I had a pistol."

"I don't know about that, my friend."

Robaire grabbed Rahimi by the sleeve, pulled him close, and gritted his teeth.

"Understand, *my friend*, thanks to you I want Saddam dead as much as you do. You simply must trust me. There's no time to argue."

Tariq said, "Another soldier is getting into the helicopter, and a small crowd is coming out of the Presidential Palace."

Robaire could see the desperation on Rahimi's face. He had come a long way to get to this moment and obviously did not want anything to jeopardize his chances of killing Saddam. Rahimi hesitated a couple of seconds before reaching under his sports coat, removed his pistol from his waistband, handing it to Robaire. "Take it, and you'll also need this." Rahimi moved to the bed and picked up a small overnight bag. Inside was a silencer. He grabbed the pistol's slide and held it steady while he screwed it onto the muzzle. As he did this, Robaire spied a key to the room on top of the television set.

"There's already a bullet in the chamber," Rahimi said. "The pistol will fire each time you pull the trigger until it empties."

"I understand," Robaire said.

"And please, only use it if you have to."

Robaire nodded and stuffed the pistol into his waistband at his right hip, so the silencer ran down the side of his leg.

"He's coming!" Tariq shouted. "Saddam's walking to the helicopter!"

"Go, man, go," Rahimi ordered Robaire. "We'll meet you in the hallway when this is over. Our luggage is already in the car." He hurried to the balcony to see for himself. Tariq threw open the cello case and removed the Stinger. He inserted a round battery into its body that started a gyro sound, and several beeps went off. He placed the weapon on his right shoulder and walked onto the balcony.

Rahimi looked through the binoculars and grinned like a schoolboy at the sight of Saddam Hussein walking to the aircraft.

Robaire seized the opportunity. He reached over to the television, removed the key, and placed it into his outer sports coat pocket. "Amir?" Robaire said.

Rahimi pulled away from the binoculars to look at Robaire, who was now standing near the door. "Yes?"

Robaire smiled. "Inshallah. Good hunting."

Rahimi gave a half-cocked salute. "Thank you, my friend. Yes, God willing, I will kill my prey." He smiled at Robaire; confident he made the right decision to have Robaire stand guard with his pistol. He placed the binoculars back on his eyes.

•   •   •

Robaire left the room and hurried to the housekeeping linen closet at the end of the hallway. The door was unlocked, and upon opening the door, saw piles of folded and used bed sheets. Satisfied, he headed for the elevators. His finger trembled as he tried to punch the button to go to the lobby. He was breathing hard and sweat began dripping from his armpits. The stainless-steel walls of the elevator portrayed his dull reflection as red and flushed. He struggled to think.

The elevator doors opened in the lobby. Standing near the entranceway was a soldier in a solid green fatigue uniform wearing a black beret and a pistol belt with a nine millimeter pistol in its holster. Robaire slid up to him.

Robaire spoke in Arabic. "Please, can you help me?"

"What is the problem?"

"There's a terrible fight going on upstairs. I think someone's being killed!"

This grabbed the soldier's attention. "Where?"

"On the twelfth floor. Please, come quickly." Robaire led the way as the soldier willingly followed him to the elevators. They got in, and Robaire pushed the number 12 button. They did not speak as the elevator whisked them to the floor. Robaire's palms were damp.

The doors finally opened, and Robaire bolted out at a fast pace.

"Which room?" the soldier asked.

"Down here, at the end of the hall." Robaire speed-walked to the end of the hallway with the soldier close behind until he stopped abruptly.

"I don't hear anything," the soldier said.

"Shhh, listen," Robaire demanded. He pointed to a room across the hall from the large linen room. "This is the room." The soldier stood in front of the door and placed his right ear to it. "Shhh," Robaire said again as he positioned himself behind the soldier. As the soldier listened intently, Robaire stepped back while removing the silenced pistol from his waistband and leveled it at the hapless soldier.

"I don't hear anything," the soldier complained. He removed his ear from the door and turned to face Robaire. He saw the silenced pistol just as it went off two times, hitting him in his chest. Without a sound, he slumped to the floor, dead. Robaire collected the two spent shell casings, put them in his jacket pocket, and replaced the pistol in his waistband. He dragged the soldier's body into the linen room, stuffing him in a corner and concealing him with used sheets. He removed the soldier's pistol from its holster, pulled the slide back to place a round into its chamber, and made sure the safety was off. Robaire was well-versed with firearms from his membership at the *Beverly Hills Gun Club*. He exited the linen room, leaving the door ajar, and quickly walked down the hallway to the room where Rahimi and his accomplices were about to make history. Robaire placed his ear to the door and listened for clues about what was happening inside. All he could hear was his heart thumping.

•   •   •

Inside, Tariq adjusted the Stinger on his right shoulder. Rahimi and Iqbal stood on the balcony and watched the helicopter's rotary wings speed up as the pilot prepared to take off. They waited for the exact moment. Anticipation spiked the air.

"Are you ready?" Rahimi demanded.

"Yes, I'm ready," Tariq shouted.

The helicopter's rotary wings reached sufficient speed to create flight, and seconds later, the aircraft lifted off.

"Is it time?" Rahimi yelled at Iqbal, who was now looking through binoculars.

"Almost," he responded. "We must wait until the helicopter is above us."

Robaire pressed his ear firmly against the door until it almost formed an airtight seal. He could hear muffled voices.

"What's taking them so long?" Rahimi asked no one in particular.

Tariq was growing impatient with him and did not answer. He had the helicopter in his sights. The time had finally come. "I'm locked on."

Rahimi took a deep breath. He watched the helicopter slowly rise and move in the general direction of the hotel. The Stinger suddenly replaced the gyro sound with BEEP, BEEP, BEEP, BEEP, BEEP. Iqbal noticed Rahimi was too close to the back of the weapon and quickly pushed him to the side just before Tariq pulled the trigger. The missile launched as flames and exhaust rushed out the back of the tube like a blast furnace and deflected harmlessly against the sliding glass door. The missile left an exhaust trail behind as it rapidly ascended and headed directly for the helicopter, seeking the heat of its engines. It struck the rear rotor within seconds, sending the helicopter into an uncontrollable spin.

As the conspirators watched, the helicopter helplessly spun counterclockwise and crashed onto the street below, throwing its parts in all direction.

Robaire heard the ignition of the missile. With the key, he opened the door and hurriedly stepped in. He had the soldier's pistol in his hand, hidden behind his back. The three men were congratulating themselves on the balcony, jumping up and down and hugging one another. When they walked back into the room, it surprised them to find Robaire standing there.

"Did you get him?" Robaire asked.

Rahimi had his arms out as if to hug Robaire. He smiled and sighed loudly, emotionally exhausted. "Yes, my friend. He is dead."

"So are you," Robaire said. He stepped back and swung his arm up with the soldier's pistol, firing off four quick rounds, striking each man at least once. The fourth round struck Tariq a second time, grazing his left ear. Each crumpled to the floor, critically wounded. Robaire was unaffected by what he had just done or the deafening noise. He was experiencing tunnel vision, focused on killing. Robaire loomed over his squirming victims and methodically placed another bullet into each of their heads. Standing over Rahimi, he aimed the pistol between his eyes. "Rot in hell, you son-of-a-bitch," and fired the pistol again.

Robaire flung the pistol on the bed and calmly walked out the door, leaving it ajar, and headed for the linen room. He looked in the hallway. No one around. He gripped the dead soldier's wrists and dragged him into the hotel room with the three other corpses, thanking God no one else was in the hallway. He positioned the soldier's body to make it appeared he was facing the three assassins.

Robaire removed the soldier's pistol from the bed, wiped it clean of his fingerprints with a bedsheet, and placed it in the dead soldier's right hand. He removed Rahimi's pistol from his waistband, wiped it down, and placed it in Rahimi's right hand, making sure his fingerprints were all over it. He removed the two spent shell casings from his pocket and dropped them on the carpet near Rahimi. Robaire stood by the door, reviewing the position of the bodies, and thought it looked perfect. He was about to leave when he remembered something important. Stepping over the soldier, he walked back to Rahimi's body and removed the keys to the Mercedes from his blood-soaked jacket. Thank goodness he remembered!

He thought of something else. What about the Stinger? Could the Iraqis retrofit it? Would they benefit from the discovery of the empty weapon? Why take a chance? He walked onto the balcony and peered over the side. An already busy street was becoming busier with increased traffic heading towards the crash scene. Robaire saw military vehicles with rotating blue emergency lights trying to make their way to the helicopter. He could not see the crash site itself, but the heavy black smoke pluming from behind a building was enough to satisfy him the Stinger had hit its target.

Robaire picked up the empty missile canister with both hands, placed it over his head, flinging it over the side of the balcony. He held on to the railing to watch it slam on the street below, crashing into pieces and sending pedestrians scurrying. He walked back into the room and hop scotched over the four dead bodies, opened the door, and turned briefly for one last look at what he had done. "See you in hell, Amir." He shut the door.

Robaire hastened to the elevator, and when he arrived at the lobby, he slowed his pace as he nonchalantly walked out of the hotel's front entrance. People in the lobby appeared to just be learning about what had happened, but the scene outside was a different matter. He pulled the collar of his suit coat up as he walked to the parking lot and got into the Mercedes.

He slowly drove in the opposite direction of the crash site and turned on the Mercedes' radio to listen to the news.

CHAPTER 34

June Cohen poured herself some iced tea and stared out the kitchen window of the desert house where Robaire's mother and sister were being held. She wore white Reebok running shoes, khaki shorts, and a loose-fitting blouse. She could feel a breeze from a small fan on her exposed legs. She glanced at her military style watch while carrying her iced tea into the living room. After reaching for the remote, she switched on the television.

A young man wearing tight designer blue jeans with a black T-shirt and hiking boots, holding onto an Israeli-made Uzi machine gun, walked into the room. He was clean cut and sported a well-trimmed military-style mustache. "You sent for me?" he said in accented English.

"Check on the women and see if they want something to eat."

The man turned around and walked up the stairs to the second floor.

June changed channels until she found CNN International. The sportscaster was speaking King's English, talking about the latest cricket match between India and Jamaica. A familiar tune and large CNN letters crossing the screen interrupted the broadcast, followed by: BREAKING NEWS. The fatherly-looking news anchor announced he had a late-breaking story from Baghdad. She gulped the iced tea and focused on the television.

The news anchor appeared caught off-guard by the sudden occurrence of such a major story. She saw a hand give him an unedited copy to read as he attempted to straighten his hair. "We have a breaking news story from Baghdad," he said again. "We are receiving unconfirmed reports a military helicopter with Saddam Hussein aboard has crashed in Baghdad. There are reports the helicopter exploded just before the crash, shortly after it had lifted off from one of Saddam's presidential palaces in the central city. Sources further state the President of Iraq frequently uses this helicopter and was scheduled to fly to a hospital on the outskirts of Baghdad, to visit sick children who allegedly cannot receive medicine due to the United Nations sanctions."

June leaped to her feet. "They did it! They actually pulled it off!"

The soldier returned to the room. "The women want something to eat."

June pointed at the man. "No time for that. Get them ready to go. We're leaving here as soon as they're ready." He took two stairs at a time to go back upstairs. June sat back on the couch and turned the TV volume up.

"We're getting confirmation now from Nic Robertson," the anchor said. "Nic's been on the ground in Baghdad for many months. Nic, what have you learned?"

Nic Robertson looked a little disheveled. Someone obviously rushed him to the scene and was winging it. The street scene behind the reporter was chaotic. Men surrounding the burned-out fuselage looked distraught and pounded their chests. Women wept openly. "Barry, the presidential helicopter crashed at about eleven a.m. local time shortly after it took off from one of Saddam's Presidential Palaces near downtown Baghdad. Saddam Hussein was scheduled to appear at a children's hospital near the outskirts of the city. For security reasons, he always takes a helicopter instead of a motorcade, but something went terribly wrong this morning. Witnesses tell me they believe an explosion occurred just before the helicopter suddenly went into a tailspin, sending it down to the city streets below. Upon impact, a huge fireball erupted. I can't see how anyone could have survived."

The news anchor interrupted. "Reuters is reporting a missile struck the helicopter moments before it crashed. Do you know anything about that?"

"There is some speculation from witnesses I have talked to a missile struck the helicopter, but so far, no one in an official capacity has confirmed that. Barry, let me be quick to add that people who claim to have seen the helicopter falling to the ground are saying the same thing: something definitely struck it before the crash. Let me repeat, I do not have any official confirmation of that, and the authorities on scene will not let foreign media close enough to see for ourselves. One man, who claims to have experience in these matters but did not elaborate, said he was certain the helicopter was struck by at least one missile, possibly two.

"I also talked to a soldier on the street who told me Saddam Hussein was on the helicopter, but I can hardly describe him as an official spokesman. I am trying to make my way to the Presidential Palace now to get some official confirmation."

The news anchor asserted himself. "Who may have been responsible for the missile attack if this is, in fact, what happened?"

"I think it would be premature to speculate at this early stage, Barry. Don't you agree?"

"We'll be waiting to hear from you when more information is available," the news anchor concluded.

A man, who looked like a soldier but dressed in civilian clothing, ran into the room, and waited for instructions from June. "Get the Land Cruiser and have it waiting out in front," she said. The man hurried off to comply.

Fatima and her daughter Leila hugged each other as they escorted them to June. "Today's your lucky day," June said. The comment brought a confused look on their faces. "Take them to the SUV." The soldier gently took them by their arms and led them to the awaiting vehicle.

June drank the remaining iced tea and switched off the television, grabbing a navy-blue canvas case. She put her sunglasses on as she walked out the door, motioning to the guards at the front gate to open it, and hopped in the front passenger seat as the first young man got behind the wheel.

"Where are you taking us?" Leila demanded.

"To Beirut. You're both about to take a little trip to the United States. Hope you like Washington."

"What's this all about?" Leila pleaded. "We're so confused."

"Quit whining, will you?" June glanced over the back of her seat and glared at the woman. "If there's anything I can't stand, it's a whiner."

"We don't understand why you're doing this to us," Fatima said.

"You're being freed, damn it. Don't you understand?" June said. "That is what's important now. By this time tomorrow, you will both be eating lunch in Georgetown, so quit griping." The SUV sped forward down the driveway and out the gate. She removed two U.S. passports from her canvas bag with their true names and photographs and handed the documents to them.

"You're giving us American passports?" Leila gasped. "We are not citizens of the United States."

"You will be by the time you arrive." June laughed. "And here is some spending money. This will keep you going until you get settled." She handed Leila a business-size envelope stuffed with crisp, new, one-hundred-dollar bills with consecutive serial numbers. "A man will meet you in New York at the airport and see you through customs and immigration. After that, he will give you airline tickets to Washington to be with your sister."

"Nadia?" Fatima asked.

"Yes. I believe that is her name," June said. She handed Leila a slip of paper. "Once you are in Washington, call this number, and Nadia will pick you up. She is waiting for your phone call."

"How did you know about my sister?" Leila demanded.

"There's not a lot I don't know about you two," June said. She settled back in her seat. "No more questions now, please. Just relax." She picked up her cell phone and dialed a number. "It's a long drive to Beirut airport."

CHAPTER 35

The temperature gauge of the old Mercedes rose steadily until it settled slightly over the halfway mark between cold and hot. Robaire drove the old car out of Baghdad as fast as the traffic would allow and headed for the nearest safe-haven, Kuwait.

He pondered what he would tell the Kuwaiti border guards. Should he show them his U.S. passport? If so, how would he explain his presence in Iraq? Would a Jordanian passport be better? Probably. Fortunately, he spoke fluent Arabic, and a host of other languages. He could only pray whatever he decided would be the right move.

He scanned the radio dial for any information about the assassination of Saddam Hussein. The three scratchy-sounding stations he could receive played recorded music by an Egyptian recording star unknown to him. Despite being raised in Lebanon, he thought all Middle Eastern music sounded the same. It lacked the variety of the Western music he had become accustomed to.

After driving all day and most of the night, daybreak was unstoppable. Not hearing anything on the radio about the assassination attempt was eating at him. No confirmation of Saddam's demise. Why didn't the government at least acknowledge someone shot his helicopter down? Had not anyone discovered Rahimi's body, or were Saddam's police officers as incompetent as his soldiers? By nine a.m. he came upon the border. The Kuwaiti soldiers were naturally curious about a man driving a Mercedes registered in Jordan. Near the border crossing, there was a U.S. Army Bradley fighting vehicle parked with several U.S. soldiers around it. He slowed down the car when he saw the border guard in the distance and let it coast silently up to them. Robaire flashed a sheepish grin to the Kuwaiti soldier, who was carrying an old American M-16A2 automatic assault rifle. His partner approached the vehicle from the passenger side and peered into the back seat.

"Passport," the first soldier said.

Robaire handed him the Jordanian identification papers provided by June.

"Where are you coming from?"

"Baghdad. I had business there."

"What is your business?" he asked.

"Carpets. I am always looking for the finest silk and wool in the region."

"I don't see any carpets in your car," the soldier noted.

"That is because I did not purchase any. These Iraqi idiots would not know a fine carpet if it bit them on the behind. I am exhausted from my journey. Nothing came of it. It was a waste of my time."

"What is your destination?" the soldier asked.

"I'm staying in Kuwait City for the evening and then on to Riyadh."

The man carefully examined the photograph on the passport and stared back at Robaire. "Open the trunk, please."

"Of course." Robaire got out and opened the trunk lid, hoping not to find any more dead bodies. He hadn't looked in the trunk since he left Baghdad.

The soldier saw two matching Samsonite suitcases that stood out from the single Hartman suitcase Robaire carried. He examined the tags and turned to him. "Where's Mister Rahimi?"

"He is home, I suspect. I was able to borrow his suitcases for this trip." Robaire complimented himself for his quick thinking.

The other soldier opened each suitcase and found the usual assortment of dirty underwear and socks. "All right," he said. "You can go, but first, see the immigration officer." He pointed to a man seated at a card table.

"Very well," Robaire said. He walked up to the immigration officer and handed him his phony passport. The frail, deeply tanned man dressed in a cotton caftan and matching white kaffiyeh stamped his passport, granting him a thirty-day tourist visa. Robaire placed the passport in his shirt pocket and returned to his car, smiling. He waved to the soldiers as he slowly drove off.

One of the soldiers walked into the small outpost office and picked up the telephone. He dialed a number and grew impatient as he counted the number of rings. A man finally answered in unaccented, American English, "Hello."

"He just entered Kuwait and says he is going to Riyadh."

"Riyadh?"

"Yes."

"Did he say why?"

"No. He only said he is in the carpet business."

The American chuckled. "Is there anyone with him?"

"No. He's traveling alone."

"Hmm. Thanks for the call," he said, and hung up. The soldier returned to the border crossing and waited for the next arrival.

•   •   •

Nadia Evans answered the phone on the first ring in her Alexandria, Virginia, townhouse. "Nadia! This is Leila! Momma and I are in *Amer-ee-ka!*"

Nadia could hardly contain herself. "Where are you?"

"In Washington, I think. However, I do not see any monuments. A nice man at the airport showed me how to use the telephone. Where are you?"

"At home, in Alexandria. Where are you in Washington?"

"At the airport. Dallas airport."

"You must mean Dulles. What airline?"

"United. We just left the baggage pickup area and walked up to the airline ticket counters to find a telephone."

"Find some seats there, and I'll be there in forty-five minutes," she said. "How did you get there?"

"It's a long story, Nadia," Leila said. "It is too long to explain now. Please hurry. We are exhausted and have so much to tell you."

"I'll be right there." She hung up, grabbed her keys, and hurried to her car.

CHAPTER 36

Robaire's heart was pounding when he entered the main terminal for Kuwait City International Airport. Robaire's heart bounced inside his chest like a racquetball. Lines were everywhere, with people leaving the country before war broke out in Iraq. Why hadn't he heard any word about Saddam Hussein's death? News reports were plentiful about the helicopter being shot down, but nothing about if the despot died or not. The Iraqi authorities would certainly disclose his death, eventually. Robaire wondered where June was and thought frequently of his mother and sister. He was exhausted and longed for a Stoli and a hot bath.

Robaire looked over his sunglasses at the young man at the Saudi Arabian Airlines ticket counter. "When is your next flight to Riyadh?" he asked.

"At fourteen hundred," he replied.

He glanced at his Omega - eleven twenty-three a.m. "Book me in first-class," Robaire demanded.

"I'm sorry, first class is filled."

"All right then, business class."

"I can put you on standby for business-class but confirm you now in coach."

Robaire became disgusted. "Coach? No civilized person fly's coach! Why don't you just make all your flights' first-class seating and be done with it? I think you have the clientele to warrant it."

The man did not answer the questions but asked one, "One way, or round trip?"

"Err, ah, one way."

"How will you be paying for the ticket?"

"Cash. You take U.S. dollars, of course."

"Of course," the man said, while staring at his computer terminal. "May I see your passport, please?"

Robaire removed the phony U.S. passport June had given him and handed it to the ticket agent.

"Mister Nasir, that will be five hundred and eighty dollars, U.S. Do you prefer a window or an aisle seat?"

"Absolutely a window," he replied, while digging into his pocket for a wad of hundred-dollar bills. He peeled off six and laid them on the counter.

The man continued to peck at his computer keyboard. "Sorry, I'm afraid there are only middle seats left."

"Then why did you ask?" Robaire howled.

"I am sorry, sir. I thought one was available, but I see from the computer there are none."

"For heaven's sake," Robaire puffed.

"Only the one bag to check?"

"Yes." He left Rahimi's bags in the trunk of the car.

The man continued his key stroking and handed Robaire an envelope with his ticket. "I am sorry about the coach seating, sir, but we will page you if a business class seat becomes available. Under the current conditions, you are lucky to get on the plane at all. In the meantime, here is a pass to enter the first-class lounge. You can rest there before your journey. I am sorry for the inconvenience."

Robaire felt like he must be the biggest asshole the man had seen all day. "Thank you, son. I am sorry I acted the way I did."

"No problem, sir."

Robaire read the gate information as he walked toward the security checkpoint. He was lumbering along when he saw him. An American looking Caucasian man dressed in cotton slacks, penny loafers, and a short sleeve button-down collar shirt. He wore a pair of black-framed Gargoyle sunglasses. He may as well have held up a sign reading, 'Hey look, I'm an American!' The man turned away as Robaire approached.

Robaire folded his sports coat and placed it in a bin after removing his shoes and walked through the metal detector. He collected his coat and walked to the lounge area. As he neared a corner, he glanced once more and saw the American talking with the security people. Robaire's palms got moist, and his heart was beating fast. He quickened his pace until he found the room marked: FIRST-CLASS LOUNGE.

Once inside, he found a comfortable chair that was strategically located so he could see the entrance to the lounge and melted into it. A waiter rolled a cart by with a variety of juices, cheese, crackers, dates, and a non-alcoholic sparkling wine, also known as *Saudi Champaign*. Also, there were a variety of non-alcoholic beers. Robaire selected orange juice and downed it. He placed the chilled glass on his forehead and rolled it from side to side. He saw a folded Arabic newspaper on the table next to him he picked up. The headline screamed: SADDAM NEAR DEATH AFTER MISSILE ATTACK.

He scanned the article reporting Saddam Hussein had survived a helicopter crash after being shot down by a guided missile. The facts were sketchy and relied heavily on the news accounts obtained by the *AP* and *CNN*. No mention made of either the dead soldier or Rahimi and his two henchmen. He reread the article, only this time slowly to absorb every word. Could it be possible Saddam survived both the missile *and* the crash? If he did, what would become of his mother and sister? He chewed on that while walking to the restroom. He turned on the cold-water faucet full blast, cupped his hands underneath, and plunged his face into it. It was difficult to get cold water from a faucet in the desert. He ran his fingers through his hair and blotted his face dry with a cotton towel from a nearby stack.

Robaire walked back to his seat and fell into it. He motioned for the waiter to bring another glass of orange juice. The stress was taking its toll. He thought Riyadh was a bad city to get lost in. It was too isolated. However, it may be perfect since no one would ever suspect he would go there. For that matter, no Westerner would go there unless it was absolutely necessary. What difference did it make? He was probably already being followed by the CIA.

When the waiter returned with the orange juice, he found Robaire fast asleep in the comfortable chair, clutching the newspaper.

CHAPTER 37

It astonished June to learn Saddam Hussein had survived the assassination attempt. She heard the news when she returned to the desert villa. *CNN International* reported that a heroic Iraqi soldier was gunned down while attempting to apprehend the three assassins, who were also killed. She was curious why there was no mention of finding the fourth body of Anwar Nasir a.k.a. Robaire Assaly, among the dead.

While June continued watching the news accounts on television, a man entered the room and announced, "You have a call on the satellite phone."

She sprang to her feet as the man handed her the oversized cell phone with a large folding antenna. She brushed aside her blond hair and pressed the receiver tightly against her left ear and stuck a finger into the other. "This is June Cohen," she said.

The voice of Donald Wilson broke the silence. "I had visitors the other day from the FBI and the DEA. They're on to you, June."

"What?"

"You heard me."

"How?"

"It seems your man, Assaly, purposely left a trail of evidence behind, just in case he was double-crossed."

"Oh? "Like what?"

"A couple of photographs of you."

Her jaw tightened before saying, "That bastard."

"And the FBI even has you on videotape."

"How did they manage that?"

"From the meeting in Los Angeles. A security camera caught you sitting in the lounge of the Bonaventure Hotel. Also, the FBI tapped Rahimi's phone and placed a video camera outside his office, which caught you going in and out."

"Shit. I only went there once."

"That's all it took."

She gritted her teeth. "What other evidence did he leave behind?"

"He took photographs of the transmitter and the digital recorder you gave him to wear, and he even got a photo of you getting into your car. He mailed all the photographs to his sister here in Virginia with instructions to give them to Gary Lowery."

"Damn. What did you tell them?"

"Nothing, of course. They were hoping I'd verify you were a Case Officer. Can you imagine? Did they seriously think I would confirm something like that to them, of all people? How naive are they?"

Her tone became serious. "What's this I'm hearing about Saddam still being alive?"

"That's why I'm calling. What went wrong?" She was lost for words. Her well-thought-out plan was crumbling all around her. "CNN's reporting the helicopter was hit, so at least that part went well."

"Yes, but he somehow survived," June said.

"That was not supposed to happen, June. And what about Rahimi and his two men? The Chief of Station says they're dead. At least *somebody* died in this deal."

"That's what I gather. It sounds like a soldier came upon them," June said.

Wilson sighed. "I'm thinking it just wasn't Saddam's time. Looks like he beat the odds again. That's the way I'm reading it until I get some specific information to the contrary. I'm having our people in Bagdad confirm all of this for me."

"I wonder where he is."

"Assaly? He's probably in Saudi Arabia by now."

"Saudi? Why would he go there?"

Wilson ignored the question. "Assaly was spotted crossing into Kuwait. He told the immigration officer he intended to go to Saudi. And he was using the Jordanian passport you gave him. They found the Mercedes we provided them in the airport parking lot, and we know Assaly purchased a plane ticket to Riyadh that left about an hour ago."

"Why would he go there?" she repeated.

"He's an amateur, and he's scared. That's a horrible combination, June. Frankly, I don't think he knows what to do."

June hated to admit it, however said, "Do you know I've released the two women?"

"Yes, I just got your cable."

"I hope you know I would *never* have released them if I knew Saddam was alive," she said. "There was every indication everyone on board the helicopter was dead," she added.

"Yes, of course. Everyone died except Saddam. These things happen, June. Don't blame yourself. I'm glad you released the women. We had no further use for them."

"What do you want me to do now?"

"Get out of the area, but make yourself available when I call," he ordered. "Somewhere like, say, Turkey. Izmir's nice this time of year."

"Yes, sir."

"Stay at the Hilton. You'll enjoy the view of the harbor. I'll call you there."

"Yes, sir," she said again, but even more solemn.

Wilson correctly sensed she was falling into a depression over the outcome of the assignment. "June, I want you to know you performed beautifully all the way. Nothing you did jeopardized the operation. You did a superb job. The FBI only just stumbled upon you, you know."

"Yes, sir. Thank you."

"And the fact the target survived was unavoidable."

"If you say so, sir."

"It was the unknown factor working against you. No matter how much detail and forethought you put into a plan, an unknown factor can rise and derail it. Murphy's law."

"Yes, sir. So, it seems."

"I also want you to know I'll be glad to run interference for you after the armchair quarterbacks upstairs read your after-action report and do their usual hatchet job on an operation."

"I would appreciate that very much, sir." She was grateful to have a friend in high places that understood shit happens.

"June, I still want you to go ahead with the second phase of the operation, just as planned."

"Are you sure?"

"Yes. Quite."

"Even though the mission failed?"

"*Especially* since the mission failed. However, I don't think it was a total failure. We've learned a lot from our mistakes, and we'll be sure to avoid them next time. Who knows, June, maybe Saddam's finally had enough and will throw in the towel and go into exile. Or maybe he's a vegetable case from the crash. Hell, maybe he'll do all of us a favor and kill himself. Boy, wouldn't that answer a lot of prayers?"

"I'm sure it would, sir," she said.

"Do you want me to start the second phase right away?"

"No. Wait about a week after you've had some rest. If anyone objects, I will take full responsibility for the decision. I'll let you know when we have Assaly settled in a location. In the meantime, take it easy."

"I'll do that sir, but I can't wait to pay Assaly a little visit."

"I can well imagine," he laughed. "I'll keep in close touch and DHL your mail to the Izmir Hilton."

"Thank you, sir."

"Enjoy your free time, June. Take a day trip to Ephesus and see the ruins. Go to Kusadasi and enjoy the seafood."

"Yes, sir. I'll do that."

"I will contact you as soon as Assaly has settled somewhere. Probably within the week. In the meantime, enjoy your holiday." The line went dead.

June folded the antenna and threw the phone on the couch. She reached into her pocket and took out a pack of cigarettes, lighting one. She placed her fists on her hips and shouted at the ceiling, "Robaire! You double-crossing, no-good, goddamn son-of-a-bitch!"

CHAPTER 38

Gary Lowery headed straight for Joyce McCarthy's home after landing at Los Angeles International Airport, glad to be away from the snow. He had phoned her ahead of time, and she had taken off early from work to beat the traffic and meet him at her condominium.

Gary drove into the complex just as the sun's huge orange ball dipped into the Pacific. He had spent a long morning at DEA headquarters hoping to get a first-hand update on the situation, but the news was not too encouraging. The best the DEA could do now was to have Robaire Assaly placed on the Interpol watch list. That way, every member nation would look for him. They would notify DEA headquarters in the event he was located. DEA sent photographs of Robaire Assaly to Interpol headquarters in Lyon, France, where they will be distributed to over 160 member nations. Gary might get lucky, and they find him.

Gary used his own key to gain entry. While entering, he winked at Joyce, who was in the kitchen mixing a batch of bone-dry Beefeater martinis.

"Just what the doctor ordered." He dropped his luggage and gave her a bear hug and a long kiss.

"Doctor McCarthy at your service," she smiled back.

He hugged her again. "I missed you."

"I missed you, too. Have you eaten?"

"No. What's on your mind?"

"Want to order Chinese?"

"Sounds good. Wanna call now?"

"Sure," she said, picking up the phone.

"I'll take plenty of fried rice with my beef broccoli," he said.

"As you wish, my Lord," she laughed, while dialing the number. She wore a navy-blue halter-top braless. Her erect nipples protruded against the cotton fabric. He stood behind her, putting his arms around her waist, and nibbled on her right earlobe.

"Stop that!" she exclaimed. "I'm trying to talk on the phone."

Gary lowered his aim to her shoulder and began to lightly stroke it with his tongue, causing her to shiver. He knew she loved it when he did that. Raising his arms, he cupped her full breasts with both hands.

"Hello, I'd like an order of beef with broccoli and your General Tso combination plate. Oh, and I'd like a side order of fried rice." She slapped his right hand.

Gary crossed his arms around her waist and ran his fingertips just inside her cut-off jeans, causing her to make a tiny shriek. She slapped his right arm again and said, "What do you think you're doing?"

"Isn't it obvious?" he replied, continuing to slide his hands down the back of her jeans."Not you, I'm sorry," she told the woman on the phone. She gave the address and yelped one more time as he passed a chilly hand over her firm butt.

"I hope the woman taking the order enjoyed this as much as I did," he laughed.

"I'm sure she did," she said and smiled. She hung up the phone, turned to face him, and gave him a lip lock.

"Think we have time for dessert before the main course arrives?" he asked.

"They said they'd be here within forty-five minutes."

"Oh, good. We can have second helpings after dinner," he said.

He poured two martinis and said, "Dessert is my favorite part of the meal." He gently nudged her into the bedroom, nibbling all the way.

• • •

They finished their Chinese food and placed the empty cardboard containers on the bedstand, careful not to drop anything on the sheets.

"That was great Chinese," she said.

He turned to her and smiled. "Not nearly as good as the dessert."

She snuggled up to his side and placed her head on his carved pecs. She ran her forefinger down his six-pack and drew a circle around his belly button. "So, tell me, Special Agent Lowery, how did your powwow go in Washington?"

"We might as well have stayed home," he puffed. "This case is really putting a dent in my workout schedule."

She raised her head and looked at him. "Why? What happened?"

"We were sandbagged, pure and simple."

"By the FBI?"

He shook his head. "No, the CIA."

"The CIA? How?"

"We paid them a visit and were politely told they didn't know anything about it."

"How can they say that with a straight face when you have a videotape of the woman and her photograph?"

"Very easy. Just deny, deny, and deny some more. Eventually, someone will believe them. We asked them straight up if she was CIA, and they flatly denied it."

"So, that's it? There's no way to confirm it?"

"Not from them."

"I'll get a court order and make them deny her identity under oath."

"Don't bother," he suggested. "The CIA will simply deny any knowledge and say you're asking to prove a negative. They're already on record stating they don't have any such employee. Can't turn back now."

She calmed down. "What makes you so sure they're lying?"

"The whole situation. The way the guy looked at us, his body language, the way he looked at her photographs. Wilson, the Deputy Assistant Chief of Clandestine Operations guy, said he'd look into it and call us back at the hotel with any information. He called within *minutes* and told Olson there was no record of any such person or operation. It would take DEA a couple of weeks to be sure about something like that, probably longer. Who's he kidding? And when I get back to L.A., I hear on the news someone tried to whack Saddam Hussein with a missile."

"Yeah, I heard that too."

"I'd bet your paycheck that was our Stinger. There's no such thing as a coincidence in this business."

"What do Olson and Rowe think?"

"They don't believe him either. They know when they're being conned from all the scams they've pulled themselves. However, I haven't talked to them since I heard about the assassination attempt."

"Why would the CIA lie?"

"That's what they do. Secrecy and all that. They don't trust anyone outside the agency. Hell, I don't think they trust each other. It shocked Wilson to see how much evidence we had. He didn't look so happy when he saw the photographs. I think he called his boss to get permission to kiss us off and did just that. What we didn't know at the time was someone was going to try to take out Saddam Hussein."

She placed her head on his shoulder and attempted to curl one of the few hairs on his muscular chest with her finger. "So, what are you going to do now?"

"I don't know. We've done all we can here. It's now a matter of finding Robaire. He's the key to locating the woman and learning what this is really about. It's got to be all about Saddam Hussein."

"Why do you say that?"

"I've had five hours to think about it during the flight home, Joyce. Tell me what you think: the CIA orchestrates the theft of a Stinger missile right under our noses. The next thing anyone knows, someone shoots down Saddam Hussein's helicopter with one. Coincidence? Not likely."

"But we don't know if that was our Stinger, do we?"

"Well, no," he admitted. "However, what are the odds? It's designed to be used against foreign aircraft. It makes sense Hussein would be in a Russian-made helicopter. Think about motive, knowledge, and opportunity. That's what you look for during an investigation. The CIA has all three."

Joyce sat up and threw the sheet around her. "Please explain again. You've lost me."

"Let's say for the sake of argument June and Rahimi are in cahoots. They kidnap the informant's mother and sister, and approach Robaire with a scheme they tell him will help get them released. Robaire takes their offer and sets us up to steal the Stinger. Rahimi and June elude surveillance and make off with it. The next thing we know, Saddam Hussein's helicopter is shot down."

She shook her head. "So, you're saying the CIA stole the missile so it could kill Saddam Hussein?"

"Exactly."

"Why wouldn't the CIA just give Rahimi one and save the million bucks they paid for it?"

"That's the beauty of it. Don't you see? This way, they can deny being involved. An Iranian and a dirty drug informant stole it, right? The president can deny any knowledge since the CIA is the only one who knows the truth, and they won't even tell him. Naturally, they'll deny the assassination plot and point to our investigation as evidence they weren't involved. We become their unwitting accomplices in the assassination. What they didn't count on was Robaire sending his sister those photographs."

"That's quite a theory."

"It gets better. Rahimi's an Iranian. Iranians hate Iraqis, right? Remember the eight-year war they had?"

Joyce wrinkled her nose. "It makes sense, in a way."

Gary found the remote to the television and tuned it to CNN. "Let's see if there's anything new."

Nic Robertson was talking about the assassination attempt and was about to recap: "Again, Iraqi officials have lodged a formal complaint with the United Nations against the United States for what they are calling a shameless overt attempt on the life of Saddam Hussein."A videotape showed soldiers displaying pieces of the empty Stinger missile tube on a table. A close-up of an identification plate of the weapon made it clear it was a Stinger missile manufactured in the United States.

Joyce looked at Gary with her mouth open. "Damn, you're good!"

The reporter continued. "The bodies of the three men apparently killed by an Iraqi soldier, who himself was killed by gunfire in the hotel room where the missile was fired, have tentatively been identified as an Iranian-American and two Pakistani nationals. Iraqi authorities said the Iranian-American had a forged Jordanian passport and a U.S. passport in different names on his person. Authorities have not released the names of the Pakistanis."

"I'll be damned!" Gary yelled. "I'll bet I know who the other two assholes were. One of them had to be the triggerman."

Joyce pounded on Gary's thigh. "That's only three! What about Assaly?"

"Shhh. Listen," Gary said.

Nic Robertson continued. "A few minutes ago, in a news conference carried live by CNN, a State Department spokeswoman in Washington denied any United States involvement in the attempted assassination of Saddam Hussein and said she had no information about the dead Iranian."

"So now the shit hits the fan," Gary said. "Everyone denies it, and the CIA comes out clean when in reality they're the ones involved from the get-go."

"And all the witnesses are dead," Joyce said.

"Not quite. Don't forget about Robaire Assaly."

"And June," she added. "I wonder where she is and what she's doing right now."

"So do I. I'd really like to get my hands on Robaire before someone kills him."

"You think he's in danger?"

"He's the only one who can verify the CIA's involvement. If they don't kill him, *I* will," Gary said, chuckling.

Joyce snuggled up again next to Gary. "So, Chief Sherlock, it looks like you've figured this one out."

"Well, maybe. That's yet to be seen. We may never know the entire story."

"Any other predictions?"

He smiled. "I predict you're about to have an exhilarating sexual experience."

Joyce threw her sheet off her and straddled him. "Right again."

"Sometimes I amaze myself."

CHAPTER 39

Robaire Assaly checked into the Marriott Hotel in downtown Riyadh, Saudi Arabia. He exchanged dollars for Riyals and proceeded to his room. The glass elevators next to a water fountain reminded him of the Bonaventure Hotel in Los Angeles. He wondered if he would ever return to Los Angeles again.

Robaire jerked his shoes off, stripped down to his boxer shorts, and plopped onto the king-size bed. He had managed to get some sleep on the airplane but still felt weary. After he switched on the television and scanned the channels until he came upon the news from Baghdad in English, French, German, and Arabic. Finally, both CNN and Al-Jazeera repeated what Gary and Joyce had heard earlier.

After hearing the news for the third time, he was bored and switched to an in-house channel showing pirated first-run movies. He noticed a listing of the movies being played that month next to the bed. Many were of the Kung-fu variety, but several were current releases. The film now playing was *The Firm*, which he had seen about twelve years before. Tom Cruise was meeting with the Director of the FBI to discuss becoming an informant. Something Robaire could relate to.

He watched the pirated film until he finally fell asleep. He dreamed about eluding his pursuers like Tom Cruise did. Escape to Bavaria? Why not?

•   •   •

The next morning, Robaire was famished. He quickly showered and shaved and dove into a plate of eggs, waffles, cereal, and juices in the hotel's restaurant. He topped the meal off with several cups of coffee while he read the news accounts about the biggest story in the Middle East since the Gulf War.

With nothing to do at the hotel, he hailed a taxi to take him to the gold markets. The Afghan cab driver spoke little Arabic and even less English but managed to get him to a cluster of small shops near a mosque.

Robaire was pleased to see small shops bursting with twenty-two karat gold chains, bracelets, rings, and the like. Each store was crowded with women wearing traditional black abayas that had their faces fully covered except for two narrow eye slits. Under the garments, however, were glimpses of gold rings and bracelets that contrasted their black elbow-length gloves. It seemed like a waste to him to spend so much money on such beauty they could only admire at home. He supposed the women secretly displayed their glittering jewelry to their female friends. Just like women anywhere, he reckoned.

He shopped for an hour before concluding all the gold merchants sold the same items at the same price. He bargained at several places and decided on a gold necklace for his mother and sister, hoping against all odds they were alive and well. The purchase would keep alive the possibility of seeing them again.

Precisely at noon, just as he was about to lay his money down for the purchase of the jewelry, the Islamic crier announced the beginning of prayer time. The amplified male voice echoed throughout the city, and all believers were being called to pray in fifteen minutes. The gold merchant, ever watchful of the Mutawa, abruptly collected the items off the counter and told Robaire to come back at four p.m.

"I'm ready to buy now," he protested, initially thinking this was only a ploy to jack up the price.

"You go now. Prayer time," the merchant said. "The Mutawa will soon come."

The Mutawa, or religious police vice squad, foot-patrol the shops looking for violators of Islamic law. All laws in Saudi Arabia stem from Islam, and this special breed of police officer assures respect for the religion. They place violators in custody and seek the suspension of business licenses of those who would defy the Koran.

The merchant gently but firmly shoved Robaire out of his shop and immediately pulled a metal door down, locking it. Robaire sauntered back to the street, depressed over not being able to purchase the gifts. He was about to hail a taxi when he noticed a considerable number of men rushing past him to the Mosque across the street. He looked around him and saw hundreds of men and boys rushing to the Mosque, lining up around a parking lot. It reminded him of a crowd hurrying from the parking lot of Dodger stadium to not miss the first pitch.

The buzz of the crowd attracted him. He wandered across the busy street to the parking lot, curious about all the commotion. He estimated there were about three thousand people gathered in the hot parking lot. Scarcely anyone was entering the Mosque. His inquisitiveness led him to join the flood of spectators who were pouring into the parking lot. Getting closer, he noticed scores of police officers in tan uniforms and black berets forming a rectangular-shaped secure area within the parking lot. These officers kept the crowd back while ten other officers created a second line of defense in a circle about fifty feet in diameter in the center of the lot.

Promptly at twelve-fifteen, the thousands of men, and some boys, dropped their prayer rugs on the asphalt and fell to their knees, facing east. Once everyone dropped to their knees, Robaire immediately spotted a man, obviously an American, standing on the other side of the parking lot. They were the only two in the crowd left standing. He wore a blue Polo shirt, blue jeans, and a pair of Ray Ban wayfarer sunglasses. The crowd had concealed him until everyone fell to their knees. The American just stood there with his arms folded, watching Robaire.

After ten minutes of prayer, the crowd came to their feet and rushed to the police lines. Swept up in the frenzy, the crowd pushed Robaire to the front of the police barricade.

Men standing around Robaire began pointing at a police van driving up. What really got his attention was a huge Saudi man who had the build of Hulk Hogan in his prime. He wore a white linen thobe and had a red and white-checkered keffiyeh on his head that looked like an Italian tablecloth. The keffiyeh was secured to his head with a black agal. The man was carrying a long, narrow scimitar. A sensation struck Robaire's stomach like a mallet. Oh my God, could it be what he thought it could be?

The back of the van opened, and the police took the first condemned man to the middle of the police circle. His hands were bound behind him, and a white hood over his head was only long enough to cover his eyes. An abrupt hush came over the crowd as two police officers, standing on each side of the man, held one of his wrists while pushing on his shoulders, forcing him onto his knees. They pushed the man's shoulders forward enough to expose as much of his neck as possible, and then quickly backed away.

Using only his left hand, the executioner raised the scimitar to a forty-five-degree angle while lifting his 300-pound frame on the balls of his feet. His sword fell swiftly. Loud moans came from the crowd as the man fell to his left side.

The police immediately led a second man to a spot about ten feet behind the first. This condemned man appeared more cooperative as the police officers gently assisted the man to his knees and pushed his shoulders forward. The executioner raised his sword again and struck the man in the same manner. The crowd became energized when the show was over and began yelling and waving their arms. The commotion lasted only thirty seconds. The crowd just as suddenly made an orderly departure.

Robaire could not move. His legs would not obey. He knew the same treatment awaited him if Saddam Hussein's secret police ever caught up with him. He watched the executioner circle around the second condemned man and grab a handful of the dead man's pants leg and ran the blade of the sword through it several times wiping off the blood.

Robaire's knees grew weak. His stomach was in suspended animation. He stood alone, watching two attendants place the bodies on stretchers and slide them into the back of an ambulance.

The executioner nonchalantly lit a cigarette and watched the ambulance attendants at work. After several puffs, the executioner walked to his awaiting BMW convertible and drove away. Just like it was another day at the office.

Robaire noticed the man in the Polo shirt walking towards him. Robaire saw a taxi approaching, flagged it down, and hopped into the back seat. "Quick. Go around the block!" Robaire ordered.

"What? Why?" the confused driver asked.

"Just do as I say. I want you to follow someone."

"Follow someone? Yessir!" The small but husky taxi driver grinned.

Once around the block Robaire said, "Pull over to the curb." He leaned over the front seat to get a better look at the American. He was jogging to a parked Chevrolet Caprice two blocks away from the Mosque. The man got into the car and drove off.

"Follow that car!" Robaire commanded.

"Yessir."

The cabby skillfully maneuvered his old Dodge station wagon through traffic to catch up with the Chevy. "Don't get too close," warned Robaire.

"Oh, don't worry, sir. I won't lose him. He cannot escape me."

Robaire sat back in his stained seat and observed the American drive west out of the downtown area to an expressway. The cabby did likewise and blended in nicely with the traffic. The American occasionally glanced in his mirror but never realized he was being followed.After about eight minutes, the American exited the expressway and drove through a sparsely developed part of the city. After traveling about two more miles, the American maneuvered into a left turn lane. Above the lane, a large road sign read: DIPLOMATIC QUARTER. "Damn it," Robaire said under his breath when he read the sign.

"Who is that man?" the cabby finally asked.

"That's what we're going to find out."

"Who are you anyway? Are you a spy?"

"Something like that." Robaire smiled. "Keep driving."

The American drove through the winding street. They passed the French, Irish, and U.K. embassies. They drove by the deserted Iraqi Embassy that had tall grass growing through the cracks in the sidewalk.

Slowing down, the Caprice turned on a street leading to the American Embassy. The cabbie continued to follow him on a street that paralleled the embassy until he reached a side gate. After honking his horn twice, the American got the guard's attention. The guard, dressed in a light blue shirt and dark blue slacks wearing an oval hat, gave the man a half-hearted salute before opening the iron gates.

"Quick! Park where I can see this," Robaire said.

Robaire saw another security guard lower a heavy metal barrier built into the driveway allowing the vehicle to pass. The man drove into a subterranean parking garage.

"He must work there," the driver said, trying to be helpful.

"He surely must." Robaire stroked his jaw in thought as the Caprice slipped out of view. "I have seen enough. Take me to the Marriott."

Within a few minutes, the cab came to a stop in the hotel's driveway. The combined trauma of witnessing a double header and being watched by a strange American was about all the excitement he could stand for one day. He did not know which traumatized him more: watching two people get their heads cut off or being followed by the CIA.

"Thank you very much," Robaire said. "You've been most helpful." He handed the man double the fare.

The man looked at the money and said, "My pleasure, kind sir. I cannot wait to tell my grandchildren someday about this."

Robaire laughed and walked into the hotel, directly to his room. He phoned Lufthansa Airlines and made reservations for a flight to Frankfurt. His plan was to rent a car and rediscover the freedom of the autobahns that would transverse him effortlessly to Bavaria. A place where wildflowers permeated the landscape, and skiing was challenging. Robaire did not complain this time there were no first-class seats. He gladly settled for an aisle coach seat on a flight scheduled for the next afternoon at five-thirty p.m.

While lying on the bed he switched on the television with the remote. He listened intently when the Arab news anchor spoke of the two executions at the square earlier in the day. They marked the 21st and 22nd of the year, and it was only late February. A Pakistani national and an Afghan were found guilty and sentenced to death for smuggling heroin into the Kingdom of Saudi Arabia. No recidivism here. Executing someone by lethal injection was one thing but decapitating them was quite another. Robaire's skin goose-bumped when he thought of the beheadings.

"And he wiped the blood off his sword with the dead guy's pants," Robaire said aloud to himself. "Unbelievable."

He laid one side of his face into a pillow and snored loudly.

CHAPTER 40

Robaire awoke after a good night's sleep and checked his watch, surprised he had slept until eight a.m. He sat on the edge of the bed and rubbed his eyes with his palms. His clothes were a mess. He stared at the telephone, wondering if he should risk making a call. Initially, he picked up the receiver and held it for a few seconds, but slowly lowered it back onto the cradle and cursed, deciding it was too risky.

He stripped his clothes off as he walked towards the bathroom and looked at himself in the mirror. Robaire pulled his cheeks to erase the wrinkles under his eyes. He thought he looked terrible. The stress of the situation had caught up to him.

"The hell with it," he said to himself. "They know I'm here."

Rushing back to the bedroom, he flipped through the telephone instructions booklet on the nightstand to learn how to make a direct international phone call. He picked up the receiver and dialed his sister's number in Virginia.

On the third ring, she answered it. "Nadia! It's me, Robaire."

Her eyes grew wide. "Robaire, dear brother. Where are you?" She covered the mouthpiece and called for her mother and sister to pick up the extension.

He hesitated a moment and said, "I'm in Saudi Arabia."

"What are you doing there?" Before he could answer, she continued, "Never mind. I'm sorry. I should not have asked. Mama and Leila are here with me."

Tears came to Robaire's eyes when he heard the news. "When did they arrive?"

"Yesterday afternoon. It was such a surprise."

"Are they okay?"

"They are," she assured him.

He let out a deep sigh. "Let me talk to Leila."

"I'm on the line, big brother."

"How's mama? How did you get to America?"

"Why don't you ask her for yourself? She's here with me."

"Please put her on." She handed the receiver to their mother.

"Robaire, my son. Where are you? Are you in any trouble?"

"What would make you ask such a question, mama?"

"I may be old, but I'm not stupid," she scolded. "The woman who took us to the airport said she released us because of something you did. Is this true?"

"Yes, mama. It's true."

"Well, what did you do to convince the kidnappers to let us go?"

"It's too long a story to go into now. This phone call is going to cost me a fortune."

"You can afford it. You're a big shot record producer in Hollywood, aren't you? Ask Michael Jackson for a loan. I'm sure he'd be glad to give it to you."

Robaire laughed aloud. A genuine laugh. The first time he had done so in weeks. "I love you, mama. I am so glad you and Leila are all right."

"Come home. We miss you. We all want to see you. When will you be coming to Washington?"

"Not for a long while, I'm afraid. I still have some unfinished business to attend to."

"Just be quick about it. We long for the day."

"I love you mama, let me speak to Leila now. I must ask her something."

"All right. Here she is. I love you, too." She handed the receiver to her youngest daughter.

"Robaire, I'm so glad you called. When are you coming home?"

"When I finish my business."

"When will that be?"

"I don't know. Soon I hope." He paused, gathering his thoughts. "Tell me, how did you and mama get released? How did you get to the airport?"

"A blond American woman drove us. She gave us American passports and plane tickets. Oh, she also gave us ten thousand dollars! She put us on a plane to New York. A nice young man met us, and we transferred to another plane to Washington, where a second nice man met us."

"A blond woman, you say?"

"Yes."

"Do you know her name?"

"No. She made it a point not to mention it."

"Was she attractive? About thirty-five years old?"

"Yes, I'd say so."

"Tell me about the men?"

"They did not tell us their names either. The first one just rushed us through customs and immigration."

"Didn't they say who they worked for?" He raised his voice. "Didn't they say anything to you?"

His sudden change of demeanor frightened her. "Do not yell, Robaire. I can hear you without shouting. Are you sure you are all right?"

"Sorry."

"Like I said, they said little except for us to follow them. We weren't about to argue. The first man gave us an envelope and put us on the plane. Inside the envelope was Nadia's telephone number. The blond woman had also given us the same number. We called her once we arrived in Washington, and she came right over to the airport and picked us up."

"The first man had Nadia's telephone number?"

"Yes. Is that a problem?"

"No. I just thought it was unlisted, that's all."

"It *is* unlisted," Nadia interrupted, still on the line. "Who do you suppose that man was?"

"It's hard to say," Robaire said. "Could be FBI, DEA, or CIA."

"CIA!" Leila said. "Is the CIA involved in this somehow?"

He ignored the question. "Nadia, did you get hold of Gary Lowery?"

"Yes. He and two FBI agents came to the house, and we had a long talk."

"Did you give him the package I sent you?"

"Yes, everything. They took it with them. I haven't heard from them since." She paused and asked, "What's going on, Robaire? What did you get yourself mixed up in?"

"I don't dare talk about it on the phone. I'll write to you soon, I promise. I'm just so glad to hear everyone is all right."

"Come home, Robaire," Nadia said. "We all miss you so much."

"I'm not sure I can yet."

"Should I call Agent Lowery again?"

"Yes. Tell him I am all right. Tell him I will call him soon."

"Can I tell him where you are?"

"No. Not yet. I'm still sorting things out. It shouldn't be long, though."

"Is there anything we can do for you?" Leila asked.

"No. I'm fine, really. I must be going before the phone bill surpasses the American national debt."

They chuckled. "You're always the funny one, Robaire," Leila said.

"Good-bye for now. I will call again."

"Soon?" Nadia asked.

"A week. Maybe two. Don't worry about me."

"If you say so," she said.

"Kiss mama for me." He hung up and had an uncontrollable urge to smile. He could hardly believe it. Despite being an unbearable bitch, June came through with her promise to free them, even though Saddam Hussein survived the attack and Rahimi and his men did not. Maybe he had misjudged her. No, she's too cold-hearted to do anything nice for someone. There must be another reason.

• • •

The man with the blue Polo shirt set the headphones down once Robaire hung up the telephone. He scribbled out his notes about the phone conversation in a notebook and penned the name "Lowery" in big letters. He picked up his own telephone and dialed CIA headquarters in Langley, Virginia, on a secure phone.

A woman answered the phone with a simple "Hello."

"Connect me with Deputy Assistant Director Wilson. This is Tom O'Reilly in Riyadh." The woman put him on hold and connected him through their secure switchboard to Wilson's home.

"Wilson here," he said.

"This should be a STU call. Is your key in?" asked O'Reilly.

"Yes, I'll press the secure button." The phone became silent, and the liquid crystal diode screen on the instrument read: GOING SECURE. About twenty seconds later, the screen on the phone read: TOP SECRET AM EMB RIYADH.

O'Reilly said, "Assaly's still in Riyadh, but he's made reservations for Frankfurt this afternoon."

"Good. What else?"

"He called his sister in Virginia but didn't mention anything about traveling to Frankfurt."

"All right. Anything else?"

"He seems genuinely surprised we released his mother and sister," O'Reilly opined.

"He ought to."

"He also wants them to call someone named Lowery."

"Oh?"

"And he acknowledged sending his sister an envelope."

"Anything else?"

"No, sir."

"All right. Keep me posted, Tom."

"Yes, sir."

O'Reilly hung up and rolled his chair over to a computer. He turned it on and began writing his report on the installed Microsoft Word software. A transcript of Robaire's entire phone conversation would soon follow and be securely faxed to CIA headquarters.

• • •

Three FBI agents in a non-descript office building in Alexandria, Virginia, rewound the audiotape of the phone call to Nadia Evans to hear it again. A supervisory special agent looked at one of his subordinates. "Call Olson in L.A. and tell him Assaly's in Saudi Arabia and it sounds like he'll be there a while."

CHAPTER 41

White House Press Secretary Ari Fleischer looked stern during a formal news conference as he answered questions about Amir Rahimi from the insatiable media.

"When did Rahimi first come to the United States?" a young reporter asked.

"I'm sorry, but I don't have that information," he said. "I'll have to refer you to the Immigration and Naturalization Service."

"Where did he get a Stinger missile?" another reporter queried. "The Iraqi Ambassador to the United Nations is claiming the United States supplied a Stinger missile to Rahimi, who is an Iranian expatriate. What can you tell us about that?"

"I don't have any information about that either," Fleischer repeated. "The allegation the U.S. was somehow involved in a plot to assassinate Saddam Hussein is absurd."

A reporter from the *Washington Post* asked, "Was Rahimi trained by the CIA or the Defense Department?" He was clearly fishing for a story.

"I don't have any information that would even *remotely* suggest Rahimi was involved with any U.S. government agency," he said calmly. "To suggest otherwise would be pure speculation and highly irresponsible."

"Are there any reported thefts of Stinger missiles from the military?" a seasoned White House reporter asked.

"Not to my knowledge," he stated. "I'll have to refer you to the Department of Defense for that information." The relentless peppering of questions about Stinger missiles clearly vexed him.

"Would the FBI have that information?" the reporter followed up.

"You'll have to check with them," he replied.

"How did Rahimi come to migrate to the United States?" another reporter asked. "I don't have all the details as of yet," he responded, wishing he had.

"Is it true he worked at the American Embassy in Tehran in 1979 during the hostage situation?" a *Fox News* reporter inquired.

"That's news to me," Fleischer replied.

"When will we know the exact contents of his immigration dossier?" a reporter from *The New York Times* quizzed.

"I don't know if any such 'dossier,' as you put it, exists." His sigh caused his face to fluster.

An *ABC* news reporter jumped up. "Come on, the government would obviously know something about a Stinger missile getting into the hands of an Iranian immigrant, wouldn't it?"

"Not necessarily."

"Can you elaborate?"

"The last count I heard from the CIA was there were hundreds of Stinger missiles still unaccounted for during the U.S.S.R. - Afghan conflict," Fleischer replied.

"Hundreds?" the reporter asked.

"Yes, hundreds."

"I thought you just said you didn't have any information about stolen Stingers?"

"That's correct," he said. "I don't know if there are any stolen Stinger missiles. However, Stinger missiles left over from the Afghan war with the old Soviet Union is another matter," he said, distinguishing between the two. "To repeat, I don't have any information about the source of the Stinger missile used in the attempted assassination of Saddam Hussein."

"You're acknowledging the loss of hundreds of Stinger missiles issued by the CIA during the Afghan war?"

"Yes, I just said that. That's old news that was first reported as far back as 1993."

Now it was the *CBS* reporter's turn. "A source at the State Department tells CBS news Rahimi was, in fact, employed by the U.S. Embassy in Tehran during the Iranian crisis. Can you confirm that for me?"

"Like I said, I cannot. I will refer you to the State department for that information," the press secretary replied, maintaining his composure.

"Well, what information *do* you have?" a reporter for the *Associated Press* asked."Not much, I'm afraid."

"When can we talk to someone who *does* have some information?"

"I don't know," he admitted. "When I have something, I'll gladly share it with you."

The *CNN* reporter fired off, "The Iraqis insist the United Nations conduct an inquiry. The foreign minister is accusing the CIA of orchestrating the attempted assassination of Saddam Hussein."

"I think the CIA was also accused of causing Hurricane Andrew," he said, bringing a polite chuckle from his audience. "I'm not going to comment on wild speculation by the Iraqi government."

* * *

Mark Olson and Calvin Rowe sat in Assistant Director Mason's office and watched the live news conference. "Look at him squirm," Mason said.

"Wait until the Attorney General has his own news conference and blows the lid off this," Rowe said. "When's it scheduled?"

"Thursday," Mason said. "I've been on the phone all morning with Main Justice. They're convinced they have a strong case against June Cohen and can show a connection with the CIA, *if* we can find Assaly. I sensed a reluctance on their part when I spoke to people in the criminal division. I'm not sure what's going on. We need to find Assaly to testify before a Grand Jury. The last we heard, he was in Saudi Arabia."

"Do we have an extradition treaty with Saudi Arabia?" Olson asked.

"Yes," his boss replied. "However, they won't act unless we have an Interpol red warrant in hand, and that won't happen unless we indict Assaly and put together an extradition package. That will take some time. Joyce McCarthy, the Assistant U.S. Attorney on the case, is waiting for permission from Main Justice to subpoena Wilson."

"They'd better hurry," Rowe said. "Assaly's obviously taking precautions."

"Can you blame him?" Mason asked. "Wouldn't you take precautions if you blew the whistle on a CIA operation to kill Saddam Hussein?"

"We don't know that for sure," Olson said. "Don't forget, we've still got to find Cohen, or whatever her real name is. That soldier in Baghdad made quick work of our other defendants."

"Except for Assaly," Rowe said. "I wonder how he got away."

"I'd sure like to see Wilson indicted," Olson said. "What do you think the chances are of that?"

"Mere knowledge is not enough. Right now, he denies everything. We must show he made an agreement with the others to violate the law to make him a co-conspirator," the ADIC reminded him. "I don't think we'll ever be able to do that unless Cohen cooperates."

"And nobody knows where she is," Olson said.

"It's a shame how often different government agencies like the FBI, DEA, and CIA, frequently work against each other while trying to achieve the same thing," Mason observed.

"A genuine lack of trust," Olson said. "No one trusts anyone anymore."

• • •

Joyce McCarthy arrived for work that day invigorated. She had time over the weekend to think about the case and how to go about prosecuting it. She decided she was going to subpoena Wilson before a federal grand jury in Los Angeles. She looked forward to the day she could grill him about his personal involvement in the conspiracy to steal the Stinger missile. Joyce had already formulated questions she intended to ask him, and she and Gary had drafted an affidavit in support of an arrest warrant for June Cohen.

Thanks to time zones, Main Justice had a three-hour head start on her. When she arrived at her office, two messages awaited her to call Grace Sugimoto in Washington. She did not know Sugimoto and was curious about the call. She dialed the number.

"Grace Sugimoto, please," Joyce said.

"Just a minute," the receptionist responded. Joyce could hear Sugimoto's extension ringing.

"This is Grace Sugimoto," a voice said.

"This is AUSA Joyce McCarthy from the U.S. Attorney's office in Los Angeles.

"Thanks for returning my call. I have some important instructions for you from the Criminal Division."

"Oh?"

"I hate to be the one to break it to you, but we're not authorizing you to subpoena anyone before the grand jury concerning the overseas matter."

"WHAT? Why not?" She was incredulous.

"Do you have access to a STU phone?"

"There's one in the building someplace. Why?"

"I'll discuss it once you call me back on a STU III. I can only discuss it on a secure phone." She gave Joyce the number.

"Give me ten minutes, and I'll call you right back," Joyce said. She hung up, mad as a hornet. She immediately called Gary's cell.

"I'm so glad I caught you."

"What's up?"

"I just got a call from Grace Sugimoto at the Criminal Division at Main Justice. Do you know her?"

"No. Never heard of her."

"She said they won't allow me to subpoena Wilson to testify before the grand jury."

"What?"

"That's what I said. She wants me to call her back on a STU. She said she can't discuss it on the regular line."

"Someone at the agency must have gotten to someone at Justice. There's more to this than she is letting on."

"What should I tell her?"

"Find out what she wants. Remind her you've got venue in the Central District of California and you're ready to proceed. Tell her when we find the informant, he'll blow the lid off this whole thing when he gives up June Cohen. We won't find out what else he knows until we can debrief him."

"That will really piss her off," Joyce said.

"Good. I hope it does. I can't wait to hear what bullshit story she tells you. Call me back the second you're off the phone with her."

"Maybe I ought to wait until tonight when I see you? I don't want to repeat what she said on an unsecured line."

"Well, hell." Gary had second thoughts. "If it's *that* secret, wait till tonight. If you can discuss it, get hold of me right away."

"Okay. Gotta go."

Joyce walked at a fast pace to the office of the chief of the drug unit who had a secure telephone unit. She got the key from him and inserted it into the phone and dialed the number. Within a few minutes, Grace Sugimoto was on the line.

"Ms. McCarthy, I called to inform you Main Justice has classified this entire case as 'SECRET.' You must store all reports, notes, and any other related documents in a classified container with restricted access."

"Does the FBI know about this?"

"Not yet. They're next on my list."

"What brought this on?" She couldn't wait for her answer.

"National security," she said solemnly.

"Bullshit!"

"Excuse me?" Sugimoto said.

"You heard me. I said, *bullshit*."

"I don't understand, Ms. McCarthy."

"Shall I repeat myself?"

"Why do you feel this way?"

"The FBI and the DEA are on to something. They know Wilson's covering someone's ass. And they suspect someone at Main Justice is getting pressure to drop the investigation."

"I didn't say that," Sugimoto said, sounding defensive.

"What do you call it when the investigation is suddenly classified? When we get gagged and can no longer discuss it openly with other agencies or with the press. Now some unknown 'national security' issue is hindering us. I can't go to the Grand Jury without credible witnesses, like Wilson, who should be compelled to testify about what he knows. What else would you call it, Ms. Sugimoto?"

"I'm sorry you feel that way."

"Who came up with this classification idea?"

The woman cleared her throat. "The Attorney General himself."

"Jesus Christ!" Joyce exclaimed. "I thought better of him."

"My instructions are to inform you of the classified nature of the investigation and to instruct you not, I repeat, not to subpoena, contact, harass, or hinder in any way, the activities of Deputy Assistant Director Wilson or anyone else in the Central Intelligence Agency. You are not to make any public statements or disclosures regarding the investigation or even to acknowledge such an investigation is ongoing. Any inquiries concerning the matter will be directed to me personally, and I will run them past the AG. Any questions from the press are to be answered in a fashion that will neither confirm nor deny the existence of the inquiry, and any further questions are to be directed to Main Justice. Is that clear, Ms. McCarthy?"

Joyce was hot. She held her tongue. "Perfectly."

"Good. If anything requires further clarification, contact me at this number. If I'm not in, one of my staffers will take a message."

"Whatever you say," Joyce said in a sarcastic tone of voice.

"Don't do anything stupid," Sugimoto said. "We're counting on you being a team player."

"What about DEA and FBI?" Joyce asked.

"What about them?"

"Are they going to continue to investigate?"

"They work for the Department of Justice, don't they?"

"So?"

"Silly question then, isn't it?" Sugimoto said. Joyce didn't like her answer. "They'll do as they're told. If the AG decides he wants to drop their investigation, that's exactly what they'll do."

"What about the informant, Robaire Assaly? Is he off limits, too?"

"No. They'd still like him located. He's got an awful lot of questions to answer."

"They?"

"That is to say, *we'd* like him to answer some questions. Don't read anything into this."

"Does my U.S. Attorney know about this?"

"Yes. The Deputy Attorney General is on a conference call with him and the FBI Director as we speak. The Acting DEA Administrator is on his way over here right now."

"I see," Joyce said. "Seems like you've got all the bases covered."

"Do the right thing, Joyce, and cooperate. There's more to this than meets the eye."

"Care to elaborate?"

"I wish I could," she sighed. "Just drop the grand jury investigation and save us all a lot of grief."

"Whatever you say," she said, but not so sarcastically this time.

"I'll contact you if there are any changes."

"Do that," Joyce said.

"Good-bye, Ms. McCarthy." Sugimoto hung up.

Joyce slouched in the chair and slowly exhaled. She could hardly wait to call Gary. She dialed his number.

"It's over," she said. "The investigation's kaput."

"What?"

"I'll explain it to you tonight. I don't want to talk on this phone."

"I'll pick you up in front of the courthouse about five and we'll have dinner."

"Fine," she said, feeling a little better.

"Bye for now." He hung up and immediately dialed Olson.

"I'm sorry, but he's in a meeting with Assistant Director Mason," the receptionist said.

"How about Calvin Rowe?"

"I'm afraid he's in the same meeting."

"Please have either of them call Gary Lowery immediately," Gary said. He hung up and pounded the steering wheel of his Beamer. "Just as we suspected. Wilson's up to his eyeballs in this!"

GREGORY D. LEE   263

CHAPTER 42

An attractive brunette German Immigration Officer at Frankfurt Am-Main International Airport stamped the U.S. passport of Mister Anwar Nasir, a.k.a. Robaire Assaly. Robaire returned her smile as he put the passport inside his sports coat pocket. After retrieving his luggage, he made his way through the customs lane and walked into the crowded main terminal. He stood out from the rest of his flight passengers, most of whom wore traditional white caftans and kaffiyehs.

A man in an olive-colored suit sat with a perfect view of the exit to the customs area, reading the latest edition of the *International Herald Tribune*. He immediately recognized Robaire from the photo Langley had emailed him. He got out of his seat and folded the newspaper holding it under his left armpit and blended in with the others in the terminal.

Robaire slowly pushed his luggage cart while looking for the exit to ground transportation.

Robaire immediately stopped when he passed a newsstand and saw a photo of Saddam Hussein on the cover of the international edition of *Time* magazine, which had the caption: WAS THE U.S. INVOLVED? He abandoned the cart and walked into the shop to devour yet another article about the assassination attempt. This one focused on the allegations made by the Iraqi government, which had no concrete evidence to support their theory the U.S. was behind the plot to kill Hussein, other than a U.S. asylum seeker had used a Stinger missile in the attempt. He was relieved to see it was still widely reported the Iraqi soldier found dead in the hotel room had shot Rahimi and his two accomplices before being gunned down himself. Robaire gladly let the soldier take the credit for the killings.

Robaire replaced the magazine, to the clerk's chagrin, and was walking back to his cart when he saw the man in the olive suit for a second time. They made eye contact for just an instant, but that was long enough to make Robaire's heart rate accelerate.

Robaire made an abrupt U-turn with his cart and headed for the airline ticket counters. He abandoned his idea of going to Bavaria. He needed to remain on the run. The variety of airlines at the airport seemed endless. Where would he go? What would he do when he got there? Could he hope to evade surveillance? When were they going to move in on him? Why didn't they just leave him alone? His questions were as numerous as the airlines servicing the airport.

He studied a huge board displaying the departures for Lufthansa airlines. London, Rome, Bern, and Paris appeared several times on the board. Boring. He continued down the listing until he saw the one that appealed to him. Perfect, he thought.

He got into a ticket line and produced his rapidly diminishing wad of U.S. dollars to purchase a one-way ticket to Caracas, Venezuela. From there, he could catch a hop to Nassau, the Bahamas. The plane was due to leave in two hours.

He checked his luggage and walked to the security checkpoint. He was subjected to a walk-through metal detector, a security agent with a hand-held metal detector, and a guard who physically patted him down.

A dark-haired woman wearing a dark blue skirt and uniform vest approached him with a clipboard. She wore glasses and was officious. She spoke in King's English. "Sir, I have some basic security questions I must ask you?"

"All right."

"Did you check in any baggage today?"

"Yes."

"Did you personally pack the bags you checked in?"

"Yes."

"Did you check in any luggage for someone else?"

"No."

"Did someone ask you to take baggage for them?"

"No," he sighed.

"Did you leave any of your bags unattended after you packed?"

"No."

"May I see your luggage receipts?"

"Certainly." He produced his Lufthansa envelope that had them stuck inside. She recorded the serial numbers. Robaire looked around and saw the olive-suited man being subjected to the same routine.

"Do you have any carry-on luggage, sir?"

"Um, no," he said as he looked away from the man and returned his attention to her.

She glanced over his shoulder and wondered who he had been looking at. "Are you traveling with anyone else?"

"No. No one."

"I see," she said, checking off boxes on a list she carried. "May I see your ticket and passport?"

"Of course," he said, trying to keep his composure.

She flipped through the documents. "I see from your passport, Mister Nasir, you were born in Lebanon."

"Yes. I'm a naturalized United States citizen."

"So, it would appear," she said.

There's nothing to worry about, he thought. He was just a naturalized U.S. citizen from Lebanon traveling on a phony U.S. passport, with a phony Jordanian passport in his boxer shorts, being followed by the CIA, and was about to board a plane for an international flight. What could go wrong? Robaire knew he could never explain away the Jordanian passport. This woman can smell a terrorist like a German shepherd can sniff out drugs, he thought. He was determined to keep his wits about him.

She handed the ticket and passport back to him. "Thank you for your cooperation, sir. I hope you understand the reasons for the precautions."

"Yes, I certainly do. Thank you." He tried to smile.

He casually walked away and found the first-class lounge. He selected a seat near the back wall so he could see people entering and exiting.

"Guten tag. Was machen sie?" the waitress asked in a friendly tone.

"Stoli on the rocks with a twist. And make that a double," he specified in perfect German.

When the drink arrived, he closed his eyes and rubbed the cold glass on his cheeks. The clear liquid soothed his nerves despite seeing the man in the olive suit making his way to the terminal gates. He was trapped and could not retrieve his luggage to escape the airport without causing a major breech of security.

He almost made it to his heaven, but Bavaria would have to wait a while longer. Paradise in the Bahamas would have to do for now.

CHAPTER 43

Ms. Garcia stood in the doorway to Bill Brownlee's office while he and Gary discussed things that were of no interest to her. "Gary, you've got a phone call."

"Take a message," he said.

"The guy says it's important. He kinda sounds like Robaire Assaly."

"What! Why didn't you say so? I'll take it in here."

"I thought I just did," she huffed, turning to go back to her desk. She transferred the call to Brownlee's office.

Bill activated the speakerphone.

"This is Gary Lowery," he said, excited finally to hear from him.

"It's me, Robaire."

"Where the hell are you?"

He responded to the question after a few seconds of silence. "We need to talk."

"We sure do. How are you? Where have you been?"

"It's a long story, but I've managed so far. You sound like you're in a tunnel, Gary."

"I'm on speakerphone in Bill Brownlee's office. He's here with me."

"Hi, Robaire. How are you doing?" Brownlee asked.

"Okay, Bill."

"Where are you?" Gary asked again.

Silence. Gary yelled at the phone. "Robaire, help me out here, will you? I can't help you if you won't tell me where you are."

"We need to talk," Robaire said again. "I have so much I have to explain."

I'm anxious to hear it, but where are you, goddamnit?"

"Can you meet me in Nassau?"

Gary glanced at Brownlee, who nodded his head enthusiastically. "Yes, of course."

"When can you get here?"

"Tomorrow, the next day. You tell me and I'll be there."

"Meet me poolside at the Atlantis Hotel on Paradise Island the day after tomorrow. Make it at noon, and we'll talk over lunch. And please don't try to find me beforehand. I'm not staying at that hotel," he lied.

"Okay, I can wait until then." Gary followed with a lie of his own.

"Good, and be sure to come alone, Gary. This will have to be a private conversation. Sorry about that, Bill."

"I understand," Brownlee said.

"Under the circumstances, I can't have it any other way," Robaire said.

"See you the day after tomorrow," Gary said. They heard the line disconnect.

"Get a hold of Olson and Rowe and tell them what's up," Brownlee said.

"Do we have to?" Gary asked, and smiled slyly.

"If we don't, we'll never hear the end of it," Brownlee said, pulling on his mustache.

"Okay, boss. Whatever you say."

Robaire passed the phone back to the bartender at the poolside bar of the Atlantis Hotel. "Another Stolichnaya," Robaire said.

• • •

A CIA operative in an office building on the other end of Los Angeles removed his headphones and placed them on the table in front of him and picked up a telephone. A few seconds later, Wilson answered.

"He says he's in Nassau," the man said. "Lowery's going to be meeting with him for lunch at the Atlantis Hotel on Paradise Island in two days. Poolside."

"Any particular time?" Wilson asked.

"Noon."

"How dramatic. I supposed he told Lowery to come alone."

"Why, yes, he did. How did you know?"

"That's always the way with amateurs. No imagination. This confirms what our man in Frankfurt saw."

"Do you want me to make the necessary arrangements?"

"No. I'll take care of them personally. That was a good job, Frank."

"Thank you, sir."

CHAPTER 44

The dual prop, six place DEA airplane Gary, Olson, and Rowe were in landed on a typical sunbaked day in the Bahamas. They had flown to Miami, where the Miami Field Division offered to give them a ride to make their journey much easier. As they all deplaned, Gary recognized Jacob Jackson, who was the DEA Country Attaché, standing at the entrance to the terminal. He was a tall black man, whose dark skin the rays of the Caribbean sunlight enhanced. He wore a bright Hawaiian print cotton shirt, sunglasses, and a Panama hat.

Gary, Olson, and Rowe walked up to the terminal, pulling their suitcases behind them.

"Hi, Gary. Welcome to the *eye*-lands." Jackson said. As he smiled, his brilliant white teeth contrasted his dark skin.

"You got the *eye*-land lingo down, *mon*," Gary said, shaking his hand. "How you doing'?"

"Great. This is paradise, you know?"

"So, I've been told. Jacob Jackson, these are the two L.A.-based FBI agents I told you about, Calvin Rowe and Mark Olson. This is Mike Morgan from the Miami air wing who flew us here."

"I know Mike well," Jackson said. "How are you guys doing?" The intros were done, and they all shook hands.

"I've got customs greased. It'll only take a few minutes to get to the embassy," Jackson said. He escorted them to an awaiting immigration officer, who smiled a toothless grin and stamped their passports. Soon they were walking to the parking lot, where they got into Jackson's new Chevy Tahoe.

"Did Gary tell you we went to basic agent training together?"

"No," Rowe said. "He didn't mention it."

"Yeah, me and Gary go back quite a ways. We worked together in L.A. until I got promoted and transferred to Nassau."

"And the DEA hasn't gotten any work out of you since," Gary joked.

"I told you to get out of that rat race and come to paradise. The hell with that hum bug bullshit in L.A."

"Maybe someday I'll wise up and get out of town."

Olson loosened his tie and removed his jacket. Rowe had already done so. They were in stark contrast to Gary, who wore a T-shirt, faded blue jeans and gray Nike running shoes. Jackson twirled his sunglasses as they drove. The road snaked along the shoreline, populated with swaying palm trees and large hotels. The breeze was picking up.

They drove into the parking lot of a three-story bank building containing the American Embassy. A guard wearing a dirty uniform with a worn-out bus driver looking hat stood up from his folding chair when he saw the familiar Tahoe pull in. He walked up to the SUV and opened the back door for Rowe.

"Leave your luggage in the SUV," Jackson said. "I'll take you to the hotel after we have a chance to talk."

"This is it?" Gary asked.

"It ain't pretty, but it's home," Jackson said. "We're on the second floor. The embassy has the top two floors."

Jackson waved to the Marine guard, who buzzed them through the security doors. He handed the visitors temporary embassy I.D. badges to wear after they surrendered their passports.

They walked upstairs to the DEA office. "Have a seat," Jackson offered once they arrived at his private office.

Olson and Rowe sat on a couch while Gary and Mike took wooden armchairs. Jackson filled his office with career memorabilia and photos of him next to piles of seized cocaine and marijuana, like big game hunters do when they shoot their prey and pose for a trophy photo. He shut the door and sat behind his rosewood desk. "So, this Assaly character's the hottest DEA fugitive around. It's not every day one of them tries to knock off Saddam Hussein."

"I suppose so," Rowe said.

"I can't believe that man's luck," Jackson said. "He survives a helicopter crash *after* being hit with a Stinger missile? I guess the only thing that's gonna take him out is the U.S. Army in a couple of weeks."

"That's about the size of it," Olson said. "You can imagine how anxious we are to get our hands on Assaly and take his ass back to the United States.

"That reminds me," Jackson said.

"Oh?" Olson asked.

"Whatever you do while you're here, *do not* let the Bahamians know you're gonna snatch this guy."

"Why's that? I thought they were cooperating with us on this one?" Rowe asked."They're cooperating, all right. However, they're kinda sensitive about sovereignty," Jackson said. "They don't like being made to feel like they're a pawn of the United States."

"Okay, got it," Olson said.

"There's another thing," Jackson said. "They just recently let us carry firearms. Did you guys bring weapons?"

"Yeah, they're in our suitcases," Gary replied.

"I'm sorry, but you gonna have to keep them here. The locals will have a cow, and they will declare all four of you persona non grata if they catch you with a firearm. But don't worry about it. No one carries a gun in town, and I keep mine locked up unless I'm going to one of the other islands. The police here don't even carry firearms."

"What's going to happen after they find out we grabbed Assaly and flew away in a DEA plane?" Gary asked.

Jackson grinned. "Once the motherfucker's out of country, they couldn't care less, especially when they learn he's an American. He's one less mouth they have to feed in jail. They just don't want to be taken for granted. They want to keep us happy, but don't want to be pissed on either."

"I see," Gary said.

"If Assaly was a Bahamian, there'd be a shit storm, but since he's one of ours, and not one of theirs, no problem, mon," Jackson said in his best Bahamian accent.

"I just hope we get him before the Iraqis do," Rowe said.

"You think they're after him?" Jackson asked.

Rowe wiped his forehead with his handkerchief. "Interpol just informed us before we left there have recently been Iraqi agents moving throughout Europe and the Middle East. Apparently, Assaly and Rahimi checked into the hotel in Baghdad at the same time. Interpol figured out Assaly is traveling on a phony Jordanian passport. If the Iraqis get to him before we do, they'll kill him for sure. No question about it."

Gary had heard all this before and was becoming bored. He stood up and walked to the window to look at the view of the harbor. "How many people do you have ready for tomorrow?"

"I'm afraid we're it," Jackson said. "My agents are all out on interdiction cases, but there'll be two Bahamian police detectives with us."

"Will that be enough?" Olson blurted.

Jackson raised his hand in a calming gesture. "Plenty. This is an island. There aren't many places he can go. Not to mention everyone knows everyone around here. Any more police than that, and we'll be raising a lot of eyebrows."

"So far, no luck in finding Robaire on the island?" Gary asked.

"Afraid not. I've checked the hotels. None showed him registered under his real name, but I never really expected him to do that. A lot of Arab types come here. I ran the photo you sent by hotel staff but didn't get any hits. Not even a nibble."

"Did you show the photo to anyone else?" Olson asked.

"I ran it past the customs and immigration officers at the airport before picking you up. No good. No one remembers seeing him come through. Osama bin-Laden himself could walk through the Nassau airport carrying an atomic bomb, and they wouldn't recognize him."

Rowe shook his head. "I wonder if he's even here. I'd hate to think he sent us on a wild goose chase."

"He probably is," Jackson said. "Keep in mind that an awful lot of tourists come through this place, and he wouldn't be noticed. To the Bahamians, all white people look alike."

"Guess you can add Native Americans to that list," Gary said.

"That's right," Jackson said. "I forgot. What kinda Indian are you, again?"

"I'm a card-carrying Lumbee," Gary said. "The tribe's in North Carolina. It's the largest in the state. None of the Lumbees have ever been on a reservation, thank God."

"Why's that?" Rowe asked.

"Ever been on an Indian reservation? They're terrible. Lots of poverty and everyone's on the government dole. The Lumbees are farmers, educators, dentists, lawyers, physicians, and bankers. But they don't have any casinos, which is probably a good thing. Did you know Heather Locklear is a Lumbee Indian?"

"No kidding? The actress?" Jackson asked.

"Yep. Locklear is a common name there, along with Lowery, Oxendine, Sampson, and a host of others," Gary replied.

"I thought you were maybe Italian," Olson said.

"Yeah, me too," Rowe followed.

"That's what most people assume," Gary said. "I'm actually a half-breed. My dad's the pure-bred. When he was in the Army stationed at Fort Ord, he met my white mother, fell in love, got married and then me and my younger brother, Jim, came along."

"Interesting," Olson said. "Well, I just hope Assaly shows up tomorrow. I'm getting tired of this cat-and-mouse game, and I'm anxious to find out exactly what happened."

"I think that's how we all feel," Rowe said.

Gary saw a cruise ship making its way into the harbor. "You can say that again."

CHAPTER 45

Precisely at noon the next day, Gary Lowery walked through the front door to the Atlantis Hotel on Paradise Island. The casino was half-full, with polite gamblers from around the world dressed in everything from suits to tank tops, swimsuits, and flip-flops. The familiar-sounding bells of slot machines paying off reminded him of his occasional trips to Las Vegas and Lake Tahoe.

Gary found the men's room to prepare himself for a long-winded conversation he didn't want interrupted by a full bladder. Jackson and the FBI agents set up around the pool. Mike Morgan, the DEA pilot, was at the airport waiting for word if there was a need for him. When Gary left the restroom and walked outside, he spied Jacob Jackson seated at a table by himself near the deep end of the pool. He removed his sunglasses and winked. Rowe and Olson were at separate tables by themselves.

Gary did not notice Robaire, who saw him when he walked out of the casino. Robaire was uncharacteristically dressed in tan shorts, a blue and yellow-flowered Hawaiian shirt, wearing a baseball cap. He was smoking a cigar and had five days of beard growth. He hid behind sunglasses and waited for Gary to recognize him. The pool was crowded with children splashing water, having fun, and making a racket. The lounge chairs and tables surrounding the pool were filled with sunbathers, people munching on sandwiches and drinking adult beverages with tiny umbrellas in their glasses. Finally, Gary recognized Robaire and walked towards him.

"Robaire! I hardly recognized you."

Robaire stood up, and they shook hands. He suddenly stepped forward and hugged Gary. "How the hell are you, Gary?"

"Never mind me. How about you?"

"I'm doing well," Robaire lied, and puffed on his cigar, blowing a smoke ring into the humid air.

"I'm sure glad to see you. You're looking good." They sat down and pulled their chairs close together.

"So are you. I'm grateful you came."

"How could I not come, Robaire? The curiosity's killing me. What have you gotten yourself into?"

He ignored the question. "My sister said she contacted you."

"Yes, and I'm thankful she did. It was clever of you sending her that envelope."

"Have you arrested June Cohen yet?"

Gary avoided eye contact with Robaire and could see Jackson and Rowe now seated at a table on the other side of the pool. "No," he said solemnly.

Robaire hit an arm of his chair with the bottom of his fist. "Damn it. That's a dangerous woman who needs to be stopped. I'm not sure whose side she's on."

"Neither am I," Gary agreed. "When did you see her last?"

"When we were in Cairo."

"Cairo?"

"Yes. My mother and sister saw her later in Beirut."

"Beirut? How do you know that?"

"I've talked to them. June personally drove them to the airport and put them on a plane to Washington."

"She did? What about the kidnappers?"

"They're dead. Rahimi and his two friends turned out to be the kidnappers."

"*They* were the kidnappers?" He settled down for a moment. "Well, I'll be damned. You didn't say that in your letter."

"I didn't know it at the time."

"When were your mother and sister released?"

"Shortly after the incident in Bagdad."

Gary had to laugh. "Is that what you call it, an incident?"

He ignored the question.

Gary glanced over again at Jackson.

"Why'd you do it, Robaire?"

"Do what, Gary? Please be more specific. Why did I do what?"

Gary leaned forward and, in a loud whisper, said, "Help steal the Stinger missile. What the hell do you think I'm talking about?"

Robaire looked relieved. "For a moment, I thought you might have thought I was somehow responsible for the death of Rahimi and his two henchmen."

Gary was confused. "I thought an Iraqi soldier killed Rahimi and the two Pakistanis? Were you involved in their deaths?"

"Of course not!" Robaire realized he made a major tactical blunder and had to lay it on thick. "Do I look like a murderer?"

"Who said anything about murder?" Gary asked flatly.

Robaire got upset at himself for his blunders, and the thought of Rahimi made him lose his temper. "They kidnapped my mother and sister. They deserved to die. Don't you think?"

"Whoa, slow down. Back up, partner. What are you talking about?"

"Amir Rahimi and his two accomplices, who do you think I'm talking about?"

"Did you whack those guys?" Gary asked.

"No!" He folded his arms and looked away, afraid to look into Gary's eyes. "But I wish I had."

"Let's start this conversation over from the beginning." Gary suggested. "Tell me about the first time you met June."

"In a minute, but first, I must do something."

"Now? What's so important it has to be done now?"

He leaned over towards Gary and whispered, "I have a sudden urge to take my daily constitution. Is that permissible?"

Gary shook his head. "Yes, of course. Hurry up, will you? I gotta hear this whole story."

"Order me a Stoli, and I'll be right back."

"Sure," Gary sighed. He watched Robaire crush out his cigar and make his way to the hotel-casino door, shuffling in his flip-flops to the restrooms.

At a bank of public telephones near the men's room, a woman dressed in a flowing white cotton sundress wearing a large, floppy hat and large sunglasses concealing a good portion of her face, pretended to be making a telephone call.

When Robaire had finished his business, he left the men's room and saw the same woman again. She smiled at him and said in a familiar voice, "Do you have any change, my dear?"

Robaire froze when he heard her voice. "June!"

June pointed her nine millimeter Sig-Sauer pistol at him she had concealed inside a folded magazine. Robaire fixated on the weapon. "Oh my God!"

She put the magazine with her gun into a canvas shoulder bag she was carrying. "Come with me." She pulled him by the belt against her body and walked him arm in arm through the casino.

• • •

Gary could see Robaire had stopped by the phone bank but could not make out who he was talking to or what exactly was happening. He hoped someone else had a better view. He glanced over at Jackson and Rowe and motioned for them to follow him. Olson saw what was happening and jumped to his feet.

• • •

"What do you intend to do with me?" Robaire asked as their walk picked up speed.

"Just shut up and keep walking." They were now in the gaming area, headed directly for the front entrance.

While still holding onto his belt, June removed her sunglasses and placed them in her bag. "This way," she commanded. A man who had assisted June at the hideout in Lebanon was sitting in the driver's seat of a Toyota Cressida when he saw them coming. He started the engine and pulled up to them. She opened the left front passenger door for Robaire to get in, gave him a shove, and slammed the door. She jumped into the back seat. "Let's go!" she shouted. The driver popped the clutch, causing the engine to stall, buying enough time for Gary, Olson, Rowe, and Jackson to come closer to reaching the car as the driver tried to restart it.

June pulled out her handgun and brandished it at them out her window as the driver continued to crank the engine. "Back off!" The unarmed agents raised their hands and complied. None were close enough to grab the pistol. "Stay the hell away from us," she ordered. The car finally started, and she smiled, giving a little wave to them as the car sped off toward the only bridge leading them off the small island and into downtown Nassau. Robaire looked more frightened than Gary had ever seen him.

· · ·

"Goddamnit!" Gary said. "We've got to get that woman!"

Jackson looked around and saw his Bahamian police detective counterparts seated in a Toyota Land Cruiser parked in front of the hotel, smoking cigarettes while reading a newspaper. He whistled and waved his arms frantically, finally getting their attention. The two detectives finally drove up. "What's happening, mon?" the driver asked.

The four men squeezed into the SUV. "Follow that Cressida!" Jackson said, pointing ahead. The Land Cruiser lurched forward and purred along, crossing the bridge a full thirty-seconds behind June.

"Do you suppose that's June?" Olson asked no one in particular.

"That's her all right," Gary said. "She's probably going to kill him." The eyes of the driver, Detective Rolle, widened. "Who's gonna kill who?"

"The woman," Jackson said. "That's the woman from America I told you about. She's come for our fugitive."

"Holy Jesus, mon," the passenger, Detective Johnson, said. He picked up the microphone to the car radio and began transmitting to his dispatcher he was in pursuit of the Cressida."Hurry!" Rowe yelled at Detective Rolle.

"Who's got a weapon?" Gary asked.

"No one," Jackson said. "Remember, the police don't carry handguns in the Bahamas. And I didn't bring mine either. I never dreamed this would happen."

"What about a shotgun?" Gary wondered.

"Negative," Jackson replied.

"What's this about a gun?" Detective Johnson asked.

Jackson leaned over the driver's seat. "The American woman. She's got a pistol and just kidnapped our fugitive. She's another fugitive we're looking for."

"May God have mercy," Detective Rolle said. "Fugitives everywhere!"

Detective Rolle drove as fast as the traffic would allow. They were several city blocks behind June, who did not hesitate to reach over the driver's shoulder and blow the horn at tourists, pedestrians, and an occasional horse-drawn buggy to move them out of the way. It was the peak shopping period of the day in the capital.

June's driver pulled to the right-side curb of the one-way street. The American agents could see the three walking fast through a city park next to a row of boat slips in the marina. She held on to Robaire's belt while her accomplice held one of his arms above his elbow. They hurried across the wooden planks of the dock as the agents got out of their vehicle.

"Come on," Olson said to the detectives. The detectives lost their enthusiasm when they learned June was armed. "We'll stay here and listen to the police radio, mon," Johnson said.

"We may receive a call," Rolle said.

Gary saw the three of them walk over a gangplank and board a sixty-four-foot yacht with her diesel engines running. The man shoved Robaire onboard while another helped June step onto the deck. "Get him below," she ordered. "Let's get underway."

• • •

June removed her floppy hat and slipped the straps of her sundress over her shoulders, allowing it to drop to her waist. She slipped out of it, revealing a bikini. Bending over, she balled up the dress, and shoved it into her shoulder bag along with her hat and tossed it through the doors leading to below deck. June made her way to a chaise lounge on the rear deck and laid down, crossing her long, tanned legs. She ran her fingers through her hair and put on another pair of sunglasses resting on a table next to her chaise. June adjusted them while she watched Gary, Olson, Rowe, and Jackson running towards her just as the ocean-going yacht shoved off too far from the walkway to jump onto. June laughed loudly and flashed them a big smile while waving goodbye.

"You bitch!" Gary yelled. June continued to wave and smile.

The motor yacht picked up speed as the rumble of the diesel engines increased.

"Did you catch the name on the yacht?" Olson asked. "It looked like it read, *Askoy* out of Miami to me."

"That's what it said," Rowe confirmed. "I've got perfect vision."

"Come on," Gary said. "There's still a chance to catch them if we can make it to the airport fast."

They ran back to the Land Cruiser and found their two counterparts sitting on a park bench resting in the shade. "Did you find them, mon?" Detective Rolle asked.

"They're on a yacht headed out to open water," Jackson said. "We need to get to the airport, now!"

• • •

They piled back into the SUV and started the twenty-five-minute trek to Nassau airport. Jackson used his cell phone to tell Mike to be ready to go when they arrived. With any luck, they could locate the yacht and call for a U.S. Coast Guard Cutter to intercept them. So far, Jackson thought, this isn't one of his luckier days.

CHAPTER 46

Mike Morgan yelled, "Clear!" from the window of the six-place Cessna. He started the turbo-charged engines that came to a roar before he pulled back on the throttle. The plane slowly rolled to the end of the runway, where Mike did his run-up.

"Well, what in the hell are you waiting for?" Gary asked into his headset. He was seated in the front right seat next to Mike. "The runway's clear," he said, pointing at the windshield.

"Engine run-up," Mike replied calmly.

It seemed like such a waste of time to Gary. He couldn't tell the difference between an altimeter and the fuel gauge. "Can't you skip this procedure just once?"

Mike glared at him, shook his head, and mouthed, "No."

Will we ever get off the goddamned ground? Gary wondered. It seemed to take forever to reach the airport, brief two Bahamian bureaucrats, and convince them to let the DEA aircraft take off without filing a flight plan. They spent more time getting on the plane after explaining for the third time how two fugitives were escaping on a yacht described as slightly smaller than the Queen Mary. Now he was waiting around while the pilot ran up his engine. How ridiculous.

"Calm down, Gary," Jackson said. "We want to make it back here in one piece."

The plane moved slowly and then rapidly picked up speed. The takeoff was effortless. Within seconds, they were over open water. Mike made a fifteen-degree right bank, which led them to the Nassau yacht club. He calculated at twenty knots, the yacht could have sailed over twenty-three miles in any direction.

The plane climbed to thirty-five hundred feet, and it soon became apparent it would be difficult to identify their yacht from the many other yachts and sailboats in and around Nassau.

For the next two and a half hours, Mike Morgan conducted a systematic grid search of the area, eliminating vessels that were obviously not the yacht in question. He flew low at times to get a better view of yachts matching the general description. Mike radioed the U.S. Coast Guard about their position and requested its assistance.

One yacht got Gary's full attention. "How about that one over there? It has the same blue stripes around the deck."

"Could be," Olson said into the microphone attached to his headset. "Let's try that one." He pointed it out to Mike.

The plane flew parallel to the port side of the yacht about eight hundred feet above sea level when Gary and Olson yelled at once, "It's her!" Olson slumped down so Rowe and Jackson could take a better look.

"That's them, all right," Rowe said. They could see June and the two men on the rear deck, but they didn't see Robaire.

"I'll make another pass," Mike said. He banked the plane into a semi-circle and headed back over the starboard side. He picked up the radio and contacted the U.S. Coast Guard about the yacht's position.

"Coast Guard, this is DEA November 1-2-3 Tango Foxtrot," Mike radioed.

"Go ahead, Tango Foxtrot," was the response.

"We've located the *Askoy,* registered out of Miami." He gave them the coordinates. "It looks to be about sixty feet long. It's white, with a distinctive blue stripe from bow to stern just below the deck."

"Roger that, DEA. We have a cutter about forty nautical miles out. I'll relay the information to it."

"DEA out," Mike said.

"Well, shit. That's quite a distance away," Gary said.

June watched them through binoculars as the plane noisily passed over. "Bring him up here," she told the men. She had almost given up on them finding her. She had something she wanted them to see.

The two crewmen went below, and in short order, brought Robaire on the rear deck. He had duct tape covering his eyes and had his hands zip-tied behind him.

"Let's make sure they see this," June said. She reached into her bag and removed her Sig-Sauer pistol. "Stand him up at the stern."

"What are you doing?" Robaire cried. "Throwing me to the sharks?"

"Not until I shoot your fat ass," she replied. "Your blood will attract the great whites even faster."

"Oh, Lord. I can't believe it," Robaire screamed.

The two men dragged Robaire to the yacht's railing and helped him to his feet. He violently shook and bowed his head in the same manner as the two men he saw beheaded. Robaire knew this was the end. He would never see his family again. Why did he ever allow himself to get involved with this evil woman? Why didn't he tell Gary about her scheme? He could hear the ocean water splash off the side of the yacht while waiting for a bullet to pierce his skull.

Just as the plane was making its third pass over, June held a pistol in a professional shooter's two-handed configuration. She stood with her legs apart, with her right foot six inches behind her, to distribute her weight evenly and minimize the weapon's recoil. With her knees slightly bent, she pointed the gun at Robaire back and slowly squeezed the trigger as the plane approached.

Robaire's head jerked sideways as if he was trying to dodge the bullets. He lost his balance and painfully fell on his butt and instinctively rolled to his right side. His whole body quivered each time June pulled the trigger. Pop, pop, pop, pop, pop.

Mike turned sharply at a twenty-degree bank and rushed back towards the yacht. The agents were stunned at what they had just witnessed.

"NO!" Gary yelled, and tightly closed his eyes.

When they made another pass, they could clearly see the two crewmembers unfolding a standard black military-style body bag and lay it on the deck next to Robaire. Again, Morgan made the steep banking maneuver to head back for an additional look.

Mike flew perpendicular towards the yacht in a slow flight maneuver. They watched the two men hoist the heavy body bag and unceremoniously toss it into the yacht's wake. June gathered up the five expended brass shell casings and threw them overboard.

"We've only got about eight percent of fuel remaining," Morgan said. "We've got to turn back *now*!"

"I can't believe it." Gary said, not paying attention. "She killed him!"

Mike turned the aircraft into the proper compass heading to return to Nassau.

"Those bastards." Olson said.

Rowe's fist hit the back of Gary's seat. "The bitch purposely waited for us to fly over so we could see her whack him. That's one evil woman."

CHAPTER 47

With the DEA plane safely out of sight, a crewman lowered the United States flag on the motor yacht's flagpole. He unfurled the blue and white flag of Israel and attached it to the rope and quickly raised it. He momentarily stood at attention and saluted.

During this time, the other man lay on his stomach and reached over the aft deck railing. He carefully removed a thin sheet of opaque plastic that had the name *Askoy Miami*, painted on it. Its removal revealed the true name of the vessel, *Illusion* with *Tel Aviv* written underneath it. The other man quickly peeled off a foot-wide strip of navy-blue plastic running the entire length of the yacht's port side. His partner did the same on the starboard side. The sticky navy-blue plastic made the vessel look striped from a distance. Together, they gathered the rolls of plastic and the United States flag and stuffed them into a tattered green army duffle bag. One man tossed several five-pound divers' weights into the bag. He secured the duffle bag and hurled the evidence of the deception into the deep, clear water of the Atlantic.

The autopilot led the yacht on a course to Bermuda to minimize the chances of encountering a U.S. Coast Guard Cutter.

June slipped on a thin white cotton robe and walked out from one of the bedrooms below to the galley. Standing there with two glasses of white wine was Donald Wilson, Deputy Assistant Director of Clandestine Operations for the CIA. He handed one to June. Seated at a table gulping his first double Stoli was a pale-looking Robaire Assaly.

"How are you two getting along?" she asked.

"We're the best of friends," Wilson said. "Isn't that right, Mister Assaly?" slapping him on his back.

Robaire was beginning to relax, but still showed telltale signs of stress from his ordeal. "What do you intend to do with me? Torture me? Kill me for sport? I won't tell you a thing, you know."

June sat beside him. "What makes you think you can tell us anything we don't already know?"

He looked at her, surprised. He didn't know how to respond.

Wilson set his long-stemmed glass on the table. "You have to believe me, Robaire, when I tell you we're only concerned with your welfare."

"My welfare?" Robaire shouted. "That's a crock."

Wilson continued with a soothing voice. "Yes, Mister Assaly. In case you don't know, the Iraqi government is making an all-out effort to find you," he said as he poured more vodka into Robaire's glass. "And if they ever do, you can imagine the unspeakable things they will do to you. We want to prevent that from happening."

The image of the two men beheaded in Riyadh resurfaced. He raised his glass to his lips in June's direction, taking a gulp, and gazed at her. "Why does my safety suddenly concern you two?"

"We're concerned about the safety of *all* our agents, not just you." Wilson said.

"Agent?" he asked. "Is that what I am?"

"Yes, of course. We recognize talent when we see it. We don't want anything happening to our people. That wouldn't be right."

"Right?" Robaire said, his voice rising. "When did the CIA start knowing the difference between right and wrong?"

"Mister Assaly, I'm hurt," Wilson said, holding his free hand over his heart. "Especially after all the trouble we went through to make you appear dead."

June added ice to Robaire's glass and poured more vodka. "We wouldn't want you to fall into Saddam's hands, would we?"

"Oh. Now I see. You think if the Iraqis catch me, I'll tell them about how you tried to kill Saddam?"

Wilson asked, "Robaire, the last time I checked, *you* were the one who tried to kill him, isn't that right?"

"Touché," Robaire muttered.

"It really doesn't matter now, does it? Nothing of the sort is going to happen to you now," Wilson said.

"What makes you so sure they'll stop looking for me?"

"They think you're dead! Those federal agents who flew over us are probably on the radio right now, screaming about how they just witnessed your murder. They'll be very convincing because they really think you're dead."

"So did *I* when that gun went off. I just naturally hit the deck. How did you pull it off?"

June looked over at Robaire, amazed. "Haven't you ever heard of blanks?" she scoffed sarcastically. "When the plane was turning around, we dragged you down here and put a body bag on the deck filled with bags of cement. When they passed over again, we threw it overboard. It was *very* convincing." She smiled deviously before saying, "I can imagine what went through their Boy Scout minds when they saw you get shot."

"How is all this going to help me?"

Wilson spoke up. "They'll forget about you before you know it. Even the Iraqis will stop looking for you after we invade. Someday soon, when Saddam is no longer in power, and the political climate changes, you'll be able to resurface. In the meantime, you'll be taking a hiatus."

Robaire remained silent. A hundred questions came to mind. Obviously, they didn't know he murdered Rahimi and the others. He wondered if it would make any difference if they did. He didn't dare bring it up.

Wilson sensed Robaire was suspicious of their motives. He gently patted his hand on Robaire's shoulder. "Look, Robaire. The days of whacking people for the sake of whacking them are long gone. You must admit, if we wanted to get rid of you, we had plenty of opportunity to do so. We could have shot you and threw your ass overboard for real. We don't do a fraction of the things people accuse us of doing." He chuckled. "This job is nothing like the trash you read in novels or see in the movies."

"Is that right? You just tried to kill Saddam and put the blame on me!"

"That's different," he said.

"Oh?" Robaire asked.

"Everything changed after September 11th," Wilson said. "We've got carte blanche to take out terrorists, but political leadership is another matter. The Iraq situation suddenly came to a head, and the president is determined to have a regime change there. However, the ban on political assassinations is still in effect. Taking Saddam out would have prevented the U.S. from having to go to war. Think of the lives that would save, mostly Iraqis. Killing one man is so much more cost effective than sending two hundred thousand troops to the Gulf, wouldn't you agree?" He paused, sipped his wine, and continued. "In any event, you can rest assured we're going to look after you until this whole thing blows over."

June followed up. "Look, Robaire, we don't use agents and toss them away like garbage. Good ones are hard to come by. We'll most likely be able to use you again. We've got a pool of talent out there to use when the time is right."

"It's the nature of our business," Wilson said. "We've learned to accept it. So should you. Just think of this little drama on the boat as the CIA's version of the witness protection program. We'll change your identity, find you a new home, and provide you with a decent stipend. The CIA doesn't expect you to find a job and work for a living like the U.S. Marshals do. We *reward* our agents for their cooperation and good work."

Robaire liked the sound of that. "What do I have to do for this stipend?"

"Virtually nothing," Wilson said. "The only requirement is for you to keep your mouth shut and don't contact any of your friends or relatives under any circumstances until things calm down."

"Why?"

"You're supposed to be dead, remember? The minute you call someone, word will eventually make it back to Iraq you're alive. The Iraqis will hunt you down for the rest of your life. They'll find your family and torture them until they give you up. Saddam loyalists will do whatever it takes to get their slimy hands on you. Do you understand what I'm saying?"

"Yes, yes, of course," he said.

"For your family's sake, you must remain completely silent," June concluded.

Robaire hung his head and stared at the table. The thought of never seeing his family again depressed him. "What happens when this war is over? Surely, Saddam will be defeated and overthrown. What happens then?

"That will change everything," Wilson said. "If that happens, assuming the president goes ahead and pulls the trigger to start the invasion, we'll reevaluate your situation. In the meantime, the money and the security will be there so long as you continue to follow instructions and keep quiet. We'll take care of you and keep you out of harm's way, but you must meet us halfway. This means you can't call your friends, family members, business associates, Gary Lowery, or anyone else. If your mother dies, you cannot attend her funeral. The minute we find out you've contacted someone from your past life, the gravy train stops, and that's when you get off. Capeesh?"

"Certainly," Robaire said quietly.

June followed Wilson's lead. "So long as you play ball, you've got nothing to worry about."

There was silence for a short while until Wilson asked, "Where would you like to go, Mister Assaly?"

"What do you mean?"

"To live, you know, reside? Where on earth do you want to live?"

"You mean it's up to me?"

"Definitely. We don't want to send you someplace you won't like. However, it must be within reason," Wilson qualified his remark, raising his index finger for emphasis. "We have reciprocal agreements with many nations. Briton's a perfect example. What do you think?"

"You want me to decide now?"

"No, no, no," Wilson said. "Sleep on it. We're still several hours out of Bermuda, and when we dock, we'll put you on a plane anywhere you'd like to go."

A rush of elation came over Robaire. "This is positively incredible," he said, shaking his head. "A minute ago, I thought I was going to be killed, and now you're offering me a whole new life?"

Wilson smiled. "This is a strange world we live in, Mister Assaly. It truly is."

"Anywhere in the world?" Robaire wanted to reconfirm. Bavaria topped his list.

"Anywhere in the *free* world," Wilson stressed. "I think moving to Tehran would be stretching it a bit."

Robaire laughed loudly, with Wilson and June joining him. It was an unencumbered laugh from their bellies. It had been a long time since any of them had laughed so easily.

EPILOGUE

May 12, 2003
Stuttgart, Germany

"Oh, Robaire, you've picked a beautiful restaurant for lunch," his sister Nadia said. "The weather is near perfect for outdoor dining," she added, while Robaire, ever the gentleman, moved her chair back for her to sit.

"Yes," Robaire said. "The weather has been cooperating since you arrived yesterday. Hopefully, it will stay this way during your entire visit." He took a seat on the opposite end of the wooden table that had a black and white checkerboard pattern on the tablecloth. Due to the black cobblestones underneath the table, it was a bit wobbly.

"I hope so. There is so much to see in the short time I have."

"You'll enjoy the castles and especially the Mercedes Benz Museum. We'll drive to the countryside and take in all the scenery Bavaria has to offer," he said.

A waitress appeared with two menus and asked about their drink preference. In perfect German, Robaire ordered his usual and ordered a glass of German white wine for Nadia.

"What looks good to you, Robaire?"

"I'm having the Jaeger Schnitzel," he said. "The chef cuts the veal so large, it hangs over the plate. It's huge! It comes with noodles and a gravy."

"That sounds good, but way too much for me. I think I'll try the cordon bleu."

"Excellent choice," he said. "Another fine dish."

The waitress returned with their drinks, took their meal order, and headed back to the kitchen. "Cheers," Robaire said as he clinked his glass with Nadia's before taking a sip of his Stoli.

"I'm so grateful you wrote to tell me where you were and that you were all right. Mother was worried sick about you."

"I didn't mean to get everyone upset, but I had to see you and find out how everyone was," he said. "I reached out to you the moment Saddam Hussein went into hiding. The American Army made quick work of his crappy military."

"What does Saddam Hussein have to do with any of this?"

"It's a long story, but the people I was working with wanted him dead to avoid America having to invade Iraq, for the second time, I might add. The bastard survived an assassination attempt, so the Americans invaded and a month later, Saddam is still in hiding. I'm sure they'll find him one day, and when they do. . ." He stuck his thumb out and ran it across his throat. "That will be the end of that despot. With him gone, I can continue with my previous life."

"I still don't understand. Maybe someday you'll tell me the entire story."

"In due time, my dear. In due time."

After eating, Nadia placed her napkin on the table and said, "Robaire, it looks like a gentleman and a lady at a table behind you are trying to get our attention."

Robaire froze. He cautiously turned around and saw Gary Lowery and Joyce McCarthy walking towards them.

"Gary!" Robaire exclaimed. He stood up so fast he knocked his chair over. "I'm so happy to see you!"

"How are you, Robaire?" The two men hugged each other. Tears formed in Robaire's eyes.

"Sit, sit," Robaire said while picking up his chair and wiping his eyes with his napkin.

"This is Joyce McCarthy," Gary said. She stuck her hand out, and to Gary's surprise, Robaire kissed it. "She's an Assistant U.S. Attorney in Los Angeles. Don't worry. We're not here on official business."

"Then what?" Robaire asked.

"What I mean is we both took time off from work and flew over here on our own dime. No one at my office knows we're here to see you. All they know is we're on a European vacation."

"How did you find me?"

Gary looked at Nadia, who had a sheepish look on her face. "Nadia gave you up. She thought it was the right thing to do."

"Oh, that big sister of mine. I'm so glad you did," he said, smiling at her.

"By the way, Robaire," Joyce said. "The entire case against you has gone away. We can't try a dead man, you know."

"I would think not," Robaire said. "But now that you know I'm not dead, what happens now?"

"Nothing," she said. "This is all ancient history. Your indictment was dismissed upon your death. There shouldn't be any issue with you coming back to the United States. You're in no jeopardy of being indicted again," she said.

"I'm so happy to hear that," Robaire said.

"We're eager to hear all the details," Gary said. "Our curiosity has gotten the better of us."

"All right," he said, while slapping his thigh. "Let's go back to my apartment and celebrate. I'll pour another Stoli, and I have lots of good German beer and wine. You'll get the whole unvarnished truth about what happened."

They all stood up, and Robaire left euros for his and Nadia's meals on the table. "Follow me to my apartment. It's not far."

"I know," Gary said. "We followed you from there to the restaurant."

"Always the investigator, aren't you, Gary?" he said, and they all laughed aloud.

- THE END -

ABOUT THE AUTHOR

Photo of the author by Florence Catania

Gregory D. Lee is a retired DEA Supervisory Special Agent and a retired U.S. Army Reserve Chief Warrant Officer 5/CID agent. In 2011, he deployed to Afghanistan on special assignment to the Special Operations Command Europe to assess the "Rule of Law" counter-insurgency strategy and worked daily with members of the U.S. Intelligence Community. He instructed for DEA Training at the FBI Academy and was on DEA diplomatic assignment to Pakistan. He was part of a team capturing 1993 NYC World Trade Center bombing mastermind, Ramzi Yousef, and testified at his trial. His unique experiences in Pakistan are documented in two best-selling non-fiction books: *Unholy Wars* by John K. Cooley, and *1000 Years for Revenge: International Terrorism and the FBI* by Peter Lance.

Please visit his website at www.gregorydlee.com
to learn more about him and his other books.

NOTE FROM GREGORY D. LEE

Word-of-mouth is crucial for any author to succeed. If you enjoyed *Stinger*, please leave a review online—anywhere you are able. Even if it's just a sentence or two. It would make all the difference and would be very much appreciated.

Thanks!
Gregory D. Lee

We hope you enjoyed reading this title from:

www.blackrosewriting.com

Subscribe to our mailing list – *The Rosevine* – and receive **FREE** books, daily
deals, and stay current with news about upcoming
releases and our hottest authors.
Scan the QR code below to sign up.

Already a subscriber? Please accept a sincere thank you for being a fan of
Black Rose Writing authors.

View other Black Rose Writing titles at
www.blackrosewriting.com/books and use promo code
PRINT to receive a **20% discount** when purchasing.

Printed in the USA
CPSIA information can be obtained
at www.ICGtesting.com
LVHW021311240824
789094LV00001B/38

9 781685 133856